D0949529

THE PRIVATE LIFE OF DR. WATSON

THE PRIVATE LIFE OF DR. WATSON

Being the Personal Reminiscences of John H. Watson, M.D.

MICHAEL HARDWICK

E. P. DUTTON, INC.   NEW YORK

Grateful acknowledgment to Dame Jean Conan Doyle for permission to use the characters created by Sir Arthur Conan Doyle.

Published in the United States by E.P. Dutton, Inc.,
2 Park Avenue, New York, N.Y. 10016

Library of Congress Cataloging in Publication Data

Hardwick, Michael
    The private life of Dr. Watson.

    1. Doyle, Arthur Conan, Sir, 1859–1930—Characters—
Dr. Watson I. Title.
PR6058.A673P7 1983   823′.914   83-5701

ISBN: 0-525-24205-8

Published simultaneously in Canada by Fitzhenry & Whiteside
Limited, Toronto

COBE

10 9 8 7 6 5 4 3 2 1

First Edition

CONTENTS

PROLOGUE

"I am lost without my Boswell."

''How are you? You have been in Afghanistan, I perceive.''

Those were the very first words addressed to me by Sherlock Holmes, in the chemical laboratory at St. Bartholomew's Hospital on the first day of the year 1881. At the time I was the triple victim of accumulated low spirits, doubt as to my future, and a hang-over. Even at my best, though, I could not possibly have recognised the significance of our meeting.

James Boswell recorded his first encounter with the Grand Cham of literature, Dr. Samuel Johnson, thus:

> Mr Davies introduced me to him. As I knew his mortal antipathy at the Scotch, I cried to Davies: ''Don't tell him where I come from!'' However he said ''from Scotland.'' ''Mr Johnson,'' said I, ''indeed I come from Scotland, but I cannot help it.'' ''Sir,'' replied he: ''That I find is what a very great many of your countrymen cannot help.''

No such exchange passed between Holmes and myself. I did not apologise for having been recently in Afghanistan, but only asked him how on earth he knew it. He brushed the question aside, and I did not learn its answer until some weeks later, on the occasion when he astonished me by disclosing that his unique occupation was "consulting detective."

"The train of reasoning ran, 'Here is a gentleman of a medical type, but with the air of a military man. Clearly an army doctor, then. He has just come from the tropics, for his face is dark, and that is not the natural tint of his skin, for his wrists are fair. He has undergone hardship and sickness, as his haggard face says clearly. His left arm has been injured. He holds it in a stiff and unnatural manner. Where in the tropics could an English army doctor have seen much hardship and got his arm wounded? Clearly in Afghanistan.' The whole train of thought did not occupy a second."

It was but the first of countless deductions which I was to be privileged to overhear, and be occasionally invited to emulate, in the course of an association extending over a great many years. My published narratives concern a selection of the most notable of them, although there are numerous others as yet unrecounted. I never ceased to wonder at his singular gift, even though, as the memoir which follows will occasionally reveal, he did not always arrive at the correct results.

It was Holmes himself who termed me his Boswell, and it was inevitable that a portion of the attention and curiosity lavished upon him by the world should have been directed towards me, his chronicler, associate in many adventures, and, I may allow myself to assert, the closest friend of one whose austere, aloof nature did not seek friendship as a need. His personality and background have been much speculated over (with varying degrees of accuracy); and there have been those who have sought amongst my writings to infer more about my own life and nature than I have hitherto chosen to reveal.

In presenting my story in greater detail, my purpose is not to claim a larger share of notice. My aim is twofold: to provide some particulars which have never been published to the world at large; and to settle, once and for all, those others which have struck my more critical reader as anomalous or lacking adequate explanation.

While the earth might not shake at the revelation of my true place of birth, my name in full, the circumstances of my family and educational background, the train of chance which led to my adopting the medical profession, the precise location of my war wound(s), or, indeed, my happening to become acquainted with Sherlock Holmes at all, I fancy that the more bizarre and sometimes exciting facets of my travels and adventures will not be received amiss. As to the wealth of meaning concealed beneath my casual but much-debated reference to keeping a bull-pup, the sensational truth (incorrectly deduced by Holmes) of my preoccupation with an unframed portrait of Henry Ward Beecher, and my justification of a claim to an experience of women over many nations and three separate continents . . . But I leave the reader to measure his expectation against the facts herein revealed.

I trust that by revealing all I shall not be considered to have diminished such regard as a kindly public has always shown me. Dr. Johnson remarked that, relieved of duties or regard for his future reputation, he would choose to spend his life in driving briskly in a post-chaise with a pretty woman. My impression of my own life during its formative years is of having done more or less that very thing.

JOHN H. WATSON

1

"Human Nature is a strange mixture, Watson."

I have often thought it indicative of something, I know not what, in the nature of the British character which has caused us down the centuries to give our magnificent ships of war names which more befit public houses. *Rose, Thistle, Bear* are perpetuations from Elizabethan times and beyond. For all I know, there may have been an H.M.S. *Rose & Crown* or *Jolly Farmer.*

It was no bearer of any such name which, on a black night in September, 1588, driven by merciless wind and awesome sea, reeled into the North Channel between Ireland and the West Coast of Scotland and was reduced to kindling against those jagged rocks. She was the *Galeón del Gran Duque di Florencia di Nombre San Juan.*

History has not recorded how many of her people survived. Mr. Ashby, at the English embassy in Scotland, wrote to his master, Sir Francis Walsingham, the head of Queen Elizabeth's secret service, that "a great shippe of Spain carrying many soldiers foundered upon ye rocks in ye vicinitie of Black Head, with grievous loss of life. She is thought to have been verie riche."

I remember being taken often, with my brother Henry, to an indentation in that coast a little north of the Black Head light, to stand and feast our fancy on the locality of drama and despair. In the gentler soughing of the ceaseless wind I would strain my ears for the ghostly cries of drowning Spaniards, the cracking of spars, the devouring of the hull by those voracious teeth of rock.

"Will they ever find it?" I always seemed to ask, wondering how my father could remain so impassive as he puffed his pipe and stared down at the creamy swirl, and why we had not brought thigh boots and shovels and other tackle with which we might be digging for doubloons.

"No, no," he would reply, in that accent as pure as single malt whisky, which merely hinted at his Scottishness. "The sea will not give up what she took that night. It was her prize money."

His poetic rationale did not satisfy us boys. Coins and other small objects had been washed up from time to time. Someone might chance to be standing there when a fortune happened to come ashore. My brother especially, with his impatient temperament, was "all for having a dig," and we did once take soundings with our tin spades, while Father sat up on the rocks, placidly smoking, unaccountably impervious to any prospect of sudden riches.

We found nothing and soon gave up. We scrambled to where Father was, to place ourselves on either side of him and join his contemplation of the water, so calm on this day, so unindicative of the tragedy which had happened at this spot.

"No," he answered, "if ever there was treasure aboard her it will be securely stowed in Davy Jones's locker now. But riches of that sort are not the only ones in life, you know. The blood in your veins owes some of its quality to what occurred here that night so long ago."

On the mantelpiece of his office in Hanover Street, Stranraer, there stood a wooden model of a Spanish galleon.

It had been made by a sailorman, passing time on a long voyage, and thrown away by relatives clearing his cottage after his death. Father, whose firm of estate agents had dealt with the property, had appropriated it. It did not represent the *San Juan* herself, but it exemplified her and those others of the mighty Armada which had been defeated against all odds by the formidable combination of Francis Drake, Lord Howard of Effingham, and God.

The reason why Father kept it had tangible witness in his features: a long, narrow face and high nose, jet-black hair and moustaches, and brown eyes, which gave him an expression of brooding melancholy. I used to fancy his tall, slender form dressed in black doublet and hose and one of those ruffled white collars: somewhat of a contrast, admittedly, with his name, which was John Henry Watson.

I myself was ever as I am: thickset, middle-sized always for my age, square-jawed, and greyish-eyed. In disposition I reflect my dear mother. My brother, Henry, inherited Father's personality. I suppose I have much cause to feel thankful for having been passed over by their strain; yet those strikingly handsome features often made me envious.

The fact is that one of the survivors from the *San Juan* lived on in the neighbourhood long enough to contribute his blood to our ancestry. They were lucky men, those sailors and soldiers who crawled ashore on our Scottish coast. They were taken in and cared for by the local people, who saw them merely as poor souls delivered from the perils of the sea, and not as agents of an alien religion. Those who reached England and Ireland were butchered without mercy.

No family papers of ours related to so early a time, but our personal legend intrigued me and I pressed Father to repeat it.

"He was an officer: of that we are fairly sure."

"An admiral?"

"Nothing so grand, I fear. More likely an army man."

"A colonel, then?"

"A Spanish colonel of the time would have been of quite high family. He would not have cut himself off by remaining here. He would have been granted repatriation.*

"His name," Father added, "was certainly Henriques."

"How do you know that, Papa?"

"Because it survived in our family name until about the beginning of this century. My grandfather was the last to have it as his middle name. I imagine he found it too fanciful for his nature, which was rather austere. He anglicised it to Henry."

"I should have liked that name," I said, savouring its ring. "John Henriques Watson."

My father laughed. "You can always give it to one of your own sons, though he would perhaps not thank you for anything so flamboyant."

"It sounds better than Hudson," I protested. "Ugh!"

"That will do, John. You must respect your mama's family name."

"Sorry, Papa. What else do you know about the Spanish officer?"

"Apparently he was severely injured in the shipwreck, which necessitated his lying up for many months. That was in one of the castles hereabouts, possibly Kennedy. He was nursed by the steward's daughter. Cupid's bolt duly registered its hit upon them both. . . ."

"What is Cupid's bolt, Papa?"

"You will find out, my boy. You will learn that answer for yourself."

"What did it do to them?"

*The first story I ever composed was entitled *The Treasure of Black Head*, with my ancestor as the only surviving possessor of the secret of the galleon's hoard. I was about seven when I wrote it. It was never published and no longer exists.

"It caused them to get married, and have children, who had Scots and Spanish blood. Now, tell me what you deduce from his descendants' being called Watson."

"I confess myself baffled."

"Come, come. You know that when a lady marries she takes her husband's name."

"Like Mama once being Miss Hudson."

"Yes, and becoming Mrs. Watson upon marrying me. What does that lead you to infer?"

"That . . . a Miss Henriques also married a Mr. Watson?"

"Precisely. It is sometimes necessary in these matters to reason backward rather than forward. Should you ever chance to come across a memorial stone worded something like 'Sacred to ye Memory of —— Henriques and his wife ——, beloved parents of ——Watson,' it will be worth half a sovereign to you for satisfying my belief that Henriques and his wife had only daughters, of whom one married a Watson, and the name Henriques disappeared from these parts almost as abruptly as it had come to them."

"Wonderful, Papa!"

"Commonplace. If you can lay your hand upon an Henriques, there's money in it."

Often and often, whilst I still lived in Wigtownshire, I pursued that quest, though without result. Our Spaniard had disappeared as thoroughly as the treasure which may have been in his ship; yet his legacy was in the features and temperament of my father and brother.

Mother's clan was Anglo-Scottish, embracing a diverse range of classes and professions. The Scottish branch, for example, the Hudsons of Garbeg, proudly traced themselves back to the Mackenzies of the Isles and that Roderick Mackenzie who sacrificed himself so gallantly for his Prince at Culloden. Their issue in my time included a gamekeeper with two sons of totally contrasting status. The elder, Donald, was a civil engineer. His brother, Angus, went into domestic service, rising to be a butler well known in the highest strata of London society.

Mother's name was Violet. Her father was a medical practitioner at Bagshot, in Surrey. When I became old enough to wonder about the circumstances which lead to mating and procreation, and the extent to which Destiny, Fate, or whatever one chooses to term it, plays a part, I asked her how she and Father met.

The conversation took place during that period in the 1860s when Mother and I were living in America, separated from Father and Henry, and consequently more intimate than before. We were seated on a bench in the new Central Park, watching the squirrels play and the rich New York gentlemen racing one another round and round the earth track on their big stallions.

"It was really quite romantic, I suppose," she replied. "My papa, mama, and I were on holiday with my sisters, your Aunts Flora and Verbena. It was the spring of '46 and we were on our way to Coleraine, by way of Stranraer, where we were to spend the night before crossing by the steamer."

"And Father was living in Stranraer already?"

"Luckily for me, he was. I had gone for a little walk by myself, down to the harbour to smell the water and look at the boats. There was a lot of noise, and I did not hear someone's warning cry. All I knew was a sudden buffet against the back of my legs, and I was stumbling forward."

"Great heavens! You were close to the edge?"

"Almost over it, before I was suddenly seized about the waist; even then I thought I should go down into the water. You know what a drop it is. But I was successfully held there on the brink and then gently withdrawn. Your father was my saviour. But for that stumble, and his happening to see and act so swiftly...well, you might never have come into the world to hear the story."

Had I been of a religious turn of mind, I should no doubt

have detected the hand of God in it. As it is, I doubt that the Almighty would have saved her with the sole purpose of my inhabiting His earth.

"Papa just happened to be passing by, then?"

"It depends what you mean by *happened*." (Mother was in her own intensely religious phase at the time of our talk.) "He had come down to buy his ticket for the same steamer on which we were to travel the next morning. He saw a porter trip on the cobblestones and lose hold of his cart, which ran towards me. Your father and it reached me at the same moment, otherwise..."

My imagination readily completed the details. "He insisted on escorting you back to the hotel, where you introduced him to all the family and told them how he had saved you. Grandpa wrung his hand and told him he hadn't words to thank him enough. You all crossed together next day and parted at Larne, already bosom friends."

Mother looked at me with her smile. "You are a romantic boy, aren't you? Perhaps you will become a writer—another Walter Scott." Then she got up and we walked on across the park, talking of other things.

They were married in the autumn of 1847, my father travelling to Bagshot for the ceremony. He took her back to Stranraer, where he had recently been made junior partner in the estate agency. My brother Henry was born in '49 and I on July 7th, '52.

We were a happy little family in our modest house, built of stone from the ruined castle, in a prime position on a hillside at the very head of Loch Ryan. We had two servants living in and a daily boy from the orphanage to do the outside work. When Henry and I were old enough we attended a dame school, conducted by a kindly old lady of pure English extraction, who set great store upon elocution and altogether deprived us of Scottish intonations, which I have sometimes thought a loss.

The real estate business was not a bustling one in a part of the world where folk tended to stay rooted and passed on their homes through their own families. No speculator had yet thought it worth his while to build villas, and there was no great holiday trade. By the time I was ten or so, a great deal of Father's work was handling affairs for absentee owners of property in the Emerald Isle. At least once a week he took the ferry to Larne, sometimes staying there a day or two. There are good golf courses at Larne, and Father became something of an addict of the game.

Regrettably, golf was not the only addiction he acquired. Larne boasted a distillery of notable Irish whiskey; and, call it Fate or what you will, one of its directors became Father's bosom companion both on the golf course and off.

2

"Some evil influence, probably drink."

"Wonderful, Papa!"

"Commonplace."

How often was my friend Sherlock Holmes to persuade me to reason in that backward-searching manner, both for my enlightenment and his amusement. Yet, as I recall his incisive promptings, I hear also the gentler, persuasive lilt of my father's tone. The uncanny conclusion is inescapable. Holmes echoed my father; Father pre-echoed Holmes.

Now that I consider it, there was more to their similarity than a method of reasoning: the tall, spare stature and frame, the hawk-like nose and keen eyes in a light-skinned, smooth-shaven face, topped by a broad sweep of forehead curving away into receding black hair. Like Holmes, Father was seldom without his pipe when at ease or meditatively disposed, and his clothing alternated between the sober morning suit which he wore to his office and the heather-toned tweed cape and cap which he favoured for outdoor pursuits. (The Inverness coat and fore-and-aft or "deer-stalker" hat which Holmes wore on many of our expeditions outside London had not yet been introduced when I was a boy; but I can picture how well-suited to my father both would have been.)

Another feature common to them was their diverse range of interests. Both were reluctant to part with documents and memorabilia, yet kept them in little semblance of order. They pasted up scrapbooks relating to any subject which engaged their fancy. My father, at one time, seemed forever to be starting collections: shells, leaves, and other botanical specimens were his favourites. He would pursue each with intense enthusiasm for a while, then abandon it for something else, in the way that Holmes would leap from one matter to another in his constant combat with the boredom of inactivity.

I can recognise now that boredom was also Father's enemy. He seemed so placid, however, and I was too immature to interpret correctly an early conversation. It was during one of our visits to the little bay above Black Head. Henry was convinced that this was to be the day when we "struck it rich." I dug with him in the channels of sand between the rocks for a time before abandoning my spade and wandering away to join Father. He was sipping from a small flask, which he capped and stuffed into his pocket when he saw me approaching. He put his pipe back between his teeth. I sat down beside him and watched him relight it.

"Have you ever been over the seas, Papa?"

"You know I go often to Larne."

"I meant *really* overseas. Foreign lands."

"No. I have not travelled."

"Shall you, some day?"

"I doubt it will be possible—now. There was a time when I thought of it. Only . . . "

"What, Papa?"

He gave a little laugh which I could sense was not wholly genuine. "Yes, I once fancied the idea of roving."

"I'd like to."

"No doubt you will have the chance."

"Didn't you get the chance, Papa?"

"I did. But it passed before I could take it."

"How do you mean?"

He patted my knee, his eyes still on the sea. "Let's just say that I met a lady, and got married, and then two fine lads came along to keep us company; and that it isn't the place of a man to go a-roving when he has a family to care for."

I see now that had Mother not nearly fallen into Stranraer harbour, and he happened to be passing by, his life would have followed a very different course. He had never, as the term is, sown his oats, and by marrying and begetting a family he had debarred himself from ever doing so.

Again, the parallel with Sherlock Holmes is extraordinary to me. In Holmes's drug-taking days, his commonest retort to my protests and warnings was that he could not tolerate stagnation. "Life is commonplace. Audacity and romance seem to have passed forever. I abhor the dull routine of existence." It was only in the grip of such despondency that he had recourse to that morocco case and the syringe it contained. Yet it needed only a letter, a telegram, or some new client's foot upon our stair to transform him again to the eager man of action, with every one of his remarkable faculties alert to a problem that promised him the only sort of fulfilment he desired.

My father had no such prospect of relief. As Robert Burns put it, "Freedom and Whisky gang thegither!" and it was from the bottle that Father sought his freedom.

A small boy, like many an adult, cannot usually recognise that a man is drunk unless he falls down. Never once did I see my father in the tragicomic role of the drunken Scotsman, by turns savage and morose. Realisation came to me only one morning in 1863, when I was almost turned eleven. He had returned from one of his visits to Larne. I heard the rare sound of him and Mother arguing in raised tones behind the closed parlour door.

I hung about in the passage, unsure whether to put my ear to the door panel or take myself out of painful hearing. While I hesitated, the door suddenly flew open and Mother dashed out, her handkerchief clasped to streaming eyes. She lurched past me, groping for the banister rail, and went off up to her bedroom, sobbing loudly. A moment later, Father came out. His unusually flushed features seemed to be frozen. He stared at me, shook his head violently as though trying to clear his vision, then hurried on up the stairs out of sight.

I became aware that my brother had come into the hallway, in his sidling way, behind me. He made a wry grimace and raised a hand to his mouth, miming drinking from a glass.

"Drunk as a piper," he said.

"Mama? Drunk!"

"No, you lummock. The old man."

Henry was cleverer and shrewder than I, and knew it. At the risk of provoking me to strike him, he was always sneering at my inability to appreciate music, at my preference for adventure stories over the plays of Shakespeare and the poetry of Byron, at my inability to find any interest in the Greek and Latin mythology which intrigued him. He condescended towards me with the lofty air our Spanish forebear probably used on peasants.

"You didn't know," he sneered. "Mama said never to tell, but I'd have thought even you would have twigged by now."

Although three years Henry's junior, I was more than a match for him physically, and did not readily allow his insults to pass uncorrected. This occasion was one of the exceptions. I was bewildered, and growing frightened.

"I don't believe you. I know what Drunken Hamish is like."

The latter was a familiar figure on our harbourside. He was an old deep-sea sailorman, deprived of livelihood by age and some disease whose nature I did not know. He drank openly and fearfully, encouraged by cronies who delighted in his outrageous songs relating to the girls of Rio, 'Frisco, Sydney, and other ports which had seen his tarry presence.

"You're silly enough for a Sassenach," replied my brother, evidently sensing that he could safely take advantage of my shocked state. He went on to explain Father's condition. "Don't you see the way he walks? Afraid to put his feet down firmly. Like tiptoeing on eggs."

I wondered how I should look Father in the eye. When I came upon him next he was in the parlour, sitting in his usual placid way, puffing his pipe. I greeted him tentatively and he answered as if there were nothing out of the ordinary. Indeed, there was not; but I could see now, with dreadful clarity, that his quiet demeanour was not tranquillity but stupefaction.

Next day, when he was away at his office and Mother had gone into town, Henry came beckoning me. I have never forgotten the unfolding horror of the tour he conducted me on of a dozen innocent-seeming places in our house, in each of which he revealed a partly-full bottle.

"I feel like smashing them all!" I declared. "Are you game?"

"What good d'you think that would do? There's plenty more where those came from."

All the same, I saw Henry's habitual impatience with me fade.

"I don't know, Jack. I don't know what'll come of it, but I reckon something's bound to happen."

He was not mistaken.

Father lost his employment that same month. Being a partner, I suppose he could not be dismissed, but had to be requested to resign, with compensation. The disaster did not plunge us at once into poverty; even so, I felt the chill of fear.

Mother hid her distress bravely. Inner strength was not apparent in her build or looks. She was quite tiny, slender, giving an impression of weightlessness, were it not for the vast skirts with which women of the last century encumbered themselves. She had very fair hair, always combed back at the sides and sometimes plaited into a girlish pigtail. Her narrow neck was remarkably long and as white as her little hands. Our bracing air kept her cheeks coloured with perfectly corresponding pink patches the size of pennies, which set off her clear blue eyes. She could not have been more different in stature, looks, and colouring from my father and brother. Even before I was twelve I was her equal in height, and more thickly-built, but I fancied I could find something of her in my features.

She knew by then that I knew, but nothing was said between us. I would go to her when we were alone and touch her, in the way that a faithful dog will put up a paw for mutual reassurance. She would gather me to her, to cling silently together for some moments, sharing feelings which could not be expressed in words.

On one such occasion she guided me into the room which she and Father shared and sat me on the edge of the bed, her arm about me.

"John, I want you to be a brave, sensible boy. I know you will."

"What is it, Mama?" I asked, instantly fearful. "Please tell me the worst."

"We . . . we might have to go to America."

"America!"

"Oh, my dearest!" She gripped me fiercely to her. "Forgive me for shocking you. I should have prepared you."

She rocked to and fro with me, breathing heavily. Her

emotion was misplaced, though. For the first time in weeks a bright prospect had been opened to me. Oftentimes I had pictured in my mind that great continent from where the winds and waves which had hewn our coastline emanated. I had read of the early voyages to it; of the colonists, the backwoodsmen and trappers, the Red Indians, the brave "rebels" who acquitted themselves so splendidly against our regulars at Lexington, Bunker Hill, Yorktown, Saratoga. I had heard stories at the harbourside (I exclude those retailed by Drunken Hamish) which had made me long to visit the land of such adventures. Yet now my poor mama was almost sobbing her pity for me.

"Don't be upset, Mama. Please."

"How can I help it? To have to drag my darling off to that place... No, no. You shan't go. You shall stay here in your homeland, with Grandpa and Grandmama Hudson."

"But I'd sooner go to America."

Mother fell silent for some moments, evidently considering deeply. Then she drew a deep breath and spoke again seriously.

"You have a right to know the situation. You see, Papa has not been... very well. He's somewhat better now, and Dr. Grieves has advised him to go abroad for a while. Unfortunately, he has become very determined that it shall be to America."

"It sounds a marvellous idea."

"I don't think it is quite what the doctor had in mind."

I hastened to reassure her. "I've got lots of pictures of America," I told her, remembering as I spoke that they were mostly of mule-trains under siege from spear-brandishing Indian braves, lone trappers being pursued by wolves in snowy wastes, and other scenes scarcely likely to kindle her enthusiasm. "I'm sure we'd be happy there."

"We'll see what is for the best," she conceded. "I'm going to Bagshot to talk to Grandpa and Grandmama about it."

"Can I come?"

"No, I'm afraid not, much as I should like to take you. I wish to think things out."

"They've discovered gold in America, you know."

"So I've heard. We shall see."

Our interview ended on that inconclusive note. I little thought that when the time came to go there it would be Mother who would prove the most eager of us all.

3

"We reach, we grasp."

In order to portray Mother's state of mind at this time, and to demonstrate how it changed, I shall have recourse to brief passages from her diaries, which came to me on her death. She wrote without pretension to literary art, and certainly without thought of publication, and therefore it may be accepted that what she recorded was the unelaborated truth.

> *July 1* [1863]: Reached Bagshot hot and weary from the long train journey. Refreshments poor and railway servants disagreeable but a blessing to the eye to see leafy Surrey again. Stranraer and its problems seem far away, but on unpacking I almost expected to find some portion of them amongst my baggage. Such burdens cannot be wholly left behind.
>
> After supper, talked long with Papa and Mama, Florrie and Verbie. All expressed horror at my account of H.'s drinking (beastly word to write!). The girls especially severe, since both are now prominent in the Band of Hope movement. There is a temperance rally in

London shortly and they urge me to go with them. Too tired and low to contemplate it.

As to America, Mama believes there is prohibition of alcohol in some states (why cannot Scotland follow that example?). Papa concerned about effects of going there on Henry and John, and how we shall manage if H. does not improve. F. told horrible story of a poor Welsh girl who became widowed in some wild part out there and had to bury her husband with her own hands. And also there is a *war*!

Why didn't I fall into the harbour and have done with it?

July 2: Well rested after a most comfortable night in the old room. Went with Mama and Papa to Cousin Heliotrope's. Percy [her husband] there, but left abruptly on urgent business just as conversation turned to work of the Church of England Temperance Society, founded last year and Helio. a keen supporter. She, too, going to the meeting. Strange to think that so many of our family will be there! They urged me again, but I fear the topic would be too distressing. Helio. very stout and expecting her fourteenth.

July 3: Can scarcely wait for tomorrow's meeting! Went with Mama this morning to see Miss Dobbs, whose father helped found the United Kingdom Alliance to press for the abolition of producing and selling alcohol. They are helping organise the meeting and have secured the *Rev. Henry Ward Beecher* to speak. This great American is in England to recuperate from his strenuous ministry in New York, where American Cousin Pansy is one of his workers. He is one of the greatest of Americans, and brother of Mrs. Stowe, the authoress, whose *Uncle Tom's Cabin* made my dear little John cry so when I read it out.

It has always saddened me that the boys did not take to that fine work of Mr. Beecher's own, *Seven Lectures to Young Men,* which Pansy sent across for Henry's tenth birthday. Perhaps it was a little beyond them, but they might have returned to it, had their father not so disgracefully thrown it to the back of the fire.

There is no man in the world whose words I am more eager to hear than Mr. Beecher's. Let Papa call him "Yankee humbug." My mind is my own.

July 5: Words of mine are inadequate to describe yesterday's experience! Exeter Hall, in the Strand, was a-bustle with people and half the clergy of England, it almost seemed. Miss Dobbs said that temperance leaders from all over the kingdom were present.

How shall I describe the great man? He will be about fifty years of age, but full of energy and spirit. Of medium height, his body well developed, though rather heavy about the middle and neck. The forehead high and noble, the face clean-shaved and inclined to redness; dark hair worn long to his shoulders and flecked here and there with grey. The eyes quick and all-seeing, the mouth seeming longing to smile (which it often does). But of all these things—the voice! Where the American twang might have been anticipated, there issued only music. I never listened to such modulations except in a singer.

In manner he was like some supreme actor in total command of his stage: the grace of movement, the expressive gesticulation, the alternation of sunshine and thunder in his countenance and tone, but, above all, that voice, perfectly cadenced and pitched, so that I afterwards found I had been too rapt in the performance to heed its substance.

How glad I am I agreed to go after all!

Mother returned to us still undecided what to do for the best. I was surprised to come upon her seated in her bedroom chair, staring out of the window at the drifting sky. Her hand was cupped under her chin, and her head cocked slightly on one side, seeming to be listening to something with intense concentration. I listened too, but could hear nothing out of the ordinary. When I cleared my throat and spoke she shook her head impatiently, as if interrupted, and I went away with my questions unasked.

"What d'you suppose will happen?" I asked Henry instead.

He regarded me superciliously, then replied, "What shall you do if Papa goes anyway?"

"Without Mama? He wouldn't."

"I reckon he will, if she won't."

"Fathers don't leave their wives and families just like that."

"What about Captain Buchanan?"

That former army officer, who had lived in Stranraer, had not only left his wife and large family to sail to Australia, but had taken their cook with him. She was gaunt, red-nosed, and quite ten years older than he. Gossip had been unable to establish an improper relationship, but he was known to care a great deal about his meals.

"He was different," I objected. "But, at the worst, I should stay with Mama and you."

"Not with me. I'd go with him."

"You wouldn't!"

"See if I don't."

I thought of going to Father and pleading with him, but did

not dare. Following a brief period of activity after the idea of going had been first mooted, he had lapsed back into lethargy. I recall this as a singularly unhappy time in my life.

Being eleven, I had by now joined my brother at the school conducted in the town by the Rev. P. J. Kennedy and his wife, a pleasant enough couple who seemed concerned by my lack of ability compared with Henry's, but never made the point in his hearing, for which I was grateful to them. It was a drear routine, though, so I was elated upon arriving home one day to hear Mother singing one of the sprightlier hymns in her clear small voice, and to find her with her face aglow.

"You are happy," I said.

"Most happy, my dear. Oh, yes, I am happy."

She almost skipped away, hymning gaily. I return to her journal to explain her new mood.

Oct. 2: Wonderful news! He is back!

A letter from Miss Dobbs this morning tells me that not only is he in England again, following his Continental holiday, but has consented to give a series of public speeches. On the 13th he is in Glasgow, at the City Hall. I have written to enquire for tickets and shall persuade H. to go with me. He needs only to hear him to be impressed, and I pray it will guide him out of his trouble....

Oct. 7: It is hopeless. H. will not budge, repeating that he will not be "preached at by any Yankee," although he added that it only wants for us to go to America for our difficulties to be at an end. I see now that if I do not agree to go to that place he will go alone, or stay and become worse. My poor little John looks at me as if to say, "Mama, I would help you, but I am only a child." It is enough to break a mother's heart.

But I shall hear Mr. Beecher, if I have to go alone.

Oct. 11: My dearest little John! "Mama, *I* will go to Glasgow with you, if you will allow it." The plucky little fellow, so unlike his brother, who put out his lip when I asked if he would escort me.

We leave in the morning.

The excitement was evident from the moment we set foot in Glasgow. Beecher's name seemed to be everywhere, on banners and posters of all sizes. "Let Scotsmen see he gets the welcome he deserves!" I read, and nudged Mama to look, though on reading the text below, we found that it was a condemnation of him for purporting to preach good will amongst men while at the same time scheming to set Britons at one another's throats by dividing their sympathies between the two sides in America's Civil War. It ended: "Turn out in force and show him what good Scotsmen think of his kind!" My interest in the meeting rose considerably.

The jam to enter the City Hall was a positive scrimmage. Our seats were only three rows from the broad platform, and the din behind us was tremendous. A portion of the crowd was singing "Scots Wha Hae" in a manner which in later years I came to associate with Rugby football crowds. When a lean, frock-coated gentleman with a clerical collar emerged and tried to deliver some introductory words he was rendered inaudible by howls and hisses. At length he made a desperate gesture towards what in a theatre I should term the wings. In prompt answer there bounded forth a brisk, beaming man, also in black, though not of a clerical style, and with a dark stock artistically arranged under an upturned soft white collar. He came almost at a run, and I should not have been surprised if an unseen band had struck up a jaunty introduction to a comic song and dance.

All the accompaniment he got in lieu was an immense barrage of catcalls, screams, whoops, and imitations of yelping dogs and quacking ducks. Mother's hand seized mine fiercely. I glanced at her to reassure her, but her burning eyes were riveted on the man who stood bowing and nodding to every corner of the "house," as if he were the Dan Leno or George Robey of his time.

While the din continued, he busied himself laying out a sheaf of notes on the stand-up desk, every now and then glancing up to beam and nod again in the direction of the worst noise-makers.

"Magnificent!" I heard Mother's thrilled voice close to my ear.

Yet still the noise continued, added to by the counter-cheers and shouts of many of the more respectable element, who had turned in their seats to face the trouble-makers. I saw clergymen waving fists and their wives their handkerchieves, and noticed what I took to be a bishop, from his purple, brandishing an umbrella.

The chairman, who had retired to a chair, where he writhed and looked ready to run for his life, ventured forward at a crouch to speak to the guest. The latter merely placed a comforting hand on his shoulder, giving him a benign smile and clearly rejecting an invitation to capitulate. Those of us in the front rows applauded wildly. We were rewarded with a nod and smile.

"Don't worry, my friends," he told us, in a voice which caused Mother to grip my arm with both her hands. "I shall be heard tonight."

Then, in a manner worthy of Leno himself, he suddenly leant sideways, as if about to fall, landing one bent elbow on the desk, his head supported on his hand and his eyes closed, perfectly miming a man who had suddenly dropped off to sleep from boredom.

It was so neatly done that it made even the rowdies catch their breath. With exact timing, he opened one eye, rolled it around the assembly, and showed his teeth in a broad grin. If ever I have heard a greater cheer I cannot recall it.

He seized perfectly the opening he had made for himself. Jerking himself upright, ignoring his notes, and stepping round from behind the desk, he said, in a voice so mild that everyone strained an ear to catch his words, "No one who has been born and reared in Scotland can know the feeling with which, for the first time, such a one as I has visited this land, classic in song and in history."

Then he stopped where he stood, his arms hanging down at his sides, his large head bowed in an attitude of total humility. A murmur of approval swept the vast audience, and I heard Mother utter a little shivering moan.

Beecher's head jerked erect, and in a voice like a bull's bellow he addressed himself to the furthermost reaches of the galleries.

"I have been reared in a country whose history is brief by comparison. So vast is it that one might travel night and day for a week, and yet scarcely touch historic ground. But I come to this land of yours which, though small, is as full of historic memories as the heaven is of stars, and almost as bright."

A sweeping gesture of his arm towards the roof accompanied these last words. "Hear, hear!" began to come from the more respectable quarters of the audience, but he ignored them.

"There is not the most insignificant piece of land or stretch of water here that does not make my heart thrill with some story of heroism or well-remembered poem; for not only has Scotland had the good fortune to have had men who know how to make heroic history, but she has reared bards who have known how to sing those histories. I come to Scotland to see those scenes whose stories have stirred my imagination from my earliest youth, yea, almost as a pilgrim would go to Jerusalem itself!"

I thought the thunder of applause enough to have silenced his opposition for good; but he had another stroke to pull. Dropping his voice to no more than conversational level, and giving a respectful little nod, he said, "I can pay no higher compliment than to say that, having seen part of Scotland, I am satisfied." One eyebrow rose humorously and the smile returned to his mouth and eyes as he added, "And permit me to say that if, when you know me, you are a thousandth part as satisfied with me as I am with you, then we shall get along together very well."

Cheers, laughter, and applause mingled in a tumult of sound. Beecher made no effort to quell it, content to stand there, gesturing, bowing, beaming in every direction. I have seen many a performer work his will upon a hostile or indifferent audience by sheer bravura, but never more spectacularly than Henry Ward Beecher did that evening. I became aware that Mother was saying something to me. Her cheeks were flushed and her eyes sparkling. Her bosom heaved more rapidly than the effort of applauding needed.

"What, Mama?" I shouted back, the heels of my own palms aching.

Tears of elation were streaming down her cheeks.

"I could follow that man to the ends of the earth!"

It did not come quite to that; but at least it got us to America.

4

"It is always a joy to meet an American."

I have never known whether it was coincidence which took us to America in the same ship as Henry Ward Beecher. It was Mother who made our reservations. Her journal is illuminating only in the cryptic entry: "Miss Dobbs writes that he will attend a public farewell breakfast in St. James's Hall, Liverpool, on October 30th. He sails for Boston in the *Asia,* and we too. God grant a calm passage."

All I can add is that, after that experience in Glasgow, there was no further doubt that go we should. She chattered of little else all the way back to Stranraer. I was overjoyed, not least by the look which came into poor Father's face when she told him her decision. From that moment he was a changed man. Once more he bustled about, shaking dreadfully for the first few days, but looking eagerly determined. His old firm made arrangements to sell our house and most of its contents. We all travelled to Surrey for a brief farewell to grandparents and aunts. It was a miserable, weepy visit, and Henry and I were glad at last to be on the train to Liverpool.

"Look!" he said to me, when we went down to the docks to

inspect the *Asia* on the day before we were to board. "Guns!"

He pointed out a stack of wooden cases with rope handles, awaiting hoisting in. A man with a paintpot and brush was obliterating the particulars stencilled on them and substituting something about mining equipment.

"They'll be for the Northern army," Henry declared. "To be run through the Southerners' blockade."

"D'you suppose we'll get intercepted by one of their men-o'-war? A shot across our bows?"

"That'd put the wind up you."

"Not at all. If the Captain calls for volunteers to repel boarders, he may count on me."

My mother's prayer for a calm passage was not heeded. For days before our sailing, monumental gales had lashed our shores. I longed to experience some part of them. It seemed to me pointless to venture on to so mighty an ocean as the Atlantic without feeling something of its elemental power. The worst had passed before we sailed, but after leaving the shelter of Ireland we began to lift and drop in the great swell. The passengers disappeared *en masse* for the misery of cabins and dormitories.

I myself felt not a qualm, taking my hearty breakfast, luncheon and supper in an almost deserted dining saloon and gladly availing myself of the extra portions pressed upon me by the stewards, some of whom looked distinctly green about the gills, especially when serving pork.

The time between meals I passed almost entirely on deck. I had found myself a place on the starboard bow, below the bridge, where the rails met. There I stood by the hour, feet braced, hands clenched upon the angle of the rails, anticipating each lift and wallow, the spray wetting my face and salting my lips. I wondered whether my Spanish ancestor had felt such exhilaration aboard his galleon. If so, it was one trait my brother had not inherited. He scarcely left his bunk, which, I had occasion to be thankful for, was below mine in our narrow cabin. Father, too, remained invisible, and if Mother had indeed contrived to be aboard ship with Beecher, it profited her little.

After thirteen days and nights we made our landfall at Halifax, Nova Scotia. Little by little, pale-faced passengers crept up from the depths to take their first tottering steps for almost a fortnight. Amongst them was Mother.

"Thank God it is almost over," she groaned. "Your poor father is too weak even to stand."

"I rather enjoyed it," I was unfeeling enough to reply. "I wouldn't mind a life at sea."

My school record was so unpromising that no obvious occupation had recommended itself.

"Look, Mama. There's Mr. Beecher."

She turned swiftly, to see him walking slowly along the deck, in conversation with another clergyman. The bland expression I remembered was gone. His cheeks and eyes were sunken, his whole face drawn, and his hair seemed to have gone more grey. His skin was the colour of lard.

Mother's hand flew to her mouth. "The poor man! He must have been dreadfully ill."

Perhaps I sensed her desire to communicate, for as Beecher and his companion came by us I spoke out.

"Good evening, Mr. Beecher, sir."

They paused, regarding me with surprise.

"You know me?" said Beecher.

"I was at your meeting in Glasgow, sir. Allow me to introduce my mother, who took me there."

Beecher's wan countenance lit with gratification at being recognised. He bowed to Mother and took her hand, and then shook mine. The clergyman bowed and walked on, leaving him to us.

"Our name is Watson," Mother explained, flushing up prettily. "I am related to Miss Pansy Hudson, of your church."

"To dear Pansy? Well, well, well! I hope you had a better voyage than I did, ma'am?"

"Not very good, I'm afraid. My little John here seems to be our family's only sailor. His father and brother are still under the weather."

Beecher gave a theatrical groan and held his brow. "You know, from the moment we left Queenstown I lay flat on my back in my berth. Such a crossing! But what, ma'am, if I might ask, brings you and your family to the New World?"

I wondered how Mother would answer this. She was forestalled by a young man in uniform who excused himself and asked if he was addressing Mr. Henry Ward Beecher. To my surprise, what little colour had returned to the great man's cheeks abruptly vanished. His eyes widened and his lip quivered as he swallowed and nodded.

The young man held out a buff-coloured envelope. I saw the tremble of the hand which accepted it. The official gave a stiff little bow and marched away, leaving Beecher turning the envelope over and over, as though reluctant to open it. All at once, he raised his head, closing his eyes and mouthing something with silent lips. I presumed it was a prayer. Then he tore open the envelope with his thumb and drew out a sheet of paper.

I feared some awful tidings, and wondered whether it might be my lot to support this distinguished man against collapse. Mother glanced at me, as we shared his suspense. Then he was smiling again, and the eyes were rekindled.

"From my wife," he said, "welcoming me home."

I thought it strange that a man should shrink in obvious alarm from a greeting from his wife. But I did not know then that Beecher had cause to fear being approached by officials.

The voyage on to Boston took two days. The sea was calm. I no longer monopolised the attention of the dining-saloon stewards. Father, whose constitution must have been a good deal undermined by his drinking, was still not recovered from the voyage and remained in his cabin. Henry was up and about, airing his knowledge of America at me, as if to pay me back for having weathered the voyage better than he.

Beecher was visible a great deal about the decks. He never passed me without a smile or a wink, and always paused to chat if Mother was with me. Once I left them alone by the rail, and found them still talking when I returned after a good half-hour. They seemed to be leaning shoulder to shoulder. I fancied they stood quickly apart at my approach.

"Such . . . such a man," Mother murmured to me later. "So understanding. So wise."

"What about, Mama?"

"Oh . . . everything. Any subject under the sun."

We reached Boston and anchored in the harbour. The tide was not right for us to go in, so we had to lie tantalisingly close to the shoreline, with its myriad lights twinkling in the early evening.

I was leaning upon the rail when I felt someone come to my side. It was Beecher, hatless, so that the light breeze played with his long hair, which he did not trouble to brush away from his eyes.

"Well, young John," said he, "wondering what our great land has in store for you, eh?"

In fact, I had been thinking about the guns, which had been unloaded at Halifax, and wondering what games were now afoot to smuggle them to their destination.

"Yes, sir," I replied dutifully.

He gave a little chuckle, and startled me by saying, "Not ships and guns, then?"

He chuckled again at my astonishment and slipped an arm under mine in the friendliest way.

"You see," he went on, gazing shoreward as he spoke, "it was ships and guns I thought about when I first came here at your age, a healthy country lad with that full, red-cheeked face you have. It was in this very harbour that I first saw a ship. I stood on that shore there and gazed upon that ship, and I tell you, Johnnie, I sniffed the sea air, and stared far out across the water, and thought of all that I'd ever read of buccaneers, of naval battles, of explorations into strange seas. Almost every week after that I went over to the Navy Yard at Charlestown there. I would go up to the battery overlooking the harbour and stand behind the guns, and just wait for one of your Britishers to dare come in sight again. Imagination was the commodore, and patriotism the gunner. I tell you, Johnnie, there have been great battles fought in Boston Harbour that nobody knows anything about but me."

I laughed aloud at this happy metaphor, assuring myself that I had shared his experience in my thoughts at Black Head.

"Where's that pretty little mama of yours, this mild evening?" he asked irrelevantly.

"I believe she's sitting with Papa. He's still not well."

"I must go down and have a little chat with him directly. Maybe get him to join me in a prayer. Nothing to match prayer, Johnnie."

I wished he would talk further of guns and the sea. I strove to detain him and lead him back to them.

"The way you handled those trouble-makers in Glasgow was terrific, sir."

"Glasgow? That was a tea-party. You should have been at Manchester and Liverpool. That was a battle. My friends in those towns seemed to be looking to me to flinch and call it off. I told them, 'I will be heard,' and I just put myself in the hands of God, and I was heard, and I got my victory. Courage in action, Johnnie. Never be afraid of a fight in life. A lot of life is about fighting, and the sooner a young fellow like you learns to stand up with his face to the front, the better he'll get on."

"Pardon me, sir," a man's voice said behind us, and I do not exaggerate when I say that Beecher almost jumped out of his skin. He spun round; and whatever I saw in his expression then, it was not courage in action.

Two men stood there, one in a dark civilian suit, the other in some sort of uniform.

"Mr. Henry Ward Beecher?" this officer asked. I fully expected his next words to be something on the lines of "This is Detective Officer —— of the Boston Police Department," and for the individual to step forward and declare, "Henry Ward Beecher, it is my duty to place you under arrest in the name of the President of the United States," or whatever formula of words they used there.

The look on Beecher's face suggested that he expected something of the same. The civilian took his step forward, but at the same time extending a hand and smiling warmly.

"Glad to see you home safely, sir."

Beecher did not physically mop his brow, but I was sure he did so mentally.

"Yes, sir," the man continued. "The Press and people of America believe that your speeches in Great Britain have changed the sentiments of the British people towards our own. Single-handed, and without official urging or assistance, you have forged and cemented an alliance of understanding between the mother country and our own which requires no written treaties to ratify it. America, sir, is in your debt."

Nothing could have been further from handcuffs and a caution.

"In the morning, sir, this here Customs officer will personally clear your baggage and pass you through the formalities of going ashore. And now I bid you good night, sir, and shall ask in my prayers that the Good Lord preserve you to render further great service to the American people."

"Amen," pronounced the uniformed official, and the two

men took their leave. I had already forgotten for the moment that strange sign of fear which I had twice seen Beecher register. Like Mother, I had fallen under his spell.

"You see?" he told me. "What if I had flinched before those rowdies' threats? Suppose I had climbed down and not said, *'I will be heard'?* The course of history can hang in such a balance. And now, young sir, I must find my friend Mr. Henderson and tell him the good news from the shore. You're coming on to New York, I gather?"

"Yes, sir. We are to stay for a while with Miss Pansy Hudson."

"Then she'll surely invite you along to Plymouth Church to hear me. Make sure you look me up—and bring that pretty little mother of yours with you."

"Without fail, sir."

Henry Ward Beecher gave my arm a squeeze and left me. I stayed at the rail for a long time, staring at the Boston lights and savouring the privilege of being befriended by the greatest man on earth.

5

"The absence of the usual feminine ululation."

Many a woman of lesser education and background than my mother would have had the instinct to deal very differently from the way she did with my father, *vis-à-vis* Henry Ward Beecher.

It cannot have done much for the spirit of a man who had just endured a fortnight of seasick misery on top of a battle against a chronic drinking habit, lying prostrate in a narrow bunk and wondering what he had done to his life and his family's, to be told that amongst the tormenting footfalls on the deck above his head were those of a paragon amongst men, all-wise and willing to come down and proffer advice. It can scarcely be accorded tactful of her to have invited that paragon to visit the cabin, where he proceeded to address all four of us on the beneficial effects of suffering upon the soul.

He worked at the theme for a full hour, addressing his words directly to Father, who lay as if mesmerised. Mother's eyes never once left Beecher's face. She looked as someone might when regarding an angel.

Henry and I sat behind Beecher's back. From time to time

he gave me a surreptitious poke in the side and a prurient leer, as, for example, when Beecher proclaimed, "If ye be without suffering ye are as bastards"; and that no man ever made wine until he had first crushed the grapes, which I felt to be an unhappy allusion in view of Father's trouble. I concentrated hard to follow his progress amongst the Christian ideals, the likeness of the superstitious ancient Egyptians to swine at the trough, the views of a German phrenologist on woman's readiness for the married state (another of Henry's pokes at that), and an all-too-brief consideration of Wellington's call for volunteers to lead the storming of Badajoz. Whenever I found myself on the verge of catching its full drift, the homily took another turn and lost me. It ended with Beecher rising to his feet and adjuring Father in his most ringing tone: "Think on these things, Christian. Say unto yourself, 'I thank the Father of mercies for the afflictions wherewith I have been visited.' "

He bowed to Mother and swept out, followed by her adoring gaze. For some moments in the cabin, silence reigned. Then Father spoke for the first time.

"Violet."

"What . . . ? Oh, yes, my dear?"

"Please ring for the steward."

"One of the boys can fetch you something. Some tea or coffee?"

"Whisky. A bottle."

Mother burst into loud tears. Henry nudged me and we made ourselves scarce.

Father did not return to the bottle, however. His call for whisky was his protest at having been made to endure what he referred to as the most stupefyingly boring gush of taradiddle he had ever heard.

A few days later found us in New York, lodging with Aunt Pansy, as we boys had been told to address her, although the actual relationship was tenuous. She was a gaunt, spare spinster who shared her house with her mother, an ancient in a snow-white cap, who laughed merrily at whatever anyone said to her, though clearly not comprehending a word of it. This provided Henry with a vulgar pastime which he would not have dared indulge within earshot of our parents or Aunt Pansy.

The plan was for us to stay there for so long as it took Father to recover completely and find work. It was not a happy arrangement. Aunt Pansy was openly disapproving of him. She and mother talked by the hour of Beecher. I could see Father's irritation growing, artfully fuelled by Henry.

A forthcoming event which was causing Mother and Aunt the greatest excitement was a grand reception for Beecher, to be held in his Plymouth Church. I chanced to be loitering in the hallway when Mother told Father of this. The parlour door was ajar, and his response was of a nature to make me stay and listen.

"Violet, I wish you to have nothing more to do with that man."

"Why ever not?"

"He is a humbug."

"Are you feeling ill again, Henry? Or are you cruelly teasing me, as you did after his kind visit to you on the ship?"

"I am not ill and I am not teasing you. The man is a fraud—a regular Pecksniff."

"He is a man of God!"

"A man of straw, more like. A blatherskite. I may have slipped down in the world somewhat, but at least I knew my way about it before that. I recognise his kind. A gift of the gab is all they have—raw talk enough to bamboozle a handsome living out of gullible folk."

"That's quite untrue. He is followed by thousands."

"Innocents like you, and doting old maids like Pansy."

I heard Mother's gasp. Throughout Father's drinking days, I had marvelled at her forbearance; she never in my hearing rebuked him or challenged his fitness to remain head of the family. Now she did both. Her usually gentle voice was raised and there was the fierceness of the provoked tigress in her attack, as she declared Beecher, a man who had unselfishly dedicated his life to the service of God and his fellow men, to be worth ten of my father.

"Take care, Violet!" My father's voice had a new, cutting edge to it.

"No. It is you who need to take care. See the light he bears. Be guided by it. Follow his example, and ye too shall be saved."

She may have added "Hallelujah!" or perhaps my ears misinterpreted the scrape of Father's chair as it was flung back for him to jump to his feet. I beat a hasty and timely retreat upstairs, from where I heard the front door of the house opened and slammed shut.

"What's all that about?" enquired Henry, who was lying on his bed in his boots, reading some trashy publication. As I told him, he continued to regard his paper in that unmannerly way of his, but I could see that his eyes did not move about the page and knew that he was listening.

"What can we do?" I concluded.

"Mind our own business."

"But it is our business."

"Well, you mind your part of it, and I'll mind mine."

I was tempted to seize his paper and rip it into shreds over him, but I was too miserable. I went downstairs to look for Mother and try to comfort her. I was only half-way down when Aunt Pansy's harmonium wheezed into lugubrious life in the parlour, to be joined by her and Mother's voices in a hymn. I went instead and sat in the kitchen, where the old lady beside the stove beamed and wagged her head up and down at me.

Father was silent when he came back after an hour or two, his well-liquored breath preceding him into the hallway. I was there to see Mother hesitate, seeming to be wondering how to treat him. Aunt Pansy put her nose in the air, took her firmly by the arm, and propelled her into the parlour, closing the door behind them. Father gave me a blank look and went away upstairs. When I went up later, I heard his and Henry's voices in my parents' room. I wondered what my brother and father could be discussing so earnestly. I did not eavesdrop this time, though. I had heard enough for one day.

Beecher's welcome back to his church, to which Mother and Aunt took me, proved a far livelier experience than I had anticipated. Its dramatic sequel served to etch the details permanently upon my memory.

Those 1860s were long before the time when Brooklyn became part of New York City proper. It was a city in its own right on Long Island, noted for its number of churches. A ferry to it operated from the foot of Fulton Street, and the answer to any stranger wishing to get to Beecher's church was, "Hop aboard Fulton Ferry and follow the crowd."

Plymouth Church proved to be large and brick-built, without steeple or ornamentation. The reception was in the Sunday-school room on the second storey, whose capacity had been extended by opening up broad doors to adjoining meeting-rooms. The throng was tremendous, but we were privileged through Aunt's influence and had reserved places near the platform.

It was a dark December day, but the room was bright from gas jets. Wreaths and flowers decorated every pillar, and a beautiful girl, who gave me a radiant smile, handed out bouquets from a great pile. I would willingly have lingered to help her, but I espied two enormously long tables bearing refreshments of all kinds (except alcoholic). People were being served by smiling ladies, so I made haste to supply myself with sandwiches, cakes, trifle, ice cream, and tea. A uniformed band was rendering a potpourri of modern dance tunes. Anything less like a church occasion I could not have imagined.

Soon after I had been summoned to my seat, swollen and a little uncomfortable, the great man made his entrance to wild applause, some cheers, and the stamping of feet to the rhythm of the Germania Band's march tune. He stood there, handsome, commanding, hands upraised like a victorious sportsman. When, at long last, the tumult ended, he sat with modest mien to listen to addresses by several speakers. His response showed him in tremendous form, by turns witty, pithy, profound, and triumphant, his audience reacting as though he were a great orchestra conductor, drawing precisely desired effects from his players. The entire assemblage, myself included, leapt to their feet to surpass even that noise which had greeted him.

Then the festivities recommenced. The band swung into a selection of pieces, amongst which, the printed programme told me, were galops and polkas and the *Flirtations* waltz of Strauss. People did not actually dance, but I am sure that some must have been tempted. I made for the refreshment tables again and had return helpings of all I had eaten before.

When I was at last sated, even to admitting that I could not manage one more ice cream, I went back to our place, where I had left Mother sitting quietly alone, looking, as the saying goes, "struck all of a heap." I was delighted to find Beecher seated beside her. He was holding one of her hands in both of his. Aunt Pansy was nowhere to be seen.

"Well, young Johnnie," he greeted me, staying seated but freeing a hand to shake mine and pull me into the other chair beside him. "Enjoying yourself?"

"Very much indeed, sir. They are very pleased to see you."

"We, dearest John, *we!*" Mother startled me with her urgent correction. "We are indivisible now. One heart, one home, one happy band."

Beecher pressed her hand to his chest, saying, "I guess, young man, we shall be seeing a good deal of one another. With the Good Lord's help, you and I will care for your pretty little mother between us, and bring her to peace and contentment."

He lifted the hand and swiftly kissed its back. Then he rose and was gone, to be claimed by others.

"Aren't you having any food?" I asked Mother.

"What is food?" she murmured.

"The trifle's jolly good."

She smiled at me, her eyes moist with tears which I knew were joyful. She squeezed my arm, and I recall her shuddering sigh.

"Well," I said, "I'll just go and have one more plate, before it's finished." I left her and plunged for the last time into the crowd about the tables.

The return ferry crossing, brief though it was, proved embarrassing to me, and I was glad to reach the house and the security of the back-yard privy. When I felt confident enough to go indoors, I was greeted by the asthmatic cry of the harmonium and the conjoined voices of Mother and Aunt Pansy in that exultant hymn "Love Divine, All Loves Excelling." I went into the parlour and lingered, judging it unwise, in my indigested state, to join in.

When they had finished singing, Mother led me to a chair. She seated herself beside me, smiling through tears.

"My dearest, you must be very brave."

"What is it, Mama?"

"Your . . . your father, and Henry . . ."

Sudden fear gripped me. I had been too busy since our return to wonder where they were in the house.

"They have gone."

For a blind moment, I thought it was her euphemism for death. Aunt Pansy chimed in, preceding her words with a long-nosed exhalation of disapproval.

"Nothing more than a note on the mantelpiece. Downright scandalous, but what one might have expected."

"Pansy, please. Not before little John."

"He must know the truth. And you should stop calling him 'little.' He's bigger than you." The nose swivelled to aim at me like a warship's turret gun. "Your father and brother have taken themselves off to California. They sailed this evening. They must have been planning this for days, weeks."

"The gold diggings?"

"Some such folly, I guess."

"Why couldn't we have gone with them?" I asked Mother.

"Because I was not consulted. Had I been, I should have refused. You would have wanted to stay with me, wouldn't you?"

I could only nod. It was what I had told Henry I should do. I confess, though, I felt a great envy of their adventure, which, given better circumstances, I should dearly like to have shared.

My condition so preoccupied me that night that I was unable to absorb the full implications. When I woke next morning, to find I had the shared bedroom to myself, my first feeling was of release.

It was a sunny morning, crisply cold. Aunt Pansy was singing in the kitchen. Mother greeted me with a smile and a firm hug, and the old lady by the hearth gave me her grin. My stomach was at peace, offering no objection to eggs, ham, hash browns, toast, and coffee. Taken all in all, life seemed tolerable enough.

6

"You were recalling the incidents of Beecher's career."

Beecher was early upon the scene, with a great deal to say to Mother and me on matters of right and wrong, liberty by bondage, and the microscopic conscience, with some observations on Nicodemus and the re-birth. It seemed to do Mother good.

On the point of leaving, he paused, frowning thoughtfully, then said, "Ma'am, I have been visited by an idea. Miss Pansy will have told you how much of my time is taken up with literary work. Bonner, of the *Ledger,* is on to me to write an article a week, and now he's pushing me to do a novel for him to serialise.* On top of that, there is the ministry and all it entails."

"It is a great load for you, Mr. Beecher."

"God's burden, from which I don't shrink. The point is, ma'am, would you care to share a portion of it with me?"

"I! What could I do?"

"Assist me. There are many things: editorial, secretarial, handling my engagements. . . ."

**Norwood*, published in the New York *Ledger*, 1867–68.

"But I am unqualified."

"'By love serve one another.' *Love,* Mrs. Watson, is the only qualification necessary. Through love, all can be achieved."

I saw Mother's doubts slip away. "Very well," she responded huskily. "Teach, and I will serve."

So she became his assistant, waiting on him daily. Or rather, he waited on her, for she found she was not welcome in his home. His wife, Eunice, was plain, stern, and as sharp and cold as any icicle. She treated the man who could sway thousands with his presence and voice like any cur. Apparently, she denied his friends admittance, squashed his enthusiasms, superintended the household budget, from which she gave him only a paltry allowance, and even opened and read all his mail. Yet they had several children. It seemed paradoxical, until I grew old enough to understand more about men and women.

So he came to Aunt Pansy's, and Mother and he spent long hours closeted together. I had been put into a school in the neighbourhood, where Aunt was a teacher. Having run home in the afternoons, I would go at once to the parlour to greet Mother. Sometimes Beecher was still with her, and they would chat lightly with me.

One afternoon, I returned as usual and went to the parlour door. It was closed and, to my surprise, locked. I knocked and called to Mother. She called back to me to wait, but it was quite some time before the door opened. Her complexion was strangely flushed. Beecher stood with his back to me, looking down into the fireplace. He did not turn with his usual brisk welcome. I thought he was meditating deeply.

"The door was locked," I told Mother.

"So it was. The key must have got turned accidentally."

A few weeks later, during an afternoon playtime rough-and-tumble, I gashed my knee. Aunt Pansy, who declared she could not stand the sight of blood, said, "You had best get along home and have your mama fix you up."

I was glad to be excused the last part of the school day, and hobbled back to the house. I thought I had better go in by the back door, rather than risk bleeding on to the parlour carpet. Aunt kept no maid, on principle, but the door was unlocked, New York being a vastly different place in those days. The old lady beside the stove gave me her silent, senile greeting.

When I had cleaned my wound, I went to the parlour. Its door stood ajar. The fire was alight and papers scattered about, as usual. Both Mother's and Beecher's chairs were pushed back from the table, at which they found it convenient to work side by side. There was an odd atmosphere.

As I stood there, wondering why I should have a strong impression that, for some reason, they had precipitately left that room together, I heard their voices. Turning, I saw them coming down the stairs, and his arm was about her.

I was unschooled in the "facts of life," except for some things Henry had told me, which I was sure he had made up to shock me. I had some notion that a lady and gentleman did not properly go upstairs together, unless they were wife and husband. Beyond that my awareness did not carry me. All I thought I saw in Mother's startled expression was concern for me.

"I cut my knee," I said. "Aunt sent me home."

Greater experience would no doubt correctly have interpreted the look they exchanged as "What shall we do?" on Mother's part, and "Leave me to handle it" from Beecher.

"Poor fellow," he exclaimed, coming quickly over to stoop and examine the injury. "Why, that's quite a gash he has here. But nothing that can't be taken care of, eh, Mrs. Watson?"

They bore me limping into the kitchen, where Mother bound my wound. Then Beecher said, "Come on into the parlour with me, Johnnie, and we'll have a little chat, while your dear mother makes us a cup of tea."

She assented readily, and he took me off. In the parlour he put me into a chair and set himself before the fireplace, rubbing his hands briskly and giving me his warmest smile.

"Yes, sir," he declared. "That's some view."

"What view, sir?"

"Why, from the landing window up there. Your mama and I were just looking out at it. You don't say you never noticed it?"

I seemed to remember that the landing window gave on to nothing save neighbouring roof-tops.

"Not really, sir."

"Tut-tut. Always use your eyes, you know. I guess that's why the Almighty gave 'em to you."

That was an acceptable proposition. "I'll go up and have a look," I said.

"No point in going specially. How's that knee feeling?"

"It throbs a bit."

"The good blood pumping. Yes, Johnnie, that's a great view from up there, but when you go to look at it you'll probably say to yourself, 'Those are only roof-tops!' " He chuckled. "Just what your dear mama said, when I took her to look. Do you know why I did that?"

"No, sir."

"Well, see, we'd been sitting here at our work when somehow we got on to discussing imagination. It's a great force, the power of imagination. There are folk who say, 'I guess when the Good Lord got around to doling out my share He found He was scraping the barrel.' They're wrong, though. It's in all of us, in full measure. All it wants is application. Take that harmonium, for example. Now, deep down, every soul on earth is capable of playing that harmonium, if he could but learn to muster his resources. I tell you, the wildest savage in Africa has it in him to master that instrument, should he be so willed."

The notion of an African native in full war-paint pedalling "Abide with Me" out of Aunt's harmonium was an appealing if unlikely one. Beecher had that power of employing the incongruous to obtain his effects.

"It's the same with imagination," he went on. "We all have it in equal measure, but only some of us cultivate it. 'Look not on those as roof-tops,' I told your mama. 'Think not of them as mere commonplaces of existence. Imagine flying out over them, gently lifting them off, peeping in at what is taking place beneath them, the dramas, the arguments, the scenes of despair and joy.'†

"That is what your mama and I were doing up there," he concluded, just as she entered with the tea-tray. I cannot help smiling now as I think how near she must have come to dropping it. But he briefly told her what he had been saying. Her aghast look cleared and she served the tea.

"Tell me, Johnnie," he resumed at length, "do you have any particular future in mind for yourself? Your life's work?"

I had no notions. Hoping to flatter him, I suppose, I blurted out, "I shouldn't mind being a preacher."

"A preacher, eh? And what would you preach?"

"The, er, word of the Lord."

"Do you know what that is, Johnnie?"

"Well, er . . ."

I strove to recall things I had listened to him saying in public and in private. I sought to picture myself in that vast hall, holding thousands enthralled with my ruminations about the metaphysical significance of roof-tops. The vision would not solidify.

†cf. Holmes in *A Case of Identity.* His and Beecher's philosophies had elements in common.

He was smiling, as he went on to address himself as much to Mother as to me.

"Tell you what, Johnnie. Why don't you just slip up there and take a look out over those roof-tops? Then come back down here and tell me what you make of them."

I obeyed. As I thought, there was nothing inspiring in that view. I could picture nothing interesting concealed by those flat and angled surfaces of dreary wood and iron. After a time I gave up and went down. Mother and Beecher were moving, as though they had been standing near together. She had her flushed cheeks again.

"I don't think my imagination is much good, sir," I admitted.

Beecher patted my shoulder. "Can't have too many sermonisers about the place, or I'd lose my congregations."

"I should like to do some good in the world," I persisted with my best intentions.

He regarded me, then raised an eyebrow. "How about doctoring?"

"Don't you have to be very clever for that?"

"Plenty get by without. No imagination needed, if that's what you mean."

"Very well," I resolved. "I will be a doctor."

"It's settled, then," he beamed. "Suit you, ma'am?"

"If you recommend it, I'm sure it's right," Mother replied. If he had told her I should one day learn to float out of windows, I am sure she would have believed him.

A few weeks after this last event, there occurred a major débâcle. A famous victory by the Northern armies having been suddenly announced, the principal of the school declared an immediate half-holiday. Aunt Pansy and I walked home together.

As on that previous occasion, the parlour was empty, the working table abandoned. I suggested to Aunt that Mother and Beecher would no doubt be found sharing inspiration from the view from her landing window. With a surprisingly grim face, she told me to stay where I was, and sped upstairs.

I was not told quite what she found. Suffice it to say that Beecher hurried from the house shortly afterwards, his countenance pale and strained, without pausing to take his usual fulsome leave of me. I heard Mother sobbing, and Aunt's voice upraised. We left the house that night, with our belongings, for an hotel.

We saw nothing more of Aunt Pansy, nor of Beecher. Mother told me only that we were going back to England, where we should live with Grandfather and Grandmother at Bagshot.

"But your work for Mr. Beecher, Mama—"

"We will say nothing more of it, or him. It does not do to allow oneself to be carried away with . . . with religious fervor."

Poor Mother's short life was drawing to a close before the "Beecher Scandal" burst upon the public, with his trial in 1875, in City Court, Brooklyn, for alleged adultery with the wife of his close friend and associate Theodore Tilton, five years earlier. The hearing lasted no less than 112 days. At the end of it, the jury could not agree upon a verdict, but the damage had been done. The American press feasted upon the details, with cartoons, lampoons, and every sort of critical comment.

It was widely reported in Great Britain, also—although, fortunately, we were able to keep the news from my mother, in her failing state of health—and similar innuendo flew. I have an approximate note of the great George Meredith's comment: "Guilty or not, there is a sickly snuffiness about the religious fry that makes the tale of their fornications and adulteries absolutely repulsive to read of. It disgusts one more than a chronicle of the amours of costermongers."

I was a medical student by this time, and a great deal more

worldly-wise. My suspicions of his association with Mother were put beyond doubt when I read that his visit to Great Britain, ostensibly in order to rest from the strain of his ministry work, had in fact been prompted by a need to make himself scarce from his own country for a time, following the deathbed confession of the young wife of another of his workers, named Bowen, that she had behaved improperly with Beecher. At last I understood his shipboard dread of being approached by official-looking persons.

I do not believe he was a lecher. He seems to have needed women's comfort and emotional stimulus, but was more susceptible to them than was good for him in his role. Like many great orators, he was sentimental and easily moved by his own words. As he extemporised, for my gullible benefit, that nonsense about the view from Aunt Pansy's landing window, he no doubt convinced himself that he meant it.

He was one of those religionists, not uncommon in the United States, who see themselves almost as chief executives of a vast corporation, whose president happens to be the Almighty. The commodity they purvey is love; and love is a product which comes in many varieties. Little wonder if the executive should find it necessary to familiarise himself with the range of goods.

''You remember,'' said Sherlock Holmes, ''that when I read you the passage in one of Poe's sketches in which a close reasoner follows the unspoken thoughts of his companion, you were inclined to treat the matter as a mere *tour de force* of the author. On my remarking that I was constantly in the habit of doing the same thing, you expressed incredulity. So when I saw you throw down your paper just now and enter upon a train of thought, I was happy to have the opportunity of reading it off.''

''Do you mean to say that you read my train of thought from my features?''

"The features are given to man as the means by which he shall express his emotions, and yours are faithful servants. Perhaps you cannot recall how your reverie commenced?"

"No, I cannot."

"Then I will tell you. After throwing down your paper, you sat for half a minute with a vacant expression. Then your eyes fixed themselves upon your newly-framed picture of General Gordon, and I saw by the alteration in your face that a train of thought had been started. Your eyes flashed to the unframed portrait of Henry Ward Beecher which stands upon the top of your books. Then you glanced up at the wall, and your meaning was obvious. You were thinking that if the portrait were framed it would just cover that bare space and correspond with Gordon's picture over there."

"You have followed me wonderfully!"

"So far I could hardly have gone astray. But now your thoughts went back to Beecher. You were recalling the incidents of his career. I remember your expressing your passionate indignation at the way in which he was received by the more turbulent of our people at the time of the Civil War. When, a moment later, I saw your eyes wander away from the picture, I suspected that your mind had now turned to that war, and when I observed that your lips set, your eyes sparkled, and your hands clenched, I was positive that you were thinking of the gallantry which was shown by both sides. But then your face grew sadder; you shook your head. You were dwelling upon the horror and useless waste of life. Your hand stole to your old wound and a smile quivered on your lips, which showed me that the ridiculous side of this method of settling international questions had forced itself upon your mind."

"Absolutely!" said I.

"Superficial, my dear Watson."

That example from my annals has been adduced down the years as a prime instance of my great associate's unique gift of observation and deduction. The truth is that his own term, "superficial," could not be more appropriate to it.

Despite our many years together, Holmes and I were never wholly frank with each other about our past lives. To have corrected him at the time would have necessitated revealing those particulars which I have just recounted. That was not our way; hence my readiness to let his erroneous theory go unchallenged.

But for Henry Ward Beecher, my life would have followed an entirely different course. I should not have been what I am; and, in all probability, I should never have met Holmes, whose career, I might modestly claim, would perhaps therefore have passed unchronicled to the world. Small wonder, then, that thoughts of that great but flawed American should continue to stir my emotions from time to time, causing my eyes to sparkle at the recollection of his wizardry with words, my hands to clench at remembering his gallantry in facing the Glasgow mob, and then, the sadness at all that had come afterwards.

My wound, like some of life's other wounds, might never have been sustained but for Beecher and the course he suggested for me. But the smile which Holmes saw quiver on my lips was evoked by the memory of joys which, by that same token, I might have missed.

I have taken Beecher's portrait down from its present place above my books to examine it closely for the first time in many years. It has no intrinsic value. It is a steel engraving, given free in 1870 by a minor American religious journal, *Christian Union,* to any subscriber who could introduce two others. I found it on a penny stall in the Charing Cross Road. Someone had taken the trouble to back and stretch it roughly, but it had no frame.

I had no money to spare for picture-framing when I bought it, and so it found its way, as such things will, on to a mantelpiece, and subsequently anywhere else it could be propped. Whenever I have thought of framing and hanging it, something has made me hold off. After writing this passage of my memoir, I know why. My attitude toward Henry Ward Beecher remains ambivalent. To take the positive step of placing his portrait on my wall would be to accord him that unreserved respect of which I am not capable.

There, Holmes: had you known as much as my reader does, could you have deduced that?

7

"Now, Watson, the fair sex is your department."

Thus it was that, in consequence of my mother's infatuation, I was led into my life's profession. My discovery of that unfortunate liaison and of the particulars of Beecher's earlier escapade did not invalidate his advice. More than ever, now, I needed to set my sights on some career that would ensure my independence of Mother's support, and doctoring seemed as good a prospect as any.

Also, there was before me the example of my grandfather, Mother's father. He owned a large house on a tree-lined avenue in the best residential neighbourhood of Bagshot, with a semicircular sweep of broad driveway to accommodate his smart carriage and those of the wealthy patients who came to consult him. It had always been my impression that he spent more time pruning his roses or reading the newspaper, or poring over the extensive coin collection which occupied several tall cabinets in his study, than attending to any sort of medical work, which he largely delegated to assistants. His income must have been more than merely comfortable, though, for the house was grandly and lavishly furnished, and he supported Grandmother and my two maiden aunts in correspondingly idle luxury, with half a dozen servants of various grades to deal with every domestic task.

He was a kind, friendly old man, stout, urbane, and silver-haired, who had never struck me as awesomely clever, yet in his day he had passed along that same road which I was to tread. If he could succeed and prosper, I believed I could.

That prospect was the one positive aspect for my thoughts to feed on during the voyage home. There was no Beecher to stimulate me this time. Mother spent most of her time in the single cabin, which seemed to me to be significantly narrower and more gloomy than the comparatively spacious one which she and Father had shared on the passage out. She went without many meals, and several times, when going to try to persuade her to the dining room, I found her with reddened eyes. I never discovered her reading or doing anything specific; she simply sat, communing silently with her misery.

It was natural that we should go to Grandfather's to live. Mother's state gave her sisters some cause to become animated, and I think they looked upon Father's defection as no bad thing. I never heard Beecher mentioned, and saw no signs of recriminations against Mother, so presumed that Aunt Pansy had at least had charity enough not to report what had occurred. But I found the atmosphere of the household oppressive and heard with some relief the news that I was to go back to school as a boarder at the recently-opened Royal Medical Benevolent College at Epsom, about twenty miles from Bagshot.

"It is an excellent place," Grandfather told me. "Founded in '55, when you would have been about three, to provide for aged medical men and doctors' widows in reduced circumstances."

"But I'm not either of those, Grandpa!"

He smiled. "You will scarcely ever qualify as the latter. As to the former, if you will follow my example you will have no need of institutions in your old age. No, the school is an addition to the foundation, to offer a general education to doctors' sons."

"I'm not even that."

"I have, ahem, a little influence with one of the governors. I was able to let him have a silver 'penny' of Offa. Eighth century. A wonderful coin, not equalled again in England until Henry VII. But come over here, and I'll show you my own specimen."

It was evidently a foregone conclusion that his fellow numismatist could influence the Board of Governors in my favour, and so I entered the college that year, 1864, aged twelve. It was a pleasant place in about eighteen acres. There were 150 of us boarders and an enthusiastic teaching staff. I determined to do my best, and in 1869 passed the Matriculation of London University in English, practical philosophy, chemistry, and mathematics, even scraping through in French, Greek, and Latin.

It was a dreary span of years, though, with the prospect of still more to be given over to medical studies. I sometimes envied Henry in the gold-fields, from where no news reached us. My restless energy found its outlet on the Rugby field. Being heavily built, I was an asset in the scrum, and I was never loath to tackle hard. Within a short time, I became the youngest member of the First XV.

There was one other "sport" for which I discovered a natural inclination while at Epsom. I have continued to play it, on and off, throughout my life. Was it not one of the old Greek sages who, when asked at what age a man ceased to be interested in women, replied that he had not yet found out that answer? Such would be my own response; and in view of my often-quoted claim to an experience of women of many nations and on three continents (more, actually), I will end my account of my boyhood by describing how it began.

Our school had a staff of maidservants. We called them by their first names, and the most presentable of them by far was Aggie. She would be a few years younger than my mother, but buxom and robust, with polished pink cheeks and shiny black hair. She seemed to me to move with the utmost grace, in her fetching black-and-white uniform.

One afternoon, when I was reading the fixture lists on a corridor notice-board, I felt a nudge in my side. Spinning round into a naturally defensive posture, I was astonished to find Aggie smiling at me. There was no one else about.

"I seen you," she said in a low tone. Her mode of speech did not match her looks.

"Seen me what, Aggie?"

"Givin' me the eye."

"A . . . a cat may look at a king. I mean queen."

"There's looks and there's *looks*."

She stood a little closer to me.

"You're a fine big chap. Be leaving soon, I 'spect."

"Not I, worse luck. I'm only in the fourth form."

"You never!"

"How old d'you suppose I am, Aggie?"

"Eighteen. Seventeen, mebbe."

"Actually, I'm fifteen."

She looked me up and down with open curiosity. "Fifteen—and never bin kissed, I bet."

She gave me a look in the eyes which froze the back of my neck, and went away with a wink. Unaccustomed as I was to such banter between the sexes, I could not fail to recognise the significance of my body's response.

The encounter lay at the forefront of my mind for days. Wherever I went I looked for her. The mere glimpse of a maid's black frock and white bands made my heart thump. When at last I saw her approaching, I was in a group of other boys, and although I looked hard at her she passed by without a glance.

"I wouldn't mind a tussle with that one," remarked Sturges, a lout with a ready fund of salacious jokes.

"She's old enough to be your mother," sniggered his friend Williamson.

"You don't look at the clock while you're poking the fire," Sturges rejoined, and they reeled about, laughing and thumping each other. Rather than risk my interest in Aggie becoming suspected, I bit back a rebuke.

At the end of the afternoons the maids cleaned the classrooms, working two to a corridor, although not in the same room together. Having observed this carefully, I lingered one afternoon until the coast was clear and then slipped into the classics room, which I had seen Aggie enter some minutes earlier. I gave the door a little push behind me, so that it swung almost shut.

Aggie was bending deliciously at her mopping. She heard me come in and looked round.

"Oh, hello, Aggie." I feigned my surprise. "I left some books. Sorry to tread on your wet floor."

She had straightened up to place her mop in its pail. She brushed back a fallen strand of the fine black hair. Her cheeks were extra-crimsoned from her labours.

"I can go over it again."

She rested her chin on the hands grasping the mop handle and regarded me.

"Don't think I haven't seen you lookin' still. I can feel them eyes in the back of me head."

"Not only there, Aggie."

"Saucy! You bin kissed yet?"

"Fat chance."

She left the mop upright in the pail and came round to me, wiping her hands on her apron. She took my hands and drew them right round her waist, in the same movement pressing her body against mine. Her arms came up to encircle my neck, and she was kissing me full on the lips.

Excitement, wonder, alarm, even, prickled through me from head to foot like an electric charge. Without disrespect to those many other ladies who have enhanced my life, no kiss has ever produced such a gamut of sensations as that first one from Aggie Brown.

"There," she said, leaving hold of me and withdrawing behind her bucket. "Now you have."

"Th—thank you, Aggie."

"'Sall right, love. Any time."

"You mean that?"

"Nice big feller like you, yes. Only I got me work to get on with, an' you wouldn't want catchin' at it, would you?"

"Certainly better not!"

"'Certainly better not.' You speak nice, too. Bet you're good at other things."

"I'm in the Rugger XV."

"I didn't mean that, love. Go on now. Get your books and hop it."

"Books?"

"The ones you came in for. Hey—you come in after me, didn't you?"

"Well . . ."

"Randy young b——! We'll see, then. Ta-ra."

She resumed mopping. Pausing only to admire her figure as she worked, I went to the door, peered out, and made my safe escape.

The reader who is familiar with my narrative *The Naval Treaty,* in which Sherlock Holmes brought about the resignation of the then Foreign Minister, Lord Holdhurst, will recall that the innocent pawn in the affair was Holdhurst's nephew, Percy Phelps, a former schoolmate of mine. I have never revealed until now how I myself made use of that same Phelps in furtherance of my adventure with Aggie Brown.

"Tadpole," as he was known at our college, was little more

than my age, but two classes ahead of me. He was a brilliant scholar who preferred swotting to playing games. This predilection, together with his boasting about his politician uncle, and how he himself could have got into Eton, Harrow, or Winchester, had he been so disposed, made him understandably unpopular. His nickname was apt, and his weediness made him a natural victim for our bullies.

I have always detested bullying and bullies. Because I was strong and useful with my fists I suffered none myself, but can say honestly that I never used my physical advantage to browbeat a weaker boy. Rather, I made it my business to reason their oppressors into leaving them alone. If they refused, I thrashed them into doing so.

One day I heard a commotion going on, and turned a corner of the chapel to find Phelps with his back to the wall, facing Sturges, Williamson, and others of their ilk. They were closing in on him, telling him that if he would not take off his trousers, they would do it for him and drive him round the grounds without them.

"Please, no," he bleated. "It's humiliating."

"Get 'em off, Tadders."

"Let's have his other things, too."

"Run him starkers past the maids' quarters."

"Nothing for them to look at."

Laughing and whooping, they surged towards him. I leapt after them, seized two by their jacket collars, and hurled them behind me.

"Lay off him, Sturges," I told their ringleader, who had turned to face me angrily.

"What's up with you, Watson? It's only Tadpole."

"Against seven of you."

"Tadders is used to a rag."

"He's scared stiff."

"Poor little swot. Izzums frightened, den?"

"I told you, Sturges—leave him."

"Spoony on dear little Tadders, are you?" Williamson leered. The next instant he was howling, with blood pouring from his nose.

"Come on," I challenged. "Who's next?"

I saw them exchange glances, considering tackling me all together. None was ready to make the first move.

"Going to put 'em up?" I demanded of Sturges. He backed off. I swung round on the rest, my fists up, but there were no takers. They broke up and trailed away, Williamson moaning and reeling with pain.

"You get at him behind my back and I'll beat the daylights out of the lot of you," I shouted after them. They made no retort.

"Thanks awfully, Watson," said Phelps behind me. "It was awfully decent of you."

"You ought to stand up to their sort," I admonished him. "Bullies are cowards at heart."

"So am I, I suppose."

"At least show some fight. Even if it means taking a few knocks, they'll give you more respect."

"It's all right for you to talk, a great heavy chap."

"You'd have found it rougher going at Eton or Harrow," I replied contemptuously, and left him.

A couple of weeks later he approached me. "I say, Watson, you wouldn't care to come over to our place at Woking next exeat? We've a croquet lawn and a billiards table, and Cook does marvellous eats."

"Why do you invite me?"

"For warning off Sturges and those others. They haven't come near me since."

"Well, I always go home to Bagshot. But I'll write to my mater and ask if she won't mind."

"Do. We'll have a spiffing time."

So I did, and a spiffing time we had. Their house, Briarbrae,* stood in extensive grounds close to the station. I had one of its seven bedrooms for that night, and my things, such as they were, were laid out for me for the first time in my life by a servant.

Although Tadpole was no player of physical games, his natural grasp of geometry and trigonometry made him formidable at croquet. I enjoyed its attendant ritual of tea, delicate sandwiches, and three varieties of cake, taken in the garden beneath a magnificent cedar tree, because a warm Indian Summer was at its glorious best just then. That evening gave me my first taste of billiards. Again, Tadpole's eye for angles enabled him to win handsomely, but I took to the game and have spent many happy hours since at Thurston's rooms off the Strand and subsequently in Leicester Square.

"Do come again, Watson," said Mrs. Phelps, seeing us off.

"I'd like to very much, thank you."

She was charming to me without condescension. Phelps himself was an agreeable enough chap, when he ceased to boast, which I suppose was his attempt to make up for lack of physique.

It was on the very next day, back at college, that I got another conversation with Aggie. This time it was accompanied by more than one kiss. I could sense that her enjoyment matched mine.

"Where do you go on your days out?" she asked, breathing hard, so that her fine bosom moved against me.

I told her. She gave me a speculative look.

"Ever bin to Cremorne?"

"The pleasure gardens? No, never."

"They're ever such fun. Bands. Dancing. Fireworks. All

*Phelps inherited it later, upon the death of his widowed mother. It was the scene of our recovery of the naval treaty.

sorts of acts.'' She leered. ''Specially in the little shelters they have for them what wants to be private.''

''You . . . you mean—''

''You fancy your kiss and cuddle. Never know your luck.''

I recall my difficulty in swallowing. ''I've just had exeat. There won't be another for weeks.''

''They'll have shut for the winter by then. My half-day's Saturday. You think about it.'' She gave me another hard kiss, then thrust me away with a loud sigh, to resume her work.

8

"What was the fair lady's game?"

Aggie was almost my only thought during the days following. Several times I was reprimanded for inattention in class. We were into the autumn Rugger season. In a practice match, sheer lack of concentration made me fumble a pass which could have sent our forwards through to a certain try. Our newly appointed captain addressed me scathingly, saying that I should have to look out for my place if I did much of that sort of thing. Yet my thoughts continued in ferment by day, and even more so by night. I imagined suspicion in everyone's glance. I realised that I had to fulfil my assignation with Aggie without more delay—but how?

Then I remembered Tadpole Phelps. Because he played no team games, his Saturday afternoons were free, and he enjoyed a special dispensation which added to his unpopularity. His late father had been a founding governor of the college, and his place had been taken on his death by his uncle, Lord Holdhurst. No doubt through this influential connection, and because Woking was so near, Phelps was allowed home on Saturday afternoons.

I sought him out. "Hello, Tadpole. Those fellows still leaving you in peace?"

"Thanks to you, Watson."

"You'll let me know if they start up again, won't you?"

"I jolly well will."

"Rely on me. Oh, er, by the way... those special exeats you're allowed at weekends—you can't take other chaps with you, I suppose?"

His pale face brightened. "You'd like to come to Briarbrae again? I can get Mater to write to the Head."

"It's deuced decent of you, Tadders. The point is, though, I want to go into London. I'm a bit mad on the theatre, you know, and there's something I particularly want to see; only I'd never get permission." Before he could ask which play it was I added, "I hate to ask, only you did say that if ever there was anything you could do for me..."

"You want them to think you've gone home with me?"

"That was the idea. I hadn't thought of your mater having to write, though."

He gave me a sly look. "She needn't."

The letter which Tadpole produced on a sheet of his mother's headed paper was a gem of imitation. He showed me one of her letters to compare the handwriting. Suffice it to say that my outing was granted. With the season not yet in full swing, I had no match next Saturday. I managed to communicate this hastily to Aggie, who whispered to me to meet her on Croydon Station, where one changed trains from Epsom to London, and to dress as little like a schoolboy as I could manage.

The wait for the appointed day was exquisite agony. I forced my attention to my studies for fear of getting my leave cancelled. But all was well, and early that Saturday afternoon, Tadpole and I left the college grounds together, soon to go our separate ways. I took off my stiff collar and tie and donned a loose cravat, an effect which I had studied before my mirror and felt made me look twenty at least.

I glanced cautiously round the Croydon platform, in case any other members of the staff should chance to be going into town. I saw none save Aggie, and thrilled at the sight of her.

She was all in green. A dark green skirt flared out from her fine hips and was hitched up at the hem to reveal a lighter green underskirt, and button-up kid boots with green tassels. A little overcoat was in another shade of green, decorated all round with green braid figuring. Her curly-brimmed hat of light green velvet was topped with a froth of green lace.

Her gleaming black hair was drawn back and up, to reveal her ears. Her cheeks were not their usual red, and I saw with a catch of my breath as I drew close that they were powdered and that her eyes were outlined with some artificial colouring. The transformation from the school maid was total.

"I say, Aggie, you look like a duchess."

"You'd pass for a young dook yourself."

"Have you been waiting long?"

"I come on the same train as you."

"I didn't see you!"

"You wasn't meant to. Best take no chances."

The expedition was becoming worthy of a tale of intrigue and adventure. Aggie was certainly dressed for one. I thought her clothes must have cost a lot of her wages. That reminded me of the financial aspect.

"By the way, I've got the best part of a guinea. I hope it will be enough for everything."

She smiled. "Special rate for you, lovey."

"But you said I wasn't to look like a school chap."

"I didn't mean the gate money."

Our train came in. There was an empty carriage just behind the locomotive, where people were afraid to travel in case of a collision. We got in readily, but just as the guard's whistle sounded a door was wrenched open and a group of loud-talking railway officials scrambled in. Aggie touched my hand with a green-gloved one and murmured, "Never mind, lovey. There'll be time enough. What time you got to get back?"

I realised with horror that I had made no arrangement with Tadpole to co-ordinate our return. It would have been difficult anyway.

"Not much after eight, I suppose."

"A lot can happen in six hours. Specially at Cremorne."

The years of the Cremorne Pleasure Gardens were already numbered. They were the last survivor of their kind, once elegant and fashionable, in the pleasant setting of what had been part of Lord Cremorne's estate in Chelsea. By the 1860s, however, they were fast sliding towards that debasement which brought their closure under pressure of complaint from neighbouring residents about the noise and misbehaviour of those who frequented them, including plenty of the Chelsea-ites themselves. The late-season attendance was thin, with some of the entertainment booths already closed. In spite of this, it was a place of excitement to me as I strolled its paths with Aggie, her green arm now in mine, pressing her green side against me and giving me little squeezes at each new vista of tawdry decoration.

"It's better later on," she assured me. "The bands really get goin', and the lights come on, and the toffs come across the river from Battersea in their fig for dancin' and what-have-you."

"You've been quite a few times, then?"

"Oh, yeh. Bit of a reg'lar, you might say. Pity you got to go back so early. The lights is real nice."

"I'm . . . not so interested in the lights."

"Ooh, naughty! You got to wait a bit yet."

We sampled a few of the entertainments. I had a go at a

shooting booth and earned her admiration, as well as the proprietor's chagrin, by the accuracy with which I won back the fee and a cheap prize, which I gave her. I bowled at skittles and knocked them all down first shot. Aggie squealed with delight and a few heads turned our way. I took her arm boldly and strutted along, feeling quite the toff myself.

The daylight was fading at long last. Gas-lamps were being lit by men with poles, creating some effect of gaiety. At least three bands were playing at their scattered locations. The arbours which I had noticed amongst the trees and shrubbery were darkening and some were occupied by entwined couples.

"Fancy a little something to drink?" asked Aggie.

"If you would."

"I could go a sherry."

"Very well. So could I."

I had never touched alcohol. It had not entered the context of my life, except in its unhappy connection with my father. But this evening was clearly one for innovations.

We entered a rustic booth, surprisingly sumptuously furnished and decorated and lit by gas jets under coloured globes. Men and women were sitting at small tables, drinking. Most of the men were middle-aged or elderly, all well dressed, wearing top hats and sporting buttonholes. The women with them looked too young to be their wives. They were as colourfully dressed as Aggie, and the artificial colouring on their faces showed up in the weird light. I saw one of them look at Aggie and me as we came in. She nudged the girl nearest her to look as well. They smiled together, and I was sure they were thinking what a fine pair we made.

A side-whiskered waiter with a very red face and an Irish accent came to take our order. He seemed to have a nervous tic, for he winked at Aggie and jerked his head.

"We will have two glasses of sherry, please," I ordered.

"Yes, sorr." Another jerk of his head.

"Big 'uns," said Aggie, frowning at him.

"Yes, A — madam."

He went away. Aggie placed her long-handled green parasol against the table and said to me, "Will you 'scuse me a sec, lovey? I just seen a uncle of mine over there, and he'll take it bad if I don't say how-do."

She got up and went away in the direction in which the afflicted waiter's head had kept jerking. A silver-haired gentleman was sitting alone, leaning on a silver-topped cane. A bottle and glass were on his table. I wondered why the niece of such a man, who could afford to dress so well, had to work as a maid and spoke so badly.

She sat down beside him and they spoke earnestly. He glanced across at me. I smiled at him, but he did not return my smile. He took out a large watch to consult.

" 'Ello, dearie," a female voice beside me interrupted my observation. "On our lonesome, are we?"

I turned to find Aggie's chair taken by a much younger woman. Her dress and hat were vermilion and her brown hair was down on her shoulders. I thought her very pretty. I was prevented from answering by the return of the waiter.

" 'Op it," said he, jerking his head yet again. The girl looked over to where Aggie and her uncle sat. Aggie saw her and rose abruptly to her feet. I heard a rustle and turned to see the retreating back of the vermilion newcomer. Aggie paused to speak finally to her uncle, who looked at his watch again, nodded, and resumed his wineglass.

"Ta, Paddy," she said to our waiter, paying him before I could ask how much it would be. He gave her his nervous wink and departed.

We drank the sherry slowly, as the darkness seeped in through the spaces in the timber walls, obscuring those areas shaded from the gaslight. More people had come in. The talk and laughter were louder and the music seemed closer. Sherry was stronger than I had imagined; I was feeling slightly but pleasantly swimmy by the time I had finished my glass. I was conscious of Aggie's foot pressing upon mine.

"Time for another stroll, eh, lovey?"

"Can't I get you another glass of sherry in return?" She had paid for our admission to the gardens and refused to let me give her my share. I had had to insist on paying for some of the amusements we had sampled.

"There's nicer things than sherry," she replied, and leant across to take my hand and lift me up. We left the booth hand in hand. I wondered what her uncle would be thinking of her behaviour in public, but he seemed preoccupied with his glass.

This time we did not saunter. Our step was purposeful as Aggie positively propelled me along one of the pathways which radiated from the well-lit centre into areas of near-darkness. The arbours were more frequent here. I could only tell that some of them were occupied by the dim gleam of faces and female giggles. At length, Aggie led me off the path into one of them. It was almost pitch-dark inside, but she guided me without hesitation to a bench seat at the rear, pressed me down on to it, and placed herself on my knees, her arms encircling my neck and her moist lips bearing urgently upon mine.

I shall not particularise the tossing and tumbling which soon ensued. I doubt whether nowadays there are readers unworldly enough not to be able to supply the sequence of events from their imagination, and I should not wish to shock those who cannot.

Ah, women, women, what you have meant to my life! Whatever emotional disturbance and even pain you have caused me you have more than repaid by your comforts and caresses and your understanding. Not even an enemy could deny that I have fulfilled myself as a man's man; but ever since that long-ago evening I have reckoned myself a woman's man, too, and I acknowledge a lifelong debt of gratitude to Aggie Brown for the perspicacious and skilled manner of my initiation.

"Oh, Aggie," said I, as we groped about in the dark, adjusting our apparel, "I love you."

"You're a sweetie," she responded gently, "but you're not to say no such thing. You're not to think it."

"But I do!"

"No you don't. It's different. You'll find out some day."

If there was still more to discover, I thought, living was an experience I should not care to have missed.

At last we were ready to quit our temple of passion. Aggie came to me and kissed me long and firmly. I would gladly have settled down again, but I had to get back to school, or risk causing trouble for myself, Tadpole, and perhaps Aggie.

"We'd better get to the station," I said reluctantly.

"You'll have to go on by yourself, lovey, if you won't mind. I promised me uncle I'd go back and have a chinwag with him."

"Oh, all right. I'm playing the next two Saturdays, but I might be able to wangle the one after."

"Lovey, listen to me, and don't take it hard, 'cos I know what I'm talking about. There isn't to be no more Saturdays for me and you, an' you got to promise you'll keep away from me at school from now on."

"Aggie!"

"Honest, I know what's best. There was somethin' you wanted, an' I don't mind admittin' I wanted it, too. Well, we've had it, and it was nice—"

"Well, then—"

"There'll be plenty more skirts in your life. One of us had to turn you into a man, and I done it. But that's where it 'as to finish."

"But why? I'll be at the college another three years. There'll be heaps of opportunities."

"I can tell you ain't cottoned on, so I'll have to spell it out.

You got your life to lead, I got mine. You're there to learn things, and I'm there to sweep up after you. Only, just now, there was one thing I could teach you. You'll know what's what when you need to, so I reckon I done some girl a favour."

"You've done me one, Aggie. Only—"

"Listen. I get me half-day a week, and that's the only time I get to be a woman. I got a few years yet before me looks starts to go, an' I want to put as much by as I can while I got the chance. Now d'you see?"

I did, suddenly and startlingly.

"You . . . you don't mean—"

" 'Yeh, I do mean. When the gardens shut, it'll be the music-halls for the winter. I won't go on the game full time, I seen too much of what becomes of 'em as does. Half-day a week's enough for clothes and the rest to put by, and I get me lodgings free at the school."

She chuckled suddenly.

"You just cost me a quid or two in lost time. Never mind, it was worth it. It was me wantin' something for meself for a change. But do you see now, lovey?"

"I suppose so."

"Chalk it up to experience. But promise."

"If I have to."

"You do. Now, one more kiss, an' I must get back to uncle. Pore old b——'ll be pawin' the ground."

I flung myself into my studies with an energy and enthusiasm which plainly astonished my masters. I became feared as one of the hardest tacklers on the Rugby field. Every minute I could fill with physical and mental activity I used to the full. The pain of denial, intense at first, began to go unfelt for longer periods.

Each glimpse of Aggie renewed it momentarily. I gave her

yearning looks, but got only little conspiratorial smiles in return. I managed to restrain myself from getting her alone and pleading with her. So I was surprised one afternoon, some weeks after our adventure, when she approached me as I was crossing the college grounds in the winter gloom. My heart leapt with anticipation.

"I come to say ta-ra," she said.

"You're not leaving, Aggie?"

"Before they give me the push. Got a bun in the oven."

"Great heavens!" I had learnt the meaning of her term from my brother.

Aggie gave me a grin and a wicked eye. "Don't worry. You ain't the baker. I bin suspectin' it for a while."

"But what will you do?"

"Uncle's found me a place to stay. Says he'll see me all right. He's a decent ole cove. Knows I wouldn't do it to him on purpose or pass someone else's off on him."

"It is his? You're sure?"

" 'Yeh, I worked it out." Her teeth flashed in the half-light. "What if it had been yours, eh?"

"I should have stood by you."

"I know you would, bless you. You're the type. Well, ta-ra, Mr. Watson."

"Wait; will you give me your address?"

"No."

She turned before I could even attempt to shake her hand, let alone risk kissing her, and walked briskly away.

Yes, I count my manhood from the autumn of 1867, and remember affectionately Aggie Brown for conducting me across the threshold.

9

"You would have made an actor and a rare one."

The adventure with Aggie Brown had left me impatient to hurry forward to embrace life proper. I faced further years in the somewhat looser bondage of medical student; but it has often seemed to me anomalous that the first quarter or third of a man's anticipated span, when his vigour and ardency are at their freshest, should be spent shackled to a desk.

I ground my way through five years in the medical faculty of London University, dulling my own faculties with botany, chemistry, physiology, pharmacy, surgery, midwifery, anatomy, and several other subjects with even less bearing upon the business of healing the sick. I watched my first major operation without disgracing myself as some of my fellows did, and quickly got over that moment of indrawn breath and hesitancy before committing myself to my own first incision. What shocked me more was the dismissive and sometimes even jocular manner with which our tutors loudly recited the symptoms, proposed treatment, and chances of recovery of the cowering patients who were made subjects for demonstration. But even this distaste wore off with custom. I found myself growing as matter-of-fact about sickness and injury as any of them, having learnt to view the human body as a machine consisting of more or less standard components, of predictable performance, with a range of remedies available for dealing with their malfunctions.

Still, those early 1870s were a good time to be a young man-about-London. Our great capital was vibrant with life. The nation itself was calm with the confidence of its superiority over all others. Let the Balkans seethe and France and Germany squabble: we basked secure in the certainty that the "personal will" of our great Queen and the policies of Gladstone amounted between them to an unchallengeable influence over the entire world.

My own situation was comfortable enough. The small allowance which Mother was able to make me was matched by an equal one from her father, proud that I was treading in his medical footsteps. It meant that, unlike many fellow students, I did not have to stint myself in order to subsist. For a little under a pound a week I had a bedroom and small sitting-room in the house of a journalist and his family in Doughty Street, not a hundred yards from the house where the mighty Dickens had come to live forty years earlier, at the height of his new-found fame. My breakfast and dinner were provided, and I lunched well for a matter of pence.

My chief indulgences were an evening or two of billiards each week at Thurston's (one shilling and sixpence an hour), a few mugs of ale (Fine Old Mild, a penny ha'penny a pint), and tobacco (one shilling and twopence for a four-ounce tin). I had taken to smoking as a matter of conformity with my fellows, but soon found I did not care for cigarettes. For my twentieth birthday I lashed out to the tune of three shillings and threepence for a briar pipe with a silver mount which smoked sweetly from the first draw, and have been a pipe man ever since.

A group of us students went about together, spending the dark evenings in cheap cafés, disputing and setting the world to rights as the young will, or, in the summer, lying propped up on our elbows in one of the parks, commenting upon the strolling girls, with many a ribald speculation of a medical nature. Sometimes we would take a river steamer down to Greenwich or up as far as Richmond. Unattached females of the shop-girl sort abounded in their twos and threes, and I soon learned that a bold approach was all that was needed to gain their company. They were of all kinds: professedly bashful, feignedly coy, genuinely nice, coarse, brazen, sometimes downright lecherous. We made much noise, laughed a great deal, split up occasionally to lie in harmless embrace, and, once or twice, sought out more private spots and went further. I found that Aggie's training stood me in good stead, although my ardours were inhibited by the recollection of her "bun in the oven."

During one of our excursions to Greenwich we climbed the hill to Blackheath. The sight of Rugby posts stirred my interest, and I lingered to watch the game. The standard of play was high, and I felt the old urge to get my head down in a good scrimmage. Enquiries revealed that the club was one of the very first to have been founded, and had attracted players from far beyond the locality.

"No hope of a trial, then, I suppose?" I ventured to ask the spectator who had told me this.

"Fancy yourself good enough?" he answered, gauging my physique with a practised eye.

I told him I had been the youngest back ever to play in my college's first XV, and that I had kept my place throughout my years there, which I had been told was also unprecedented. He pointed out an official and suggested I try my luck. The response was that there was a waiting list of hopefuls to get into the team, but that good backs were harder to find than forwards and wingers, and that I looked the right make. I was fixed up with a trial game about a month later, acquitted myself well, and after only a fortnight was summoned by telegram to substitute for a man who had broken a leg. I played many times for Blackheath thereafter, taking part in several of the keenly contested matches against our arch rivals, Richmond, both at home and on their Deer Park ground. The hard play and the beer and comradeship which followed left an indelible impression on my memory.

Speaking still of recreations, perhaps there had been some prophetic element in that little falsehood which I had used to enlist Percy Phelps's co-operation in my escapade with Aggie. I had had no interest whatever at that juncture in the theatre, in any of its forms, and reached the end of my schooldays without having seen more than an occasional Christmas pantomime. As a student, I found myself rapidly making up the deficiency.

The "legitimate" theatre was undergoing its passage of transition from a crude melodramatic style to a quieter, more thoughtful genre, attracting a better sort of performer and audience, and, through the influence of actors such as Irving, Kendal, and Squire Bancroft, and actresses of the respectable status of Helen Faucit and Ellen Terry, was gaining a degree of tolerance hitherto denied it by the mighty middle class.

It was not that form of theatre which attracted me, however. Its striving for drawing-room gentility made me shift restlessly in my seat. At the other extreme, the opera struck me as grotesquely absurd, with fat, shrilling sopranos trying to pass as consumptive heroines, and swaggering, vicious-looking Italian males opening their mouths to full stretch in order to express supposedly romantic sentiments.

The ballet, at first sight, seemed more promising. As the curtain rose on a swirling line of girls, I caught my breath and held it until I realised why my head was swimming. The pink flashes of limbs, as diaphanous short dresses and petticoats lifted with each pirouette, was delicious. It was far removed from the way women dressed and disported themselves generally in those days, when even a momentary glimpse of an ankle was enough to arrest a man's attention. I equipped myself with opera-glasses, and I paid several visits before the appeal wore off. Those titillating forms became a species of frustration, representing a mirage-like illusion in which I could have no active share; besides which, I found ballet itself tedious and such story as there was attached to it incomprehensible.

What I and my fellows desired was a sort of entertainment in which we could take part. We found it in the singing-parlours of some public houses, and in the music-halls, where we could sway and bellow and bang our tankards in unison with the songs of such good-hearted favourites as Jolly John Nash, Arthur Lloyd, Arthur Roberts, and Annie Adams, one of the first of that sterling band of singing comediennes.

"Are You Gazing on This Little Beauty?" was one of Miss Adams's most popular numbers; and while she was neither so little nor so remarkably beautiful herself, there was plenty for us to feast our eyes upon in the way of dainty-limbed dancers, every bit as well shaped as the girls of the true ballet, though more enticing, with their painted faces and saucy looks, instead of wan cheeks and insipidly ethereal stares.

"Which one's your eye on, Watson?" asked Hooper, the second-year man beside me one evening, leaning close to my ear to be heard above the tootling band and the breathy chorusing of the girls, who were required to dance and sing simultaneously. I had been trying to follow the movements of a black-haired little thing in a pearl-grey dress with silvery sequin edgings, but kept getting distracted by one and another of her sisters as they flitted across her. I told him.

"Fancy your chance with her, could you?"

"What chance?"

"I'm in the funds. Old Ted, on the stage door, knows me. See if we can't get her and coppernob along the line to make an evening of it."

"You believe they would?"

"If we get in before any of the other johnnies. Here, you don't tell me you haven't been round before?"

"'Round'?"

"God save us from you Rugger chaps! I suppose a cold bath's your idea of fun."

I set him straight on that score and, shortly before the performance seemed to be drawing to an end, followed him out and down to the stage door, where a coin into the old door-keeper's palm produced a wink and a nod of his head towards a dark and cluttered passageway. Hooper led the way along it, until we fetched up in the wings, with a side-on view of the limelit stage, where the entire cast was down for a noisy final medley of songs, in which the largely male audience was participating with gusto.

This was my first sight of theatre folk at work, as opposed to the illusory view of them from out front. It was a revelation. Although their bearing towards the audience was so carefree, all flashing eyes and teeth, the studied movements of feet and limbs were from here quite apparent. I could hear their panting breath, and I noticed how the bosoms of girls and men alike heaved from the effort of their work. For the first time I realised how hard that work must be, especially considering that some of these artistes performed several times nightly, at different halls across London, for as little as a shilling or two a show. I heard the slap of their feet and caught the painful grimace when a step was missed. I noticed the little snowfall of sequins from their costumes, twinkling in the limelight. For the first time I inhaled, in its full potency, that ineffable odour of size, paint, dust, perfume, and perspiration, which is one of the most evocative of all smells, along with wood-smoke, the sweetness of new-cut grass, and the beckoning aroma of breakfast.

The music ended with a squealing triumphal flourish and a cheer from the unseen audience. Shirt-sleeved men standing near us were busy now, hauling on ropes, causing the heavy curtains to swish to. The cast on stage hastily regrouped itself just in time for them to open again. Bows and curtsies were made in response to the applause and thunder of beer glasses on table tops.

After two more calls, chiefly for the benefit of the principals, the curtains stayed shut. With the limes and footlights no longer on them, the performers seemed diminished. The row of overhead gaslights was extinguished, leaving a single flare for illumination. The costume colours were dulled, faces shadowed, the hollows of eyes and angles of jaws and necks deepened. Shoulders seemed suddenly to sag, as animation and disciplined tension gave way to fatigue.

I had imagined them pouring from the stage in a laughing, chatting throng; but they came surprisingly quietly, with little conversation. The men brushed past us without a glance. I was aware that Hooper and I were not the only outsiders waiting there. As the girls approached, other men in street clothes stepped forward, doffing hats and leaning down in exaggerated bows towards the painted creatures, whom I saw to be indeed much smaller than they had appeared from the distance of the circle. The splendid busts and thighs seemed to have melted quite away. The colours which had made cheeks seem to glow with health and vivacity proved to be bright blotches, heavily applied and now ravaged by courses of perspiration. Dresses which had looked so pristine in the glare of light were, in fact, worn and grubby. There were darns in tights and splits in some of the shoes.

My eyes sought my black-haired prize, and almost slid past her without recognition. The hesitation cost me any possibility of her company. Another man was stooping to her. She regarded him unsmilingly; then, with resigned weariness, replied to his invitation, "All reet. Ah'll see thee outside t'stage door." Her North Country accent was thick and brittle, and as she passed me to go to the dressing-room I wondered how on earth I could have been attracted by her.

It was another of life's lessons learned, however, and I have encountered far worse deceptions than the tricks of the theatrical trade, which could transform an undernourished, overworked, and ill-paid provincial girl into the semblance of a flitting moth of many colours, and make her an object for men's desire by requiring her to paint her face and flaunt her body. No wonder that, in those days when almost any woman who worked for a living was considered degraded, it was taken for granted that dancers and actresses were automatically prostitutes. Many were, wilfully or because they were flattered and grateful for an hour or two of luxury offered by a stage-doorer, and repaid it in the way expected of them. Those who might have wished to stay virtuous cannot have found it easy.

Hooper, my companion, had gained the attention of the red-haired girl he had marked down for himself, and no longer had any thought for me. I left the place feeling somewhat cheapened and ashamed of myself. But it is not much in the nature of medical students to brood compassionately on the human condition, and I soon became adept in the role of "stage-door johnnie." During the rest of my years as a medical student I was a familiar figure in the wings of theatres and music-halls. The Toms and Bobs and Charlies who kept the stage doors pocketed my half-sovereigns knowingly and secured me introductions I sought. All I will claim in self-mitigation is that I never wittingly gave a woman less than her due of respect, and never exploited one's misfortunes.

The theatre folk generally came to know me. To a degree they made me one of their own. I drank deep with the men and toyed with the girls, both in public supper rooms and, with greater abandon, in their lodgings. It was all most instructive, physically and psychologically, although it would be hypocritical to pretend that my purpose was anything higher than the fulfilment of fleshly lust.

I graduated from the girls of the chorus and corps de ballet to some of those actresses who hired themselves out to amateur groups to take rôles which middle-class ladies could not properly fill, even had they had the ability. My next step was into the wings of the legitimate theatre, where some daughters of army men, doctors, lawyers, and such had penetrated in their determination to banish old taboos and make the stage their career. It all gave me a fine understanding of stage people and why their often silly, vainglorious occupation held them in thrall, despite its insecurities and generally wretched conditions. There was even a very brief occasion, a little later, when I was able to sample their mode of working.

I had made my first acquaintance with the combined talents of the new and native composer and librettist, Arthur Sullivan and W. S. Gilbert, in April '75, when I had gone along to the little Royalty Theatre in Dean Street, Soho, to see Offenbach's short operetta *La Périchole,* and found myself unexpectedly treated to an additional entertainment by them, *Trial by Jury,* which had been put on to fill out the evening. Like everyone else in the audience, I had found their piece funnier and more tuneful than the Frenchman's, and inexpressibly English in its brilliant burlesque of the courts of law.

One day in the early summer of '77 I was approached by my then landlord, Macgregor, a journalist, and like many of the best Fleet Streeters, a Scot. His manner of speech tended to reflect the headlines and sub-headings which punctuated his printed writings.

"Sullivan and Gilbert working up new piece. George Grossmith, former reporter, Bow Street Court, hired as comic magician in take-off of Italian opera. Love potion in tea administered to English village populace. Hilarious!"

"Sounds promising," I agreed.

"Gilbert takes charge of production. Impresario D'Oyly Carte agrees interview and illustrations. Exclusive!"

"A nice job for you, then."

"You keen on stage. Tag along?"

"To the Royalty?" My response was cautious because I had formed a slight attachment to a dancer there whose intensity towards me was giving me concern.

He shook his head. "Carte floats new company at Opéra Comique. Bright hope for English operetta."

"Then I'd be delighted to go with you, if it's possible."

He winked. "Render assistance with artist's equipment. Tuesday morning."

Thus it was that, in the theatre off the Strand, subsequently pulled down during the Aldwych development, I met those two immortals whose works I would not exchange for Puccini's, Verdi's, and Wagner's put together.

The new work, *The Sorcerer,* was that which it is said became the mould from which their subsequent triumphs were formed. Gilbert had recruited players corresponding to the characters of the story, rather than as singers in their own right. Grossmith, as John Wellington Wells, was a case in point, a former journalist turned reciter and piano-entertainer. He stayed on for many years, to create the leading comedian's rôles in many more of their works.

He proved to be a slight figure, with receding hair and rimless pince-nez giving him a scholarly appearance. He knew my landlord from his newspaper days and shook my hand affably when I was introduced; but he left us anxiously when a general hush amongst the company heralded the entry into the auditorium of the autocratic Gilbert.

He was turned forty, military-looking, with severe moustaches, sandy sideburns, and a frowning brow. He marched, rather than walked, head back and chin up, wholly purposeful and without greeting to right or left. I caught the formidable glint in his eye, and wondered how such a man could possess so wonderful a gift for expressing the ridiculous.

Sullivan entered with him and seated himself at the piano. He was a smaller man, with bushy black hair and a monocle. He smiled encouragement at the performers, whom Gilbert proceeded to chivvy relentlessly, though always to purposeful effect. He seemed to have worked out in advance everyone's precise movements and gestures. It was plain that all respected his firm direction.

The day's rehearsal was devoted to the scene in which the villagers and several of the principals fall under the influence of the love philtre unwittingly dispensed by their vicar, Dr. Daly, from his teapot. Complex ensemble singing, groupings, and dancing were involved, and I watched fascinated. The men were overcoated against the unheated theatre's October cold, and the women were also in coats, hats, and even gloves, with never a vestige of paint or disguise; yet such was their art and the magic of the piece that I saw them only as the simple-hearted populace of a West Country village, attending the summer nuptials of their squire's son and his betrothed.

At length Gilbert called a break for luncheon. My landlord, who had been keeping quiet beside me and the artist, darted forward with his notebook to avail himself of the fifteen minutes' interview he had been promised with producer and composer. I wandered out into the street and followed some members of the company into an adjoining public house. A throng of them were there, and I soon struck up that easy acquaintance to which theatricals welcome outsiders who will buy them drinks and uninterruptingly listen to their talk about themselves.

After some forty minutes, during which several glasses went down, accompanied in the case of the more prudent by pastries and pies, someone called from the doorway that it was time to get back. We drank up hastily and moved to the door. I noticed one man hang back, though, and gesture urgently to the potman for a final drink. He caught my eye.

"Bit off-colour," he explained. "Touch of fever, I reckon."

He was served with a glass of spirits which he drank straight down before joining me to follow the others. When we got into the fresh air he took a deep breath and immediately staggered, so that he had to seize my arm. I hastily searched my knowledge of fevers.

"Be. . . be all right," he mumbled. But inside the theatre he tripped on the stairs, and when we reached their top he sank on to a basket and slumped sideways.

"Oh, lor'!" exclaimed a girl's voice behind me. "Percy's off again."

"He has a touch of fever," I explained.

"We know what Percy's fever is," she returned grimly. "The stupid fool. If the guv'nor sees him like this, it'll be curtain-down for him."

"Will he be wanted straight away?"

She nodded. She was a pretty little thing, with a healthy colouring and firm figure. "It's the bit where we all wake up after sleeping off the potion, and think we're in love with the first one we see."

"Lucky that one," I essayed, giving her my eye. I had learned by now to seize my chances. She looked at me, and I smiled back in my winningest way.

"Do him a favour," was her unexpected response. "Stand in for him while he dozes it off."

"I?"

"You're not so different, if you keep your coat and hat on."

"But I'm no singer."

"You don't need to be. It's just character work. There's the whole crowd of us."

"Then one won't be missed, surely."

"Yes he will. We've got to be paired off for when we wake up, see. The man stares at the girl next to him and they go spoony on each other."

She gave me that look with which women open men's hearts and purses and said, "Please help, dear. Poor Perce'll be right as rain in half an hour."

"All right," I said. "Perhaps when you've finished for the day you and I could, er—"

She nodded abstractedly and seized my hand. "Come on, quick," she urged, and hurried me out on to the stage.

The villagers were arranging themselves in recumbent postures on the boards, two by two. I shot a glance towards the pit, where Sullivan's piano stood. I was relieved to see that he and Gilbert were in deep discussion over the score.

My companion lay down swiftly, pulling me with her. I made to manoeuvre my head on to her breast, but she fended me off. I felt ridiculous, lying there with my bowler hat on, though I dared not take it off, for fear the keen-eyed Gilbert might spot a stranger.

"Who the hell's this?" hissed another man *sotto voce,* craning his neck briefly to stare across her.

"Percy's tight again."

"Bloody idiot!"

"This chap offered to stand in."

The man gave me another stare.

"You know the lines?"

"He can just move his lips," answered the girl. She had said nothing about any lines, but I was trapped on the stage now. She turned her head to me and added, "Keep your eyes on Claude here and do what he does."

"It won't work," Claude prophesied darkly. "Eye like a gimlet, Gilbert."

"It's the only chance for Perce. We can't let him down."

"I'll do my best," I assured them, looking her meaningfully in the eyes. "If you'll just give me an idea of the sort of thing."

Claude said, "On cue, we all sit up like we've been snoozing under the drug. You know, rubbing our eyes, stretching and that. Then it's, 'Why, where be oi, and what be oi a-doin', a-sleepin' out, just when the dews du roise?' "

I repeated it after him. "Then what happens?"

My lady friend was about to reply, but there came a sharp rapping from the direction of the piano, calling us to order, followed by Gilbert's commanding voice.

"All down, now. Eyes closed. Perfectly still. And . . . !"

The piano struck up. I lay there semi-petrified. I heard a single male voice, which I recognised as Grossmith's:

"But stay—they waken, one by one . . . "

A spasm of fear shot through me. "One by one!" How should I know my turn?

"The spell has worked—the deed is done.
I would suggest that we retire
While Love, the Housemaid, lights her kitchen fire."

I became aware of a general rustling round me. Risking a squint between half-shut eyelids, I saw my fellow rustics beginning to move. I sat up and began rubbing vigorously at sleep-caked eyes with the backs of my hands.

"No, no, no!" came Gilbert's cry over the piano, which

stopped playing. I peeped out again. To my horror, I found that I was the only one sitting up.

"A bad dream, I take it?" I heard his acid tone. "A nightmare, perchance? Or is it your unalterable habit to wake up like Jack springing out of the box?"

"I am sorry, sir," I muttered, as anonymously as I could make it sound.

Fortunately, he seemed to be in a good humour.

"Sleep again," he ordered. "And a pleasanter dream to you this time."

I lay back thankfully.

"Keep it slow," hissed my female partner. "Follow me."

The piano sounded again, and again Grossmith sang his cue lines. Risking all, I partly opened my eyes and saw the others stretching and writhing, as though emerging from deep sleep, then gradually sitting up to stare about them. I did likewise, and thought I carried it off pretty creditably. The piano suddenly soared into a triumphant few notes, and the male voices about me burst into loud song:

"Why, where be oi, and what be oi a-doin',
A-sleepin' out, just when the dews du roise?"

I did my best to get out a few of the ill-remembered words, but once more there came the loud rapping. The piano ceased and the girls' responding line straggled into silence. I saw with horror that Gilbert's eyes were full on me again.

"I find it a pity," said he, "that a gentleman who seemed so eager to waken from his slumbers should do so to so little purpose."

My dread increased as I saw him moving towards the flight of steps leading up to the side of the stage. I was almost tempted to jump up and run for it.

He came to where I sat and stood glowering down at me.

"Kindly," said he, in a tone which I felt rather than heard, "give us all the benefit of your solo interpretation of your rôle. Pay attention please, ladies and gentlemen. We may yet learn something."

There was nothing to do but brave it out. Beyond him, as he had climbed on to the stage, I had glimpsed the errant Percy standing in the shadows of the wings, with an appalled look on his face. If only I could satisfy Gilbert enough to make him retreat back to his place beside the piano, I might make my escape behind his back and hope that Percy might be able to slip into my place.

I lay still again, my eyes closed. Once more the piano started and Grossmith gave his cue. I squirmed and stretched as I had done last time, and slowly sat up, hoping I might have done enough. But the piano went on uninterrupted and soared into that dreaded passage. I croaked forth:

> "*Why, what be oi, and where be oi a-doin',*
> *A . . . a sleepin' here until . . . where the dews*
> *do . . . do . . .* "

The music ceased and a terrible silence prevailed.

"The question is," said Gilbert, "who the devil be you, and what be you a-doin' in my theatre?"

I rose to my feet and answered with what vestige of dignity I could muster, "I am very sorry, sir. There is nothing I can say."

"There isn't, eh?" he retorted, and his gently sarcastic manner was abandoned for venom. "Well, I have a few words. You, sir!" he snapped, swinging round to point at my landlord, who was looking aghast in one of the pit seats. "You brought this fellow in. I saw him with you. Whatever your cheap journalistic intention was in meddling with my rehearsal in this way, I can tell you I found it out from the first moment. I hope your wretched assistant will feel that whatever you are paying him for this prank will be compensation for making a fool of himself. As for yourself, I withdraw entirely my permission to write about this production. Print one sentence, and I shall have you in court. Now, take yourselves out of my theatre before I am tempted to violence.''

He turned abruptly towards the wings, where Percy cringed.

''And you, sir, come here. Before you crawl away to richly-merited unemployment, I have something to say to you, too.''

My landlord turned me out of his house with scarcely time to pack my belongings, having described my behaviour in headlines of a sort no decent printer would have set up.

On several successive nights in my new abode, a lodging-house in another part of Bloomsbury, I awoke in terror from dreams of being alone on a stage, before a full house, with no lines save those I could make up as I went along. Professional actors and actresses have since told me it is a dream familiar to them.

The experience was not enough, however, to destroy my love of the theatre. I attended a performance of *The Sorcerer* in later years and quite enjoyed it; but at that juncture where the villagers were discovered asleep an apprehensive shudder ran through me.

My lady companion squeezed my arm and whispered, ''Did someone walk over your grave?''

''Just recalling something Gilbert once said to me,'' I murmured nonchalantly, and received her admiring stare.

10

"A medical student, I suppose?"

In the year 1875 I had passed my final examinations for the degrees of Bachelor of Medicine and of Surgery. I was visiting my grandparents' house when the results reached me. Poor Mother, whose health had not been good for the best part of a year, wept with brief happiness for me. It was the last time I was ever to see her joyful.

Grandfather beckoned me into his study afterwards. He and Grandmother, too, had expressed their pleasure in my achievement, but his expression was grave as he closed the door and motioned me into a fireside chair.

"Well, John, what is it to be next for you?"

"I'm not sure, Grandpa. I thought I'd better wait and see whether I'd passed before making any plans."

"Mm. Your results were not what might be termed sparkling, but you are through at first attempt, which carries its own merit."

"Thank you, Grandpa. As to what I'm to do now, I should certainly value your expert opinion."

He seemed to hesitate, as though he had something ready

to say, but was holding back. There seemed a reluctance to look me in the eye.

"I dare say," he managed at length, "you wish to go on and get your doctorate?"

"I might as well," said I. It meant yet another two years' work, but I supposed an M.D. would stand me in greater stead than the mere M.B. and B.S. "The question is, how best to go about it."

"Well, there are the usual alternatives. You can walk the wards of a hospital—Bart's, Guy's, or the Westminster, in the case of a London man. Or you could get into a practice, which would be less bother. I dare say I could find someone to take you on."

"Thank you. Only, I'd like to travel. A couple of years in the army or navy medical service would qualify me. I'm inclined to go for one of those."

He sighed, and at last looked me squarely in the face.

"I thought that would be your choice. I mean it as a compliment when I say it seems typical of you. There are drawbacks, however."

"What are they?"

"Principally, most of your work would be with men. You would get comparatively little to do amongst females and children. When you did eventually decide to set up in general practice, you might find the lack of that experience a bit of a nuisance. There is, ahem, money in women and children."

"I suppose so."

"You would also find the life less alluring than you might expect. There is no war, nor likelihood of there ever being one. Should you be tempted to make one of the services your career, you would find advancement very slow and conditions often tedious and uncomfortable. Believe me, there is a better living to be had here at home."

"But at least there would be the chance to see the world,

Grandpa. I've hardly been anywhere yet. I'm afraid of putting down roots too soon, like—''

I had been on the point of instancing my father. His example of frustration due to premature domestication remained vivid to me, although he himself had quite vanished from our lives.

''John,'' sighed my grandfather, ''you have asked my advice, and I must be frank with you. In normal circumstances, I think I should advise you to follow your instinct. I gather that the Army offers a gentleman a decent enough way of life.''

''Why do you say in normal circumstances, sir?''

''Because I have to give you some grave news. As a medical man yourself, you will have recognised that your mother has been showing no signs of getting back to full health.''

''Yes. But she bears up quite well, doesn't she?''

''It is what we have been telling ourselves. Unfortunately, my belief that there is a regression has been confirmed by her specialist. I'm afraid we must brace ourselves for the worst.''

I was horror-struck. The specialist had earlier declared so firmly that Mother was only suffering from a morbid state, from which she might recover quite suddenly, at any time. Now Grandfather was telling me that she would not.

''You will hear no mention in your studies of the broken heart,'' he said. ''It is a romantic term, not a medical one, yet the complaint is as old as any known to history, and one of the least easy to cure.''

For a moment a blind anger against my profession welled up in me. I recalled those jesting remarks of our tutors; their offhanded asides about suspect symptoms; their cynical assurances that most sickness existed only in the imagination, and that ninety per cent of the calls we might anticipate when we were in practice would prove not worth leaving our beds for. I thought of my own simile for the human body as a mere machine, needing only a mechanic's care, and felt disgust at its glibness.

"Is it . . . Father?" I asked, scarcely able to articulate.

"He has much to answer for. Your brother, too. There has been something else as well, I fancy, only she will not discuss it. It may be to do with her religious phase. It is all very exalting to acquire so sudden and strong a fervour as hers, but the loss of it again leaves a dreadful vacuum which had not existed previously, and which it is almost impossible to fill."

There seemed no point in my telling him about Beecher. It had not been the man's fault that Mother had been so ready to clutch at what he could offer her, spiritually and in other ways. My mind's eye pictured her as she had been in our Stranraer days, so fresh and bonny, before Father's drinking had riven our family apart. I had often pitied him, and even despised him, but never actually hated him until now. The ugly feeling swept through me; yet, even as it did, I remembered our Spaniard and the legacy from his blood. For all I knew, it might be dormant in me, too, ready to erupt some day and strike me down.

"There might yet be a miracle," I heard Grandfather saying. "If your father and Henry were to return suddenly . . ."

"I will go and look for them—find them and bring them back. Surely they would come if they knew the situation."

"I admire your spirit, John, but the notion is impractical, I am afraid. It would take you months to locate them: a year, possibly. Your very absence from her would be the final hurt she could not withstand. Don't you see, that is why I hope you will not choose a service career. As to travel, there will be plenty of chance for you after . . . later. You appreciate what I am saying?"

"Of course, Grandpa. I shall say no more of going."

"Good boy. Settle for a hospital, then. You can easily detach yourself when you feel free to do so. I pray, for your mother's sake as well as yours, that she will be delivered from her unhappy lot, one way or the other, before too long.''

Thus it was that, with a heavy heart, I made my application to the three teaching hospitals associated with London University for a place as a house surgeon. I was accepted by Bart's, and took up my duties there at once, wishing to busy my thoughts, and determined to use such knowledge and skill as I possessed to take away a little from the sum of human suffering. There was nothing I could do for Mother, beyond letting her know that I was not far from her, and seeing her whenever I could; therefore, I would make up for it to other unfortunates.

The work proved suitably demanding, and I felt better for applying myself conscientiously to it, under the tutorship of such eminent consultants as Howard Marsh and A. E. Comberbatch. I filled my leisure hours to the full also, continuing to play Rugby for Blackheath and keeping up my theatre-going. The resilience of youth insulated me against the tendency to brood on Mother's condition, and the wild anger against my father for having brought her to this, and not being at hand to comfort her, gradually subsided.

Mother died not long after Christmas. Her passing left a great void in me. Something like panic seized me when I considered how alone in the world I now was. My grandparents did their best to treat me as if I were their son, and the aunts rallied round in a sisterly sort of way. But it was artificial, as we all knew; a substitute for what should have been.

I was now free to give up hospital work and set forth upon my travels. That I did not do so was for two reasons. Mother had never been told how grave her condition was, in the certainty that the information would affect her for the worse. She had made no will. By law, Father was her automatic beneficiary, but because his whereabouts were unknown, her assets were declared frozen while enquiries proceeded. As the only member of our family still in England, I felt I should remain at hand, both as a duty and in order that the lawyers should not feel wholly unsupervised.

However, a new interest absorbed a good deal of that time which might otherwise have hung heavily during the late spring and part of the summer of 1876. It also brought me into association with another giant of the Victorian age.

W. G. Grace, the greatest cricketer of all time, entered Bart's in the same year as I, coming up from Bristol Medical School. He was a number of years older than myself and most of our fellow students, past his mid-twenties, already married, with an infant son, and, unlike any of us, famous throughout the kingdom and beyond the seas. As a batsman he had scored thousands of runs and many centuries, and as a bowler had taken several hundred wickets. He had become the first cricketer ever to score a century and bowl a hat-trick in the same match. He was captain of Gloucestershire, and he had toured with teams to the United States, Canada, and Australia. His father and two elder brothers were doctors. A sportsman's career is a relatively short one—though "W.G.'s" lasted far longer than most—so he pursued a medical career as a second string to it. "Pursued" is perhaps scarcely the verb for his case, though. His studies were so much interrupted by his cricketing that it was to take him, in all, twelve years to qualify fully, as compared with my own seven, although I do not put that forward as any claim to superiority.

He was a gigantic figure, well over six feet tall, barrel-chested, and proportionately burly. I believe his boots were size fourteen. He wore a thick black beard, and the eyes under his bushy black eyebrows were dark and intense. In contrast with his physique was a high-pitched, almost squeaky voice, which sounded quite incongruous issuing from him, as though he were a ventriloquist pretending to be someone else.

He was not a particularly popular student: I think he was held in too much awe; besides which, his opinion of himself was acute and he liked his own way, off the field as well as on it. But I did him a small favour by lending him some lecture notes, and he lingered for a chat.

"I hear you're the Blackheath Rugger man," he said.

"One of them. Of course, I know all about you."

"You're a cricketing man yourself?"

"Only from the sidelines, I'm afraid. I've always loved the game, but I could never get the hang of playing it. Perhaps if my college coach had taken me up—"

"School coach be blowed! My mother taught me everything I know, in our back garden. You're a strongly-built chap, and you must have a good eye to do well in your game. Try cricket. Best sport in the world."

He was for ever getting up teams, travelling all night, if need be, in order to get in a day's play. It was as if he knew that cricket was his fulfilment, and that he must cram as much of it into his life while he was able. In fact, he made his last appearance in a first-class match in 1914, when he was sixty-six, and died little more than a year later.

"Come on," he said to me one day, "I'm taking an XI of Medical Men across the river on Saturday to play a mob of Non-Smokers. We'll give 'em smoke, all right."

"You're offering me a game?"

"You'll be worth at least four or five of them, I'll be bound. We'll have some fun."

I duly played, in borrowed white flannels. I cannot claim to have distinguished myself. I went in seventh wicket. The first ball I received struck my bat on its edge and hurtled away to the boundary of the South London ground where we were playing. Grace, who had been occupying the crease since the start of our innings, and had already scored his century, squeaked, "Well done, well done! That's the style!" I was clean bowled next ball. Our side mustered a total of 167, of which Grace scored 133. He then proceeded to bowl out the opposition almost singlehanded for 42, and came off the field complaining that the game had finished early, while there was plenty of daylight left.

On two further occasions he invited me to play. The more notable of them was an away match against Edinburgh University, on their ground. Once again I failed to come up to his hopes for me, scoring but a single run, although I must record in my defence that not another member of our side got into double figures, other, that is, than our mighty captain, who rattled up another of his hundreds and would doubtless have doubled it, had he not run out of partners. The Edinburgh team, whom he personally bowled out for a negligible score, presented each of us with one of their club caps as a souvenir and had us photographed wearing them in a group with them.

I kept my cap proudly as a memento of having thrice appeared on a cricket field with the immortal W. G. It led Sherlock Holmes, some years later, to make one of his instant deductions when he spotted the cap's emblem reproduced on an envelope which arrived for me through the post. My reaction to its contents showed him correctly that it was an appeal for a contribution to a bazaar being held to raise funds for the enlargement of Edinburgh University's cricket field. Perhaps it was his mordant wit which made him pretend to mistake the cap as that of my own old college team, for he went on to twit me further about lacking full medical credentials, which he knew was untrue. But it is characteristic of the sort of gaps which yawned in his seeming omniscience that he knew nothing of cricket and failed, where any schoolboy would have succeeded, to recognise the unmistakable features of W. G. Grace in the group photograph.*

*I tell this little story in a fragment entitled "The Field Bazaar." It was published in the Edinburgh University *Student* in November, 1896.

That game at Edinburgh was my last. I have watched cricket ever since, though, and often, seated at Lord's or the Oval and overhearing ill-informed judgements on the play, I have been tempted to lean across and say, "You do not appreciate what it is like to be out there. It is a different game, watched from here." The retort would surely be, "And what do you know about that, sir?" enabling me to return nonchalantly, "Actually, I turned out a few times for W. G." That would make them catch their breath, all right!

In the summer of 1877, soon after my encounter with that other contemporary genius, W. S. Gilbert, Grandfather showed me what could truly be termed "a Letter from the Diggings." It had arrived at Bagshot, addressed to my mother, by then deceased for more than a year.

Having never been a recipient of letters from my father, I did not at once recognise his hand. If I had been familiar with it, I imagine I should have been shocked to find it deteriorated to this shaky scrawl. I could not help feeling glad that Mother had been spared seeing it, and reading its painful message.

It was a chronicle of mishap and despair, expressed in terms of alternate penitence and self-pity. Evidently the high hopes of a fortune to be found on the American gold-fields had come to nothing. Father and Henry had moved from field to field, ever believing that the next would yield their fortune, ever finding that it did not. They had toiled night and day for no more than mere subsistence, and sometimes had starved. In time, they had been reduced to hiring themselves as labourers to the more successful miners, until "circumstances prompted us to obtain passage to Australia," where brighter hopes were thought to offer. It sounded to me as though there had been some trouble which had forced them to leave America in haste.

They had reached Melbourne destitute and made the long trek on foot to the diggings at Ballarat, seventy-five miles away, from where the letter was penned. It was clear to me that they had arrived in Australia, as in America, too long after the actual gold rushes when men had scooped nuggets from little below the surface of the earth. The speculators had moved on, leaving behind the few who were prepared to work hard for modest yet steady returns from the established claims. Most of these were Chinese, with the infinite patience of their race and used to living on little. In final humiliation, Father had abandoned all ambition of his own and had hired himself to one of these, working interminable hours alongside the coolies and living in squalor.

What had prompted him to write his only letter after so many years' silence, however, was his desertion by Henry, against whom he proceeded to rail bitterly for leaving him in his hour of greatest need. He did not say where Henry had gone, or what he was doing.

The long last paragraph of the letter made embarrassing reading, with its mixture of self-reproach, attempted justification of what he had done, and pleas for forgiveness. It gave the impression of being the last testament of a man at the end of his tether. Despite my revulsion at its tone, I felt a surge of pity for the disintegration of the fine man I had once considered my father to be.

"It is a sad document for you to have to read, John," Grandfather said gravely, when I handed it back. "It would have finished your poor mother at an instant if she had been alive to receive it."

"I was thinking that very thing. Do you suppose there might be time to do anything?"

"A draft of money? It occurred to me at once, but you will see that he has given no address, other than plain 'Ballarat.' I dare say something would reach him somehow. He cannot be unknown to someone in authority there. But it would be risky sending money at such chance."

"How long has the letter taken? I didn't notice the date."

"Nearly two months."

"That means another two at least before anything could reach him."

"I know what you are thinking, my boy. What will have become of your father in that time? I cannot pretend that the omens are good. He would scarcely have broken his long silence now, unless he were in dire straits."

"Nevertheless," said I, making up my mind upon that instant, "there must still be some hope. I shall go there and try to find him."

Grandfather gave me a startled look; then he stepped forward and gripped my arm, and I fancy his eyes had moistened.

"You are a good fellow, John. But there comes a time in the lives of most of us when we are entitled—nay, it is our duty—to put our own interests first. You have less than a year to go to complete your studies and qualify. Think carefully before you consider squandering so much work."

"If it had not been for Father," I replied, "dear Mama might have been killed, that day in Stranraer. You and Grandmama would have suffered the grief of losing a daughter, and I myself should never have come into the world. Surely, we owe him that much?"

"You're right, of course. Yes, I confess we were delighted when he later asked for her hand. It made it all the more puzzling that he should have gone off in the way he did."

I hesitated a moment before replying, "I have a theory. You will think it half-baked, no doubt; only I believe there is something in our blood. The Watson side, that is. I am sure it is some black legacy from our Spanish ancestor of long ago."

He did not show surprise. He was regarding me keenly, and said, after a moment, "I will tell you something, John, which you may or may not know. Your Great-grandfather

Watson rid himself of Henriques as a middle name because he believed it perpetuated something which he wished eradicated from your line. Did you know that?"

"No. Father told me it was because he thought the name too fanciful."

"It was nothing so whimsical as that. I had the true reason from your mother, to whom your father confided it before they were married. She sought my advice."

There was an ominous ring to this that chilled me. Clearly, there was more to my notion that some sinister element dwelt in our blood than mere romantic imagination could account for. I swallowed, and said, "I'm a grown man, Grandpa; a medical man. If there is something you know, I should wish to hear it."

He indicated a chair and took his own.

"There is not much precisely known about inherited characteristics. A lot of superstitious belief has attached itself to the subject, though, such as your great-grandfather's, in thinking that he might effect a purge by simply changing a name. Men and women have been persecuted and even executed by others who have suspected them of inherited evil and supernatural powers. A wealth of legend has grown up, particularly amongst backward and ignorant people. There is more to their custom of driving a stake through certain dead people's hearts than the irrational dread that they might otherwise rise again. It is a symbolic act against the evil spirit which is imagined to lurk within them. It is the stuff of which belief in such things as vampires is largely made."

The drift of his explanation was starting to alarm me. What was coming next? Surely not the revelation of a Watson vampire connection!

"Should you ever decide to specialise," he was going on, "it could be a fruitful field of study, in which you might make your name. You could start from your personal association, in that your mother doubted the desirability of her producing offspring."

"You . . . you are saying I came into being undesired!"

"No, no. You must not entertain any such belief. The fact is, your father confided in her aspects of his ancestry, so far as he knew of them—certain cases of irrational violence, some distressful consequences of weakness for drink, a touch or two of insanity—nothing major, I hasten to assure you, but—well, you will have caught my drift. Your mother was much attached to your father, but wondered whether it might be best to eschew a family. I counselled otherwise, and, looking at you standing there, and having listened to your noble wish to rescue your father, at the cost of inconvenience and possible setback to your career, I am glad she accepted my advice."

I hope I blushed at this. A thought had entered my mind, though.

"Henry . . ." I began.

Grandfather sighed. "Your brother is another matter, I fear. I could always see the signs in him."

Again, my own impression was confirmed. It brought me insufficient comfort, though.

"Grandpa, do you think that I . . . What I mean to say is . . . Could it be possible that . . . ?" I could not express the doubts which were seething in my mind.

"I think you need have no such fears, John. Insofar as any study has been done of the subject, it seems accepted that such traits as may come out in one member of a family might never show themselves in another, however close by blood. It is not proved, mind," he added (and I wished he had not, thinking at the same time that I should not care to be one of his patients if his bedside manner were as clumsy as this). "All I can say is that you appear to me to be as normal and healthy as could be, whereas, in the case of your brother and father . . . But you understand me. We will say no more.''

It was certainly not a matter I wished to pursue, either. Implications were already troubling my mind, as they were to do often in the future.

I said, ''It makes me more determined to go. Mother loved him and chose to risk whatever it was to bring me into the world. I can't repudiate him for failing to rise above his own nature.''

''She would have been proud to have heard you say that. Of course you are right. In fact, it occurs to me there is a way for you to go about it without risk of hindrance to your career. Get a passage as a ship's surgeon.''

This was more to the point than his morbid musings.

''Does that count?'' I asked eagerly.

''If the appointment is official, and your superiors certify that you duly carried out your duties, it is the equivalent of working in general practice ashore.''

''I couldn't sign on for an entire year, though. I might have to spend weeks in Australia, looking for him, and after that who knows what.''

''You could nevertheless accumulate the time. A couple of months' duties on the way out; the same on the way back—there is a third of your required year already. Any other opportunities you might find of practising would all count, so long as you produce the certificates.''

For a discreditable moment, I confess, my mind flashed to Tadpole Phelps's counterfeit penmanship. With his help, I could account for the entire year. The notion appalled me abruptly, and for a horrified moment I wondered whether I had not just suffered an exemplary manifestation of that Henriques legacy.

''There will only be the matter of your thesis to consider.'' Grandfather's words broke into my thoughts. ''But I'm sure you could mug up something or other.''

"I'll give it thought," I assured him hastily, and left. I had heard enough, and suddenly longed for action and movement and the purifying influence of the sea to reaffirm my wholesomeness.

I made enquiries about getting a seagoing appointment, and was relieved to find that there was a general demand for such services as I could offer. There was great competition between the shipping lines at the time, and the footnote "Carries a Surgeon" was a desirable adjunct to an advertisement for a sailing. I felt well enough qualified to tackle any emergency which might come my way during the voyage. I duly put myself forward, was interviewed and accepted without demur or delay, and within a fortnight was sailing out of Liverpool for the second time. On this occasion, however, I was no wondering child, eagerly anticipating an unknown future, but an experienced sailor, dressed in the uniform of an officer of the steamship line, which I felt suited me admirably.

There is nothing of importance to record about the voyage to Australia. The vessel was carrying several hundred passengers, the majority of whom were Irish emigrants, and my duties consisted largely of prescribing fresh air and food as the est cure for seasickness. When a violent storm struck us one night, several people were flung from their berths and three of them sustained fractures, which I was able to deal with satisfactorily. There were no grave medical cases, and only one childbirth.

Much of my time was my own, and I was able to indulge again in the practice of standing at the rail by the hour, revelling in the whip of the wind and the salt taste of the spray. It brought poignant memories of that previous voyage. I pictured my poor deluded mother, infatuated with religion and with Beecher, its personification for her. The train of thought led me to that heartless desertion by my father and brother. I found myself feeling less animosity towards Father, now that I knew he had been brought so low and might even be already dead. Henry's was a different case. I had suspected that his self-interest had been behind his persuading Father to leave us, and now he had evidently perpetrated a second betrayal. I vowed that I would find him and give him the thrashing that was the only means of retribution available to me on my own and Mother's behalf.

My musings were curtailed after some ten days out. I was not impervious to the admiring looks we officers received from the lady passengers, and I observed that one in particular seemed to be all eyes for me. When she took the seat next to mine at supper in the first-class dining-saloon I quickly discovered, from the touch of her foot against mine, that I had not misread her glances. She proved to be the wife of the shipping company's chief representative, at Sydney. She had been visiting her aged parents in Wales on her own and was now returning to her husband, with a call at Melbourne en route. Her official connection entitled her to sole occupancy of a cabin which would normally have accommodated a couple, and, to cut the story short, it was soon doing so again, as often as I could spend a few hours with her. She was a good few years older than I, and far from beautiful, of burly build and with a rather commanding manner; but, as the saying went amongst us sailors, any port in a storm, and I spent little time at my solitary station on deck for the rest of the voyage.

As we bade one another a tender adieu, the night before our ship was due to reach Melbourne, she told me that if I should find myself in Sydney I was to call and perhaps dine with her and her husband, who, it occurred to her to add, was sometimes absent on business for several days at a time. I assured her that I should not fail to take up her invitation, should my Australian sojourn bring me to New South Wales.

11

"So and so of Ballarat."

My knowledge of the geography of Australia, or of the conditions there, was scanty. I had intended working it up during the voyage through conversation with passengers who were returning, but although most of my spare time was spent in the company of one of them, our conversation somehow did not come round to the subject.

I was agreeably enough surprised upon disembarking at Melbourne to find it busy and bustling, its size quite belying the fact that it was still only some forty years old. New construction seemed to be going on everywhere. I noticed two theatres, and what little time I had to spend looking into shop windows showed me that everything obtainable in London seemed to be here, at much the same prices.

One thing which it had occurred to me to ask my fair friend, although I did not confide my purpose to her, was how I should get from there to Ballarat. She answered that Australia already had an extensive railway system, and that she was sure there must be a line to so important a mining centre, only seventy-five miles from the capital city of the State of Victoria. For the best impression of the scenery and nature of the country, though, I should "go up by Cobb," by which she referred to the horse-drawn coaches of the American-founded Cobb and Co., Australia's equivalent of Wells, Fargo. That would take longer, however, and my quest would brook no delay. I signed off from my appointment and exchanged the uniform for my own suit. There was a train to Ballarat that morning, and I was there by the middle of the same afternoon.

Though of only four hours' duration, the train journey was tedious. The terrain was flat and featureless, with little to relieve the empty scene, save for patches of gum-trees and an occasional lonely shack-like building. Almost the only living things I saw were sheep and many magpies. I looked out for kangaroos, but saw none.

The people with whom I shared the carriage were a heterogeneous mixture of squatters, as they termed men who had acquired land from the government, and other sorts of colonists, representing various trades and professions. It did not escape me that dress and apparent affluence did not necessarily correlate to breeding or manners. Some of the more expensively dressed were quite uncouth in language and personal habits, whilst my immediate neighbour, who was middle-aged and pleasant-featured, but positively shabby, spoke in a most cultivated tone and disclosed that he had read divinity at Oxford.

"You will find this topsy-turvyland," he told me quietly, while the prosperous-looking ones snored noisily with mouths agape. "Take my advice, sir, and never openly compare anything you see with how things are back at home. They do not wish to be reminded that there they were mere labourers, living in slums. Gold has made them men of property, but they have acquired no graces along with their expensive clothes, and do not care a fig. Their wives and daughters put on grand airs in their fine gowns, but their manners in private are those of the back streets."

"I suppose they came out as convicts," I observed. A pained look came over his face as he glanced about.

"That is something to which one never refers under any circumstances. One can no more judge a man here by his coat than by his way of speaking. The one you may take for a gentleman may be a scapegrace or even a villain, while your man sporting a nugget on his watch-chain, yet who picks his teeth and spits, may be a decent fellow who has not been afraid to work hard and has got his reward. He will not seek refinement, however, for it doesn't do for a man to set himself above his fellows. He may flaunt his wealth—that is acceptable—but he must keep in his place. Can you imagine, sir, that there was a time when fellows would eat five-pound notes between bread and butter, to show off how rich they had become?"

"You don't say!"

"I have seen it done. All the capital a man needed in those days was a spade, a tent, and some tea and coffee and biscuits and preserved meat. The gold was there, so near the surface that a child could have dug it with his tin spade."

His allusion reminded me of Henry's eagerness to dig for the Spanish treasure at Black Head. Gold-prospecting must have seemed to him like a dream fulfilled—yet something must have gone wrong. My neighbour supplied the explanation.

"The philosophy in those times, fifteen or more years ago, was, 'There's plenty more where this came from. Easy come, easy go.' But quite suddenly the surface gold ran out. They struck quartz. They broke their shovels on it. Those with diligence and a business turn of mind combined into companies and bought machinery to dig shafts and crush the rock after it had been quarried with explosives. Some of the shafts now are hundreds of feet deep. When you hear complaints that Ballarat is no longer what it was, it will mean that a miner has to work hard to earn a wage of about forty shillings a week, paid by a company. He can no longer hope to pick up a fortune by driving his heel into the earth. Thousands have left the town and moved on to such places as Bendigo, where the pickings are easier."

He fell to musing. I wondered what his own story had been, but did not venture to ask. I said, "I understand there are a good many Chinese nowadays."

"That's so. They can subsist on very little and have all the patience in the world. They are happy to fossick amongst the rubble left by others and reclaim whatever has been overlooked."

"I seem to have heard that they employ some Europeans who failed on their own account."

"Oh, those. Feckless wretches, most of them. Down-and-outs, drunkards. There is a living of some sort in this country for any man who will put his pride aside; but those are the dregs."

It mortified me to know that he was unwittingly including my own father in this category. I recalled the trim stone house at the head of Loch Ryan, and the outwardly serene man in his parlour chair, pipe alight, eyes fixed on something unseen. There seemed no possible association with this place into which the train was now jolting us; this weird, disrupted landscape of mine-shafts and great mounds of turned-up earth, littered with pieces of timber and rope and rusting tools which must have been flung down by exasperated diggers who could get no further with them, or else had made their pile and needed them no more.

I had not asked my friend his business. I doubted whether an Oxford divinity student with his cuffs frayed and the uppers of his boots straining from the soles would have welcomed the enquiry. As to myself, I volunteered to him that I was a ship's officer between voyages who fancied seeing a little of a strange land. He showed no curiosity and we parted with a handshake.

Outside Ballarat railway station, I stood with my belongings about me. In contrast with those desolate outskirts, I saw before me a large and prosperous town of substantial buildings of every sort. The men, women, and children who thronged the street were for the most part decently dressed. If I recognised my father, I hoped it should not be by his rags.

"Hotel, sir?" enquired a voice, and I saw a beady-eyed little man regarding me hopefully. I nodded. He gathered up my entire baggage in his hands and under his armpits and led off at a shambling trot. I was more occupied in scanning the bewhiskered faces thronging the sidewalk than in concerning myself about what nature of hotel he would find for me. In the event, the place looked decent and proved to be very well appointed.

It was too late in the day to start pursuing active enquiries about Father, but as soon as I had washed and put out enough things for the night, I was drawn, as though by a magnet, back into the bustling street. I wandered about until it was time for dinner, which was at an early hour, but saw none save strange faces there.

The meal was surprisingly good: soup, sole, chicken, and a light pudding. I drank some sherry and some wine. Only one thing marred the repast for me: the waiter who served it was my companion from the train journey. He had changed into waiter's garb, but wore those same broken boots. He was neither familiar nor mockingly deferential. He went about his duties, which he performed skilfully. When I rose, I handed him his tip, as I would have done to any other waiter. He gave a little bow and thanked me. As he had said, there was a living to be made for any man who would put his pride aside, and he was evidently his own witness to that. I turned in early, in philosophical mood.

Next morning, with a hearty breakfast inside me and feeling brisk from the keen air—Ballarat, I learned, was two thousand feet above sea level—I began my rounds of all those places where I thought that Father's name might be known. It proved a depressing task. The clerks in the administrative offices showed me little sympathy or patience. They seemed to care nothing for the whereabouts of a prospector unless he happened to owe money. "Watson? Dozens of 'em," was another attitude, and I learned also that no great store was set upon names, since so many men there went under assumed ones, for a variety of reasons. When I mentioned that he had last been heard of working for the Chinese, I got only sneers.

I tried instead those shops where miners' gear was sold. There flickered a gleam of brief hope when one man thought he knew to whom I was referring, and felt even more sure when I added that he might have had his son with him. But it had been months since, and the population of Ballarat had turned itself over several times in between. I went into drinking parlours, of which there were a great many, but came out again with the strengthening impression that unless a man were in some way impressive, either for the richness of his strike, the prodigiousness of his thirst, his capacity for violent behaviour, or some memorable eccentricity, he remained anonymous, as many wished to be.

The entire morning passed in this fruitless search. I determined that, after luncheon, I would go on to the diggings and look for white faces amongst the yellow. I turned my steps in the direction of my hotel. A stretch of wooden sidewalk led past a pawnshop, and I stopped to glance over the motley collection of items displayed without arrangement in its none-too-clean window: rings, brooches, tiepins, lockets, watches, chains, and every other conceivable sort of personal jewellery. My fellow passenger in the train, who doubtless would shortly be serving my luncheon, had told me how men had been willing to part with their last and closest possessions, rather than give up the search for gold and settle to a steady job for a regular wage.

As I looked over that detritus from fevered ambition, my

heart gave a sudden great thump. Among the watches lay one that was unmistakable to me: it was my father's, and I knew at once that the day he had pawned it would have been the same day that he wrote the despairing letter which had brought me all this way. It had been his wedding present from my mother's parents, and nothing short of desperation would have let him part with it.

I hurried inside. An old Jew behind the counter glanced up at me from a book in which he was writing figures.

"Ve don't do no slops 'ere," said he.

"Slops?"

"Ole clo'. You got to go to rag-fair for 'em."

"Who said anything about old clothes?"

He smirked. "Can't go on the diggin's in them smart things. Go down to rag-fair, aside the station. Get all you wants there."

"What I want, my good man, is that gold watch in your window. Or rather, I wish to know who deposited it with you."

His eyes turned shifty. "Gold watch?"

"The one with *H.W.* engraved on its back."

"Who says there's anything on the back? You can't see that through the window."

"Because I should know that watch anywhere, merely from looking at its face. Kindly get it out and see if I'm not right."

He moved reluctantly to obey. "Vot are you? A rozzer?"

"I am a ship's surgeon, and I have come here from Melbourne to look for my father, whose watch that is. If you can tell me anything of him, I shall be much obliged to you."

He was turning the watch over in his hands.

"I got it straightforward. A pledge, it was."

"For how much?"

"Ve don't tell that. Principle o' the trade."

"Look here, my name is Watson. The initials are my father's, Henry Watson. I am perfectly willing to redeem the pledge on his behalf, if you will tell me how much it is for."

"It ain't allowed, vithout the ticket. Anyways, it's time-expired."

"Lapsed?"

"It's generally the way. Not many of 'em ever comes back."

"Then the watch is for sale?"

"That's right. Fifty quid."

"Fifty! I suppose you lent five against it, at the most."

He tapped the side of his nose with a forefinger. "Didn't get it back, did I? Out o' pocket four month. Anyways, it's a nice gold watch, this 'ere, an' if you say there's some sentimental value as well . . ."

"I will offer you ten."

"That's a joke, ain't it?"

"I am entirely serious. Ten pounds, cash."

"If you say twenty-five I might just 'ear you."

I got out my pocket-book and examined its contents. I had not much over forty pounds, and my hotel bill to pay. Buying back the watch might force me to curtail my time in Ballarat and limit my search, but I could not risk losing it to some stranger. It had doubtless been on display for many weeks, and had not been sold, yet the very next person to enter the shop might take a fancy to it.

I took out twenty pounds and laid them on the counter, looking him significantly in the eye. He hesitated, then shrugged and pushed the watch across to me.

"Thank you," said I. "I am sure you have done well enough for yourself. Now, if you can tell me anything at all which enables me to trace my father, I will come back and add something to that before I leave the town."

He gave me his sly look as he scooped up the money and placed it in a drawer.

"Unless you got a father young enough to be your own brother, I reckon you're wastin' your time lookin'."

My startled mind struggled to grasp the implications of this. Either he had died and Henry had returned to Ballarat to claim his possessions; or one of his fellow workers had simply made the watch his own. There was another, far less savoury possibility.

"You remember him?" I asked.

"Do, now I look at you. Havin' me on, wasn't you? Not your ole man you're lookin' for. Brother, more like."

"I am after them both. They were here together, only I understand my brother moved on and my father stayed." A thought occurred to me. "You must surely have a note of the date on which the watch was brought in."

He answered merely with a nod, and I saw his thumb and forefinger rub meaningfully together. I took my pocket-book out again and produced a single note.

"It is all I can afford at present," I told him disgustedly.

He took possession of it, then went to the ledger in which he had been writing when I came in. He flipped back a good many pages, before bringing his finger to rest against an entry. He turned the book so that I could read for myself. My fear was realised. The watch had been pawned a full fortnight before the date of Father's despondent letter. I knew in my heart that, in reciting his woes, he had spared us the shameful detail that not only had Henry deserted him, but he had taken the watch with him.

I found Father that afternoon. It proved so simple that I need not have spent the morning so fruitlessly. I went on to the diggings where the industrious Chinese worked and lived in canvas tents, and made simple enquiries of such Europeans as I found there. After a few headshakes I encountered a tall, lean man, an American, who said he had worked alongside Father and Henry. He was able to tell me all I needed.

"Took it real hard when that young rat-bag skedaddled. Told me he didn't care no more whether he lived nor died. Know how he felt. Been that way myself sometimes."

"What . . . what has become of him?"

I dreaded the answer. It came with a shrug. "Last I heard, they took him into the Benevolent. Month or more ago. Went on one bender too many, I guess, and got picked up off the street."

"You have made no enquiries?"

He shrugged again. "Guys just come and go. The day they take me in, I won't be expectin' anyone askin' after me. It ain't the way out here."

"His son—my brother. Have you any idea where he might have gone?"

"The b—— was always talkin' big about movin' on up-country. Bendigo, Mount Korong, Mount Alexander, some place like that. I guess that's where he'd make for."

A sharp summons from one of the man's Chinese employers terminated the interview. There was nothing more to ask, anyway. I made my way back into the town and soon found the Benevolent Institution. It was a well-ordered place for the care of helpless old people and the many babies and infants who were found abandoned by their unmarried parents, and even, I learned with horror, by married ones, lured on by the gold fever to other places and not wishing the encumbrance of children upon their wanderings.

The superintendent proved to be a Dr. Ramsay, a Bart's man himself, though of a generation before mine, and we shared a little general chatter before I told him of my quest. His pleasant expression turned grave.

"You are only just in time, I'm afraid. He has been here almost a month, but we have been able to do little for him. He has no will to live. You know how crucial that is."

"Do you think he is capable of talking to me?"

"He says nothing to the staff, and can no longer be persuaded to eat. It may be that the sight of you will make him bestir himself. I must warn you, though, that there is no hope of his rallying. He has gone too far for that."

He led me personally into the ward where the old men lay awaiting death. My medical training had not prepared me for the shock of seeing my own father so debilitated. His eyes were great hollows, his cheeks sunken to the bone, his once-raven hair turned a dirty white. He had a thin, ragged beard. Yet, even in this state, I could see the Spaniard in him, as perhaps he had appeared on his own deathbed. I was reminded of a *memento mori,* carved in the stone of a Tudor tomb.

His eyes were open, but he showed no recognition as I leaned across.

"It is I, Father," I said. "John."

The superintendent touched my shoulder and went away. I sought one of the long hands lying inert on the sheet and took it in one of mine. It was icy cold and felt like a bunch of dead twigs.

"I came to find you," I said. "Thank God I have been able to."

Still he did not stir. I rambled on, hoping against hope for a miracle.

"If you will only eat again, and get your strength back for a fight, I will stay here with you. However long it takes, I will help you battle through and will take you back home with me."

With my free hand I took his watch from my pocket. I drew his hands together into a bony cup and placed the watch in it.

"Mama forgave you," I said. "So did I, long ago. I only wish you had written sooner. I would have come."

He still did not move his limbs, but I fancied I saw his eyes change. Looking closely, I saw it was because a tear had formed in the corner of each. One of them spilled out, to trickle down his left cheek; and then I knew he was gone.

12

"We plunged away at a furious pace."

My one thankfulness at this melancholy time was that I had been able to save my father from a pauper's grave. The friendly Dr. Ramsay, a well-fed man in his forties with an engaging smile, gave me an introduction to an undertaker and a stonemason.

"I'm afraid it will have to be something modest at first," I replied, referring to the headstone. "By the time I've settled with the hotel and paid for my ticket back to the coast, I'll be down to my last few pounds."

"Why not leave your instructions for a permanent stone, and remit the money when you get back home?" he suggested. "O'Reilly will deal fairly with you. Send me a line, too. I'll make sure that it's carried out properly, and have the grave photographed for you."

"That's more than decent of you," I said, shaking his hand gratefully.

"As one Bart's man to another." He shrugged. "But, look here, I've a better idea. I'll stump up the money now and you can repay me."

"You would trust me?"

"If I can't trust a man who would come all this way to give his father a decent send-off, whom can I trust? Make it fifty pounds, eh? You've got to live until you're back aboard ship."

This unlooked-for kindness and generosity, on top of my emotion over Father, came close to unmanning me. My first impulse on his proposing a loan had been to offer to leave the watch with him as security. I was thankful I had not. It would have been almost an insult to the spirit of his gesture.

He went further still, inviting me to dine with him that evening in his bachelor apartment in the Institution. The meal was served by a pretty young Irishwoman, who I fancied was rather more to him than mere cook and servant. She retired discreetly after removing the things, leaving us to smoke and yarn away a most agreeable few hours, lubricated with a bottle of excellent whisky.

"How do you intend getting back?" he asked, as I was at last preparing to take my leave.

"I came up by train, rather than lose time. If there had been less haste, I think I'd have taken a friend's advice and used the coach."

"That's what I was going to suggest. Get a far better feel of the country that way, and you might as well, since you're here. In fact, if you've time to spare, why don't you carry on up to Mount Alexander, and perhaps Bendigo? You'll see plenty to interest you, and the direct run from those parts is far more spectacular than going back from here. Two or three days will fit it in easily, if your bones can stand the shaking."

"My liver will be grateful for it, after all your whisky." I laughed, and we wished one another a cheerful good night.

I had recognised the names of those places from that American digger's laconic speculation as to where Henry might have gone. There was just a chance that I might run across him. I had been thinking about him as I went about my melancholy arrangements that afternoon. One part of me insisted that it was my duty to try to find him. He was obviously destitute, and, much as I despised him, now more than ever before, he was my only close kin. If I could persuade him to accompany me home, there was surely hope yet for his redemption. He should not, however, go unpunished for his callous abandonment of Father; he should have the hiding of his life from me. It was that resolution which made me hesitate to go after him at all. I was unsure whether I could trust myself not to half-kill him, or worse. The black taint which I was ever conscious might some day overturn reason, if only momentarily, might precipitate me into violence beyond my control; I did not wish to have my days ended by a colonial noose, condemned for fratricide.

Father was buried next day, in a graveyard already unduly thronged, I thought, for so young a settlement. Most of the inscriptions which I paused to read on tombstones that ranged from the most expensively elaborate to mere wooden crosses related to men in their twenties and thirties. Their numbers were matched by the many other mounds which bore no identification. The elderly parson whose services I had managed to obtain was my only companion at the graveside, where we were watched by two bearded labourers, leaning on long-handled shovels and smoking clay pipes. As soon as the undertaker's men had lowered the coffin and strolled away, chatting and spitting, the waiting sextons moved forward and commenced shovelling in the earth in great clumsy clods, which thumped down on to the plain wood. I was thankful to turn away. It was so far removed, in decorum as well as distance, from our Stranraer respectability of so few years ago. I looked forward to telling Henry as much, and emphasising it with my fist. Perhaps that would bring him back to his senses in a way that persuasion could not.

I decided there and then that I would make the brief excursion which my friend had suggested. If I chanced to meet Henry, it would be because I was meant to, for both our sakes, and I must prove myself capable of controlling my wrath. If our paths did not happen to cross, however, and a simple search not bring him to light, I would accept it as Fate's decree and leave him to his own life. Whether he finished up a nameless corpse, as Father had so nearly done, or a gold millionaire, would be Providence's responsibility, not mine.

I had an obligation to fulfil before quitting Ballarat. It took me back to the pawnshop where I had found the watch. The Jew was behind his counter, scrutinising something closely through an eyeglass. He smirked triumphantly on recognising me.

"Ho! Come to pop it again, have you?"

"Certainly not. I promised you that if I succeeded in finding my father, I should come back and add something to what I paid. I did find him, and although it was not directly due to you, I feel I owe you some gratitude."

He looked astonished, and on hearing my account his look softened and I fancied his brown eyes moistened.

"God rest 'is pore soul," he said huskily. "It vasn't none of my helping that you found 'im, though."

"I think it was a last comfort to him to hold the watch in his hands, and to pass out of the world not wholly disenchanted," I explained. "I am grateful for that at least."

"Maybe, maybe, but I don't vant nothin' more off you."

"Well, I'm not exactly flush, as I told you. I did wonder, though, whether you might be able to sell me an albert to go with the watch, so that I may wear it myself?"

There had been no chain with it when I had found it, and he had told me then that there had never been one. My guess was that Father himself had parted with his plain gold one when down to his last extremity, but had balked at getting rid of the watch itself. The pawnbroker delved into a drawer under his counter and brought out a whole fistful, which he deposited on the counter in a heap.

"There's plenty more," he said.

I rummaged through and quickly found one quite suited to the watch. It was of some yellow metal, not gold, unelaborate in pattern, and looked as though it might not be too expensive.

"This would do nicely," I said, demonstrating the effect. He nodded approval.

"How much, then?"

He took the watch from me and expertly attached the chain. "To you, nix."

"No, no. I insist."

"Listen, I got dozens. First thing most o' them pops ven they gets 'ere and 'as to buy tools and things. They never comes back. They strike it lucky, they gets fancy ones made up, to show off their nuggets. They don't strike it, then an albert's the last thing they've got tin left to spend on."

"All the same, I came here to give you money. I can't walk out with a free watch chain instead!"

He tapped his nose, grinning slyly. "You ever 'ear somebody sayin' Jews is a pack o' Shylocks, jest you tell 'em there's some as ain't."

I shook his hand heartily and left his shop.

I would not have missed the experience of riding on Cobb and Co.'s coaches for the world. Of course, in that part of my life before the advent of the motor vehicle I had been accustomed to travel in many types of horse-drawn vehicle: gigs, traps, waggonettes, post-chaises, cabs of various sorts, and, in London, the lumbering knife-board omnibus. The stage-coach of yore was a romantic subject of my imagination, as was the frontier coach of America, the rugged Concord which had carried the successors of the Californian

"Forty-niners" through the Sierra Nevada to the gold-fields beyond the high passes. It was a thrill I had coveted, to ride on the box of such a vehicle, drawn by a team of dashing thoroughbreds, controlled by a leather-skinned, hard-swearing driver of the old school. I hurried eagerly to the booking-office, a substantial brick and granite edifice whose stone balustrades punctuated with classical urns contrasted with billboards below listing the coach routes and fares. I reserved a place for Mount Alexander on the following day.

There was nothing elegant about the "Cobbs," and virtually no resemblance to the "olde English" stage-coaches of the prints and Christmas cards. They appeared deceptively light, but were enormously strong, the larger ones able to carry fourteen passengers and a great deal of luggage and freight, which occupied the roof and open boot. Solid wooden benches were the only inside seating, and there were neither doors nor windows, only rolled canvas blinds which could be let down to keep out rain and cold. Comfort came last for Australians in those days.

"Set for'ard and hold yerself loose," was the advice I received from the lanky, long-boned driver beside whom I sat on the box seat of the Mount Alexander coach next day. I was apprehensive at first of being pitched out head-first, but soon got the knack and began to enjoy the drive.

I had paid the extra for the privilege of the driver's company, rather than ride inside. I gathered that these men were great characters, highly skilled at their trade and ready raconteurs when in the mood, as mine proved to be. Like so many of them, evidently, he was an American, self-introduced as Long Jim Clucas, tempted to Australia by word of mouth of the high wages Cobb and Co. were willing to pay to expert drivers able to establish themselves as favourites of regular travellers, and of the rich pickings in tips to be made on the side.

"Stands to sense," he told me from the side of his mouth

nearest to me, seated on his left; the right seemed to be reserved for the emission of great squirts of tobacco juice. "Treat 'em pally, and they'll stay travelling with the line. Ruffle their feathers, and they'll take their asses to somebody else's seats, then maybe you've lost 'em for good. Bosses don't like that, so they pay you good for to keep smilin', like me."

He turned and demonstrated a broken-toothed leer. I had been about to ask him where donkeys came into this, but realised what he meant in time to prevent his adding another anecdote to the repertoire from which he kept those regular passengers happy.

" 'Sides," he went on, "you're the first they remember when they've struck it rich and are coming back all liquored up and their pack full o' dust. Right open-handed they can be then to someone they count their pal."

"You will be owning coaches yourself one day," I suggested.

"No, sir. Not me. There's them as has tried breaking off on their own, but the big lines soon run 'em off the road. They pay high for you to keep loyal, but they sure get mean if you try hivin' off their trade. Me, I'm happy. Don't I look happy?"

Long Jim gave me his leer again.

"Extremely," I assured him. "It must be a hard life, though."

"It's a man's work, I give you that. Set up here hours on end, in all weathers. Gotta keep to time, for the company and the Post Office. Reach the next stage and find your durn relief's gone sick, you jest gotter keep goin', like Jack Peck, the night he had to take the Bendigo mail on from Castlemaine to Melbourne without a wink o' sleep for sixty hours afore he set off. Said he slep' all through the Black Forest, that's six mile, and din't wake up till they ran off the corduroy and he felt the motion change. It was freezin' cold, and all the passengers was huddled together inside. He made 'em come up by turns and set beside him on the box, to stick a woman's durn great hatpin in him whenever he started dozin' off. You got the mail to get through on the dot, an' the passengers' lives is all in your hand.''

He held up his great left hand in which the reins controlling the five-horse team lay. I could judge from the callosities on the thick fingers that there was no exaggerating the hard work of controlling the surging beasts who drew us at a never-flagging pace, their hooves and our wheels throwing up a cloud of dust which we drew like a white banner behind us.

Suddenly he cried out, ''Daisy, ye lazy bitch!''

He swung the great whip which lay in his right hand's grasp, like a fly-fisher making his cast. Its twelve-foot thong seemed merely to touch the neck of the wheeler he had addressed, causing it to make a spurt of extra energy, to which its companions responded.

''Lazy bitch,'' he repeated, but I sensed affection in his tone.

''You don't need to use the whip much, I see.''

''Naw. They knows me, an' they knows I know them. Play up all their tricks jest out o' devilment, they will, but they knows they'll get tickled up for it. It's their way o' not gettin' bored.''

''Do you always have your own team of nags?''

''All the way through. Fresh team every ten mile or so, but all reg'lar to their own driver. Goddamn it, you bitch, didn't I jest tell ye?''

But I think his roar was more for my benefit than any genuine rebuke, and the horse momentarily turned its head to its nearest companion, as would say with a look, ''There he goes, showing off again!''

In this style we bowled along at a good ten miles an hour or so, our vehicle swaying rhythmically on its taut springs, but with none of the lateral movement which I had heard from my elders was the bane of coach travel in England, with the constant risk to those outside of being jerked overboard, and needing to hold on grimly all the way. Those Cobbs were first-class examples of the coach-builder's craft. Their drivers, from the brief experience I gained of them, were of correspondingly high quality, tough, dedicated, and the best of companions. Travelling that dusty, rutted road, between alternating stretches of empty countryside, scrawny, brittle bush, and delicate glades of eucalyptus trees, under an immensity of sky seemingly only matched by that over sea, I felt that here was a land where a man might prove his manhood and garner a store of experience to comfort his old age with the feeling of fulfilment.

The driver raised a stubby little horn to his lips and blew a penetrating flourish. Then he tickled up all three leading nags in one deft sweep of green thong. I saw a little settlement ahead, and smiled to recognise the way he had summoned up that last extra spurt, to enable him to pull up with bravura effect before a low wooden shack with a veranda. The passengers beneath me tumbled out and ran, women and men, not through the open doorway but round the back. I realised their purpose, and followed suit, and was able to enter the building at last and take my place at table feeling able to concentrate fully on my meal.

The outdoor facilities had been primitive, and this dining-room was austere: merely some long tables and benches, and a bar at the end. The service, however, would have done credit to any city rooms. A meat soup was already before us as we sat down, with a thick hunk of delicious bread at every plateside. An immense rattling behind a screen in the corner heralded the speedy appearance of plates of roast meat and potatoes, and then, in their turn, more bread and a jelly-like jam which a neighbour told me was prickly pear. The serving and consumption of the entire meal cannot have occupied half an hour, yet the only waiter at table had been a young man in waistcoat and rolled shirt sleeves, and the cooking staff who at length emerged to receive congratulations and exchange compliments with the regulars was one pretty, perspiring young woman, several months in the family way, who proved to be his wife. They ran this changing station together, along with the wife's brother who served as groom, and, I gathered from Long Jim afterwards, could so rely on the punctuality of the coaches that the meal would be fully ready to start serving up at the sounding of that approaching horn.

I paid my shilling and went outside to stretch my legs briefly. A fresh team of horses was already harnessed to our vehicle and our driver was checking the security of the gear. Nearby, in fenced stockades, dozens of other horses took their rest or waited their turn for their particular driver to come along. I could only marvel at the organisation and efficiency, all the more unexpected from the generally unconcerned manner I had come to associate with the settlers of this sparsely populated land.

A suggestive tootle of the horn summoned us back to the coach, and we were on our way again. We had covered the sixty miles from Ballarat to Mount Alexander by late afternoon. Long Jim was driving on to Bendigo with the third new team of the journey, but I chose to stay overnight in a modest hotel, on the chance that I might run into Henry. Although I roamed the thronged, noisy streets until a late hour, as I had done at Ballarat when searching for Father, I looked about me in vain. It would have been pointless to make enquiries. I wondered whether I should even recognise him if Fate did send him across my path; but I thought that however hard living and adversity might have changed him, I should know those Spaniard's eyes of his anywhere.

Following a good night and a surprising breakfast of *filet de boeuf à la Parisienne,* eggs, more excellent bread and butter, and rich black tea, I took my place in the next available coach for Bendigo. Two men were already in possession of the box seat with the driver, so I had to ride inside. The company and the experience were by no means as agreeable as the previous day's. A disagreeable boy child's clamour and his mother's monotonous but ineffectual scolding combined with a commercial traveller's rank cigars and the dust which swirled up from hooves and front wheels to cause me profound relief that this journey was of only twenty miles, with but a single change. On arriving in Bendigo I went straight into the coach office and asked for a box seat for the through run to Melbourne starting next day. It was a distance of one hundred miles, and I was determined to make it as enjoyable as I could. The clerk tried to convince me that inside seats only were available. I drew upon my little store of money, whereupon he discovered with effusive surprise that he had been mistaken, after all.

I had booked for next day with almost certainty that I should not find Henry and need to stay there longer. This proved to be the case. I am sure that Bendigo and its celebrated diggings, far more extensive than Ballarat's, and peopled with men and women of every nationality and costume, would have made a fascinating study, had I been in the mood. But I felt I had seen enough already, and looked forward to returning to the coast. Reaction to Father's death had been delayed through the exhilaration of the ride with Long Jim. Now it was upon me, and I realised that in fact I cared scarcely a jot whether I found Henry, and what I should do with him, other than thrash him, if I did.

I was glad to wake next morning knowing that I should soon be on the road again; and gladder still when, on arriving to take the coach, I found the driver to be none other than

Long Jim Clucas again. I scrambled up beside him and assumed the prescribed forward-drooping posture like a veteran. His bugle sounded, the long whip snaked in the air with a pistol-like crack, and five white horses heaved forward as one.

The morning's air was crisp and keen. My direction now was towards the sea and homeward, with the hope of a sporty interval with my buxom Australian friend before setting sail. I was turned twenty-five. All life awaited me. The fresh energy of those white horses seemed to correspond with what I myself felt as I drew my collar high about my face to shield it from the penetrating cold.

Little did I imagine that I should shortly be living in a nightmare.

13

"What you would call over here a highway robber."

Long Jim was singing beside me:

"He was scarcely sixteen when he left his father's home,
A convict to Australia, across the seas to roam,
They put him in the chain gang in the Government employ,
But ne'er a chain on earth could hold the Wild Colonial Boy.

And when they sentenced him to hang to end his wild career,
With a wild shout of defiance, bold Donahoe broke clear.
He robbed the wealthy settlers, their stock he did destroy,
But no trooper in the land could catch the Wild Colonial Boy."

"I understood it wasn't done to speak the word 'convict' out here any longer," I joked when he had done.

"Ain't even strictly legal to sing that there ditty," he replied. "Shows how little they know of human natur'. They hadn't gone and put a ban on it, Jack Donahoe'd 'a bin forgot by now."

"Just as well, from the sound of him. Who was he?"

"Like the song says, a wild colonial boy. Shipped out from Ireland in the 'twenties or thereabouts. Took to the bush and lived by cattle-rustling and bailing up folks for whatever they was carryin'."

"A bush-ranger?"

"That's right. Frank Gardiner, Ben Hall, and Fred Ward—Cap'n Thunderbolt, he liked to call himself."

"A desperate crew, eh?"

"Some, I guess. They treated them convicts real hard, though. Can't say I wonder they'd go on the run and chance gettin' shot down, sooner'n get took agin. At least they was men."

"Pretty well died out as a breed, have they?"

"These parts, yes. There's the odd one crops up now an' agin, but they're more New South Wales an' Queensland way now, by all accounts."

"Have you ever been held up on the road, Jim?"

He spat copiously. "Once or twice. Nothin' serious."

"Is it true that some of them have a sort of code of honour, like the highwaymen? Letting a lady keep her jewels in exchange for a kiss, and so forth?" I had come across something of that nature in my boyhood reading. Long Jim laughed.

"Never heard tell of that meself. There was Cap'n Morgan, though, bailed up a homestead once an' made one o' the womenfolks play 'Home, Sweet Home' for him on the pi-anner. Didn't do him no good. Surrounded the house and shot him down like a dog, they did. Put his corpus on show at Wangaratta. Folks used to pose with it for their photographs, till some nosy medico took his head off to pry around inside it."

He spat again, with unmistakable contempt.

"You have a bit of a soft spot for some of them?" said I.

"Cain't be no life, on the run in all weathers, no one to trust, no woman to tend to you, every day like to be your last.

Sure, they were thievin' skunks, a lot of 'em, but there ain't many folks wouldn't give one a square meal and let him go on his way, if he didn't do 'em no harm. Like back in the States, folks here ain't that keen on having the Government and police tell 'em how to run their lives."

Remembering an engraving from one of those adventure books, I asked, "I suppose all the gold is brought down in armed convoys?"

"Sometimes. When there's a deal of it to be shipped at once."

"You mean that smaller amounts are sent by ordinary coach? I wonder there isn't a bush-ranger waiting every mile along the way."

He patted the seat between us. "You're settin' on some now. It's hid under a bag o' wheat in here. They ain't after gold, most of 'em, though. You cain't eat gold, an' they cain't cash it in, 'cos they'd be twigged at the assay office. Money and clothes and the sort of valuables they can pop without questions asked is more in their line." He gestured briefly. "That gold ticker on your chain there. That's their style."

I resolved hastily that, should anything untoward occur to us, I would waste no time in cramming the treasured watch down behind the box. For a mile or two, I watched the margins of the road more carefully, alert for any watchful figure erect on a motionless black horse, moving only to raise the dark neckerchief up over his lower face before stepping his mount forward from the tree shadows. I saw no such being, however, and soon forgot about the subject as Long Jim, loquacious as ever, proceeded to regale me with salty yarns picked up from the commercial travellers who frequently rode with him. If only a quarter of the anecdotes were true, the women of the lonely homesteads evidently led a busier and more varied life than their remote situation implied.

With the satisfaction of knowing that every mile we

travelled was taking me nearer to the coast, I enjoyed this drive as much as I had that first day's run out of Ballarat. Some of the scenery was spectacular, not necessarily in the sense of panoramic grandeur, but for the stately stands of gum-trees, mimosa, and other colourful plant life growing thick and wild on the steep banks bordering the roadway. Brilliant-hued parrots and other birds strange to me flitted and swooped and gave curious tongue. It was quite the most exotic land journey I had ever taken.

We changed teams and enjoyed another hearty meal. I felt quite dozy after it, and might have nodded off, had we not reached a section where logs had been laid side by side laterally to form the surface of the track for some hundred yards, over which the wheels bumped infernally. For once I was forced to hold on to the railing of the box seat. Above the racket it caused, I could hear the lamentations of the inside passengers.

"Durned corduroy!" Jim spat. "Plays old Harry with the wheels. Still, I guess it's better'n a waterlogged track for weeks on end."

He had regaled me with some fearsome tales of flooding and bush-fires. This was an in-between season, so I could endure the shaking-up philosophically. He had also told me of various kinds of mishap, from both experience and hearsay. We were not long off the so-called corduroy section, and starting to descend a long steep incline, when there came an occurrence which jerked me instantly from my complacency.

The brakes, I had observed, were worked by his feet pressing on long bars in the floor on either side, causing a bar beneath the chassis to bring brake blocks to bear against the back wheels. Now, as Jim's long legs bore down, one of them suddenly shot forward with a crash against the boarding; the pedal's resistance had failed and it had given way. At once our vehicle began to gather speed.

"God damn!" Jim yelled, and to my surprise jerked the long whip from its socket beside him. There was no playfulness in the way he used it on his team this time. In place of sharp, stinging little flicks, the great thong of kangaroo hide lashed into their backs, causing them to toss their heads from the hurt, but to surge forward with an access of speed. I could not understand the wisdom of making an obviously brakeless coach on a steepening downward slope go even faster, but it was no moment for asking questions.

A horse neighed under the lash. The inside passengers gave different voice now, mingling cries of alarm from the men and a woman's and child's screams.

"Hold on like hell!" Jim shouted to me, not shifting his eyes from the road. He was making no effort to rein the horses in, but drove them on ever faster, his whip arm swinging to and fro. The sight and sound of the lash falling on the poor beasts' backs made me wince, despite our danger.

It needed only an abrupt bend in the track ahead and we should be doomed. We could never get round one at that speed. We should topple over on to the track, or be dashed against the roadside overhang, with almost certain fatalities. I resolved to try to jump clear at the last moment and hope for relatively minor injury.

Luckily, there was no such bend, as Long Jim must have known, for he uttered no warning, merely concentrated all his effort on making his team fly hell-for-leather down that slope. Gradually, the incline began to ease, and at last levelled out. Only now did Jim start to increase his pressure on the reins, drawing them back firmly against his chest, slowing the horses to a canter, then a trot, finally halting them altogether. Before I could congratulate him, he had leapt down from the box and was caressing the animals in turn, rubbing their tossing noses to calm them, offering them endearments and apologies in a manner that was positively touching.

The inside passengers paid no heed to this. As one, they had tumbled out and made for what cover there was on either side of the track, eager to relieve their anxiety in separate privacy. I thought I had better take the opportunity, too, but first I had to thank Long Jim for saving us.

"Knew there wasn't no bends." He shrugged, rubbing down his sweating animals with an old towel. "Still, it only wants for one animal to go down, and you're a sartin gonner."

"Is there less likelihood of that the faster they gallop?"

" 'Tain't that. See, goin' downhill, the coach is sartin to run into the polers if it catches up with 'em. On'y thing is to keep 'em at full stretch so's they stays ahead. Means layin' into the poor b——s, but there's no ways else."

"You're making your peace with them, at any rate."

"First thing you gotter do. See, a horse can on'y think of one thing at a time. He knows you're a-hurtin' him, and he don't know why. Now they knows I'm pettin' 'em, an' they're calmin' down already, see? They'll have clean forgot their lashin' soon. But if you leave it, an' don't make up to 'em soon's you can, they go on rememberin'."

My respect for Long Jim Clucas and his kind swelled. This understanding between beast and man seemed a demonstration of something basic and elemental which had been left behind in lands where progress had gone more apace than here. It occurred to me how the "horsy" set back home would look down their snobbish noses if a man such as this were to presume to present himself amongst them; yet how much he could teach them, assuming that they should even care to learn!

My fellow passengers were straggling back now, chattering excitedly and coming to cluster round Long Jim and praise his skill. I took my turn to go behind a bush. Before I was quite ready to return, I heard a call of "Mail up!" which I took to be the mail-coach equivalent of "All aboard!" I hurried back to the road, not wanting to incur Jim's displeasure by further disrupting his precious schedule; but just before breaking cover, I stopped suddenly and stood quite still.

The grouped passengers stood facing me, as did Jim, automatically still stroking the nose of one of his wheelers. Between us, with his back to me, legs planted firmly apart, stood a man with a shot-gun.

I knew at once that he was a bush-ranger. That cry I had heard must have been "Bail up!"—the bush-ranger's equivalent of "Stand and deliver!"

He wore leather breeches and heavy boots and leggings. His thick shirt was of the typical digger's red-flannel sort, and he had on his head a floppy wide-awake hat. At the back of his neck I could see the knot in the dark neckerchief which concealed his face.

His gun was held against one hip, ready for use. I hesitated, wondering what to do for the best, as he advanced on the group, holding out his other hand. To my surprise, the passengers obediently began rummaging about their clothing, producing money and small objects of value which they meekly proffered to him. There was no move by Jim or any of the other menfolk to tackle him.

I looked round cautiously, wondering if he had accomplices, unseen to me, who were covering the group from other points. I saw no one. Obviously, he had been lying in wait at this place, planning to take a coach before it could get up speed after the careful slow descent of the hill down which we had careered. Our having had to stop completely had given him his perfect opportunity, but he had held back until he had thought all the passengers had returned from the bushes and he had them in a compact group. Somehow, he had failed to spot me entering the bush just as he emerged.

From the others' mild acceptance of the robbery, it seemed to me that they had no intention of opposing him, and that he would be feeling complete master of the situation. His shotgun barrel dropped unchecked towards the ground as he busied himself cramming his pockets and a leather wallet at his belt with their contributions. I tiptoed from cover and made towards him as rapidly as I dared.

Jim Clucas saw me coming, but gave nothing away. One of the two women put a startled hand to her mouth, but the bush-ranger did not seem to notice. The others all saw me, but somehow managed not to let him see it.

When I was within some six paces of him, the only child passenger gave a sudden cry and pointed at me. As the man whirled, I sprang.

The gun barrel jerked up, but I had got it under my arm before it went off with a bang, which set the women and child screaming and made my ears ring. It could not harm me, though, and I used all my strength to squeeze it against my side and wring it from his grasp. Only now I saw a sheathed knife at his belt. I took a quick double step forward and grasped him in my arms, pinioning both of his. He had not my physique, and I was confident that I could deal with him. Long Jim was moving forward to assist me, but I called to him to keep back.

My intention was to employ the old schoolboy trick of hooking a leg behind one of his and shoving him backward, giving him a tumble. Suddenly, though, he went limp in my arms. I thought it was a trick to make me hesitate. Taking a chance, I let go of him, stood back slightly, and gave him an almighty straight right between the eyes. He went down flat on his back like a falling log.

I reached down and dragged him up again. As I let go, he started to crumple. I crashed my left into the pit of his stomach and followed it with an upper-cut to the jaw which sagged towards me. He struck the track with a loud thud, dust billowing up about him.

I stooped to pull him up for some more. Blood was gushing

from his nose, and his eyes were shut, but my blind fury took no account of that.

"For God's sake, man!" I heard one of the other men expostulate.

It would not have stopped me, but I felt myself seized by both arms and dragged backwards. Jim Clucas had me by one of them, and a passenger by the other.

"Get off me!" I yelled at them. Their grip tightened.

"For the love o' Pete, you'll murder the guy!" shouted Jim. "Can't you see he's out for the count?"

"I don't give a damn!" I raged. "Let go!"

"No durn fear," Jim replied. "I'm driving this here coach, and I'm responsible to the law. I ain't having no killin' done, specially of a guy what cain't defend himself, an' with women an' children lookin' on."

I made a final struggle, but the two of them together were too much for me. And suddenly the crimson mist of rage cleared. Dementia receded, leaving me chilled and trembling, grateful suddenly for their grasp, without which I might have fallen.

"Well done, sport," I heard another man say, and a general murmur of congratulation took him up. The hands holding me slackened and left me swaying where I stood.

The two women had gone to squat beside the inert form. They drew the blood-soaked neckerchief from over his nose, revealing black moustaches and beard.

"Is it Captain Moonlight, Mama?" the child piped.

"Naw," Long Jim answered for her. "Nothin' like."

I pulled myself together with an effort and made to go towards the still figure. A man quickly stepped into my way, his expression outraged.

"It's all right," I assured him wearily, "I am a doctor."

I knelt beside him and felt his pulse. It was strong. I saw that I had not broken his nose or jaw, though it would be some time before he would breathe or eat with any comfort.

"Poor fellow. You could have killed him," an elderly woman said, looking up with eyes full of reproach. There was a murmur from the others. There were scowls and head-shakings now. I thought what topsy-turvy loyalties must prevail in this extraordinary land.

"Can you spare some water?" I asked Jim. He nodded and fetched one of the leather flasks. I poured some of it over the forehead, already swelling into a great lump where my fist had landed with all my strength behind it. With my wetted handkerchief I wiped his brow and eyes and cleared away the blood from his nose and lips.

He groaned and stirred slightly. His eyes flickered open, closed, and opened again. I watched them focus on mine.

I got to my feet.

"He'll be all right," I said, and turned away, shaking anew, to sit on the iron coach step, the bloodied handkerchief forgotten in my hand.

I felt it withdrawn, and saw Long Jim looking down at me, frowning with puzzlement.

"You didn't have to do any o' that," he said. "The poor guy on'y wanted some cash and bits an' pieces. Like I told you, live an' let live."

"I'm sorry," I muttered. "I'm not used to your ways."

"You meant good. Pretty handy with the dooks for a medico. But, Christ, pickin' him off the floor and layin' into him again when he was already out . . . What you want to go at him like that for?"

"Because he's my brother," I said.

14

"I expect . . . that I shall share your downfall."

"*Because* he's your brother!" Long Jim echoed.

"What will happen to him?" I asked, not wishing to be drawn further.

He creased his leathery brow. "I dunno. Don't usually arise. They jest b——r off back into the bush, and that's the last you see of 'em—unless there's a reward poster of 'em outside a cop shop. Next thing you get to hear, they've been taken or shot down. They don't last long."

"You would let him go?"

"Sure. Don't go offerin' 'em no free rides at Cobb and Co.'s expense. Look, mister, we got to get movin'."

"Will you be reporting this?"

"Not me. Us drivers prefers to keep our noses clean, case they get to hear and remember and come shootin' next time. Mind, someones else might say a word, on'y it looks like if they all got their stuff back off him, so mebbe they won't."

The passengers had indeed been plundering Henry's pockets and wallet as he sat there in the dust, holding his head with one hand and his stomach with the other.

"Do me a favour, please," I asked, getting up. "Keep it

from the others that he's my brother. I'll take responsibility for him."

"You'd have done him in if we hadn't a' stopped you."

"I owed him what he got. It's too long a story to go into, but it's out of my system now. If you'll take him along on the box with us, I'll pay."

He was shaking his head. "Nothin' doin'. On'y wants us to come across a trooper out lookin' for him, and it'd be the end of Jim Clucas where Cobb and Co. is concerned. Turnin' a blind eye's one thing. Aidin' a criminal's another."

"How far are we from Melbourne?"

"Fifty mile."

"If he and I get to the next posting station, where they may not know of him, can we get on a coach like any ordinary passengers?"

"No one ever got on or off there in all my years on this road. Ain't nobody livin' local save the old couple as keeps the place, and the troopers call reg'lar."

I looked across at Henry. He still sat in the dust, ignored now by the passengers, who were waiting for Jim to get moving. He was skeletal under the shirt. His face was gaunt and aged, as Father's had been, its darkened skin and black whiskers accentuating the Spanishness of his eyes. Our ancestor must have looked something like this, cast up on the rocks, certain his time was come. I might have known, I thought bitterly, that, having taken all this trouble to find him, I should let Henry land me in a mess of these proportions. I could not leave him now, though. He looked so defeated, as Father had sometimes done after losing his job. He must have been truly desperate to have sunk to this level. Were I to desert him now, it would be on my conscience for ever.

"Very well," I decided. "I'll stay with him. We'll take our chance together."

"Suit yourself. I guess I'd be leery of being left with you if I was in his shoes."

"All aboard, folks!" he called to the others. They began climbing in, without a backward glance at Henry.

"Don't let on it was me told you this," he said, "on'y I reckon your best bet is to keep to the bush near the track till you hear a waggon come along. Ain't many out this far, but you may find somethin'. He'll likely give you a lift for a quid or two, and no questions asked. Hide you 'mongst whatever he's carryin', mebbe. On'y, make sure it is a waggon, afore you shows yourselves. If a trooper sees two guys on their lonesome in these parts he'll surely take you in on suspicion. And get rid o' that there gun. Get caught with that, and you'll risk swinging."

"Will you take it?"

"Nope. Don't want no explainin' to do. Come on, I'll hand your bag down."

"What about the others?"

"They won't say nuthin'. Like I say, folks out here don't care to get mixed up in police matters."

He climbed on to his box and handed down my small valise. He also gave me one of his water flasks. I reached up and shook his big hand.

"It's been a pleasure to ride with you, Mr. Clucas."

"Mutual. Thanks for jumpin' him, by the way. Guns make me nervous."

"You!"

"Prefer the peaceful life. So long, mister."

A jerk of the reins, a shout; the horses' broad shoulders strained and the coach began to move. I turned away to Henry, wasting no time.

"Now, you skunk," I said. "Let's get you out of sight of the road, then you're going to exercise that jaw."

I hauled him to his feet and shoved him unceremoniously up the bank and out of sight of the track. When I let go of him, he sank to the ground and broke into sobs, his shoulders heaving. I knew he was not shamming.

I had not considered the possibility that he might have accomplices. It seemed unlikely; they would surely all have taken part in the hold-up. When he eventually ceased blubbing, which I left him to do without interference, he surprised me by sniffling, "Just . . . in here a way . . . bit of a camp."

It proved to be a pathetic shelter made from boughs and leaves, a mere place to huddle, whose covering would have kept out neither rain nor wind. Its sole furnishing was a grey blanket, and there was a worn knapsack which sagged half-emptily. A billycan hung from a triangle of sticks over a small unlit fire. It was empty.

"For God's sake, Harry!" I cried. "Are you off your nut or something?"

"I'm all to smash, Jack," he admitted miserably. "Cracked up." He flung himself down on to the blanket and hid his head in his hands. He certainly looked all in.

"I'm at the end of my tether," he muttered.

Anger made me lose patience with him. "You'll be at the end of a rope, and me with you, if you don't pull yourself together and make an effort." I reached over and roughly dragged him into a sitting posture. "Listen to me. Have you used this gun on anyone?"

"No. I wasn't going to. Honestly. I stole it from a homestead up the road. I thought I might shoot something I could eat."

"You were ready enough to hold up the coach with it."

"I swear to you, Jack, I only did it from desperation. I've had nothing to eat since yesterday morning. I've seen nothing to shoot at save birds, and I knew I'd never hit any. I was lying here, wondering whether to put the muzzle in my mouth and finish it all, when I heard the commotion and looked out and saw the coach pull up. It was like a gift from the gods. I didn't stop to consider—just picked the gun up and went out and took my chance. You'd have done the same in my place."

"I should hope not!" I retorted—yet I wondered what that strain which my blood shared with his might not have let me do in extreme circumstances. The more I considered my brother, the more I became inclined to think that there, but for God's grace, went I.

"Are you saying you're not already a criminal, then?"

"I swear it."

"You stole the gun, though."

"Stealing isn't a crime." There was a hint of the old arrogance in that. "If a man's desperate, he's a right to do something for himself. Those people wouldn't have missed the few bits I took off them."

"Any more than Papa missed his watch?"

He stared at me, his wide-eyed gaze travelling slowly down as I drew it from my pocket and dangled it on its chain.

"How—"

"That'll keep. If I tell you it now, I might work myself up again, and there's no one to hold me back. Suffice it to say that Papa's dead, and no thanks to you for standing by him."

"He was too far gone. Believe me, Jack, he was finished. I took the watch off him to stop him selling it to buy booze. What he'd have got for it would have gone straight down his throat, and that would have been the end of everything."

"You always were a lying sneak, Henry."

"It's the truth!" he insisted. "He kept saying he would sell it. I persuaded him not to, but this time he was determined."

"So you sold it yourself!"

"*Pawned* it. It was safe from him there."

"What happened to the money?"

"I . . ." He fell silent.

"Exactly," I sneered. "You didn't want him to have it, but you weren't so particular yourself. Couldn't you at least have used it to help him?"

He answered brokenly, "I lost it. I'd worked out a system for two-up—"

"Two-up?"

"A game with two coins. They all gamble on it here. I reckoned if I could double my money, or better, it would give me time for one more try to get Dad off the drink and eating properly, and . . . Only, I lost."

"Always the smart aleck. Thinking you know better than anyone else."

The dark eyes flashed with sudden spirit as he retorted, "What do you know about being at the end of your line, how you might behave? What if you'd found me and Dad in a mansion on Muck Hill somewhere, with servants and horses and a string of shops bought out of our lucky strike, and we'd turned you away from our gate because we'd made our pile and you'd got nowhere? There are rich men in this country who were near starvation just before they washed that one lucky pan of dirt. You never give up. Always one more go, hoping that'll be it. Only, for us it never was."

My anger welled and my fists bunched.

"Yes," he said, seeing them. "Solve anything that way, can't you? Your answer to anything. Go on, use them. Make a better job of it this time. You'll be doing me a favour."

I didn't strike him. I seized him in my arms and clutched him to me as he dissolved into the sobs which had broken his last utterance. My own eyes were more than moist. His rebuke had borne it all in upon me: the tragic way a happy little family in comfortable circumstances can be riven apart as ours had been, disintegrated and destroyed by a chain of events which we had not had the collective ability to break. Because Father had chanced to rescue Mother from drowning, he had denied life to himself. By letting herself become infatuated with Beecher, she had driven him past his limits; but who was to apportion blame between them for the end result? Henry, too, had played his part, taking advantage of their rift to further his own desires. And what of myself? I might plead my youth at the time as the excuse for having done nothing to try to save our situation. Yet how smug even to feel tempted to sit in judgement on the rest of them!

My reader may imagine my emotions when, years later, I sat down to recount that investigation of Sherlock Holmes's to which I gave the title "The Boscombe Valley Mystery," with its background of this same Australian territory, the holding up of a coach, and its legacy of hatred and violence shared between outwardly respectable and law-abiding men. As Holmes had remarked then: "God help us! Why does fate play such tricks with poor, helpless worms?" As I wrote those words, I remembered with pain the time when I myself had had cause to wonder.

The upshot of our interview was that I assumed command and dictated our plan of action. I had money, but we were without food; I was thankful that I had had two square meals that day, but Henry was clearly weak from hunger and privation. On his assurance that he was not actually a wanted man, I decided that our best prospect would be to come out into the open and take our chance. I could honestly answer any questioner that I had come from England in search of my distressed father and brother, only to find Father on his deathbed and Henry tramping towards the coast, disillusioned with the gold-fields and unable to pay a coach fare. There seemed no reason why any enquirer should not leave it at that.

I made Henry cover up all traces of his having camped there, while I pushed my way farther into the bush and buried his shot-gun. His few remaining cartridges had been taken by the coach passengers, along with their own things. His half-empty knapsack contained nothing but some rags of underwear and socks. I slung it over my shoulder and he bundled his blanket under his arm and took up the billycan.

Ensuring that there was no one in sight, we stepped out on to the road and began walking.

We had not gone far, largely in silence, before Henry turned to me and said, in a very changed tone: "Listen, Jack, I've been thinking. Why not cut across Mount Alexander way? I reckon there may be a track not far along from here."

"There might be something to be said for it," I accepted readily. "I'd prefer us to get off this road, in case someone has said something about your hold-up. On a different route we'd stand less chance of being suspected."

I had been growing more uneasy about that prospect. We would look an odd couple, he in his digger's gear, I in my suit and light boots and with money enough in my pocket. Questions would undoubtedly be asked as to how I had found him, and where, and why we had chosen to walk instead of picking up a coach.

"We can lie up in the timber for the night somewhere," he continued, beginning to sound positively enthusiastic. "Push on to Alexander early and be there by nightfall. There are plenty of places to doss down decently there."

It was a relief to hear him beginning to perk up. His natural sharpness had not left him and could be an asset to us.

"Agreed," said I. "Perhaps we can get you some decent things there, and then take a coach down to Melbourne."

That was what we set out to do. The track across appeared soon after, and we made good time along it through what remained of the daylight. We bivouacked amongst bush and trees and spent a hungry, uncomfortable night, glad to move on again at dawn's first glimmering. My boots were inadequate for the job, compared with his heavy ones, but there was nothing to be done but plod on grimly, a progress not enlivened by Henry's narrative of Father's and his misfortunes in the years since they had deserted us. It was no satisfaction to hear how bitter had proved the harvest they had sown for themselves.

It was a warm day, and tramping was thirsty work. No coach came by, or I should have risked asking if it could take us up. At about midday, we came to a place where a wooden bridge spanned a small stream. We were glad to get down and scoop the water to our mouths and faces.

"Better fill the billy and take some with us," I said.

"Take off your boots and socks and dangle your feet in the water," he advised, doing so himself. "It's an old dodge against blisters."

The sensation of the cool water running between my toes when I spread them was delicious. I could have luxuriated there for longer, but hunger was becoming a driving force.

"Come on," I ordered. "We must keep going."

He had been about to say something just as I spoke. He hesitated, then returned to it.

"Jack, what would you say to staying in Alexander awhile and trying to make a go of it together?"

"A go of what?"

"The diggings. You've got cash for gear and things. That was the trouble with Dad and me, we never had anything. A few quid would be enough at first, and there's an old working where I'm dead sure there's more waiting to be dug out. . . ."

His voice trailed away as he saw my face.

"Haven't you learnt yet?" I said.

"Honestly, Jack," he pleaded rapidly, "there were so many in the early days who just scratched the surface and got lucky and kept moving on. They didn't bother to go deep, just moved on. It stands to reason there's plenty they overlooked."

"Just to oblige you," I observed sarcastically. "They left it there for you to come along at your leisure and pick it up. You, the greatest gold-miner of them all."

"There's no call for that. I'm prepared to work as hard as any man."

"A fat lot you have to show for it."

"By the law of averages, I'm due for a turn. To walk away from it all, just when my number's ready to come up—it would be crazy."

"No crazier than believing any such rubbish. Father's gone. You're at rock-bottom, desperate enough to resort to crime. If I hadn't found you, you'd soon have had a price on your head and got shot down or stuck in some jail for years. And you haven't the nous to see how it's all come about."

"Who d'you think you are to talk?" he flared back suddenly. "What have you got to show? A few borrowed quid in your pocket and half a qualification at doctoring. You a doctor! You can't even read a label, if it's in Latin."

The last of self-restraint deserted me in that moment. We were both still seated, half-way to resuming our socks and boots. I threw mine aside and grasped him by the shirt-front with my bunched left hand, drawing back my right. He ducked his head sharply, though, and my punch whistled over the back of his neck. The momentum of it pulled me across him. He gave me a great shove, sending me tumbling helplessly into the stream.

I still had him by the shirt, though, and he went in with me. There we wrestled in the shallow water, splashing and cursing. He had never been any match for me, but he threshed and struggled, giving me no opportunity to use my fists on him.

My strength prevailed at last. I got him onto his back, my full weight bearing down on a knee crushed into his stomach, and his arms pinioned. He had to arch his neck up to keep his face from submerging.

"For God's sake!" he spluttered. "D'you mean to drown me?"

"Shouldn't do that, sport," a loud, drawling voice behind and above me called. "Might finish up doing a rope-dance."

15

"Some particulars of the voyage of the bark."

There were two of them, uniformed in tight tunics, riding-breeches, and tall boots. They had on gleaming leather shoulder-belts and hard-peaked little pillbox hats. I knew that they were state troopers.

They were leaning on the bridge rail, as casually as if pausing to watch ducks gambolling. Their mounts wandered nearby, nibbling at tufts of the wiry grass. The tumult of our struggle in the water had altogether swallowed up the sound of their approach.

As I dragged myself to my feet and gave Henry a hand, I inwardly cursed once more the misfortune which I seemed doomed to suffer in connection with him. He had become my bad penny, certain to buy me incalculable mischief.

Both men had produced pistols by the time we came towards them. They put them away in their big leather holsters when they saw we were unarmed, but left the flaps significantly unbuttoned. From the braid on his cuff I took the elder of them, who was bearded, to be an officer. The younger was a sergeant.

"Right, my lads," said the former, leaning his back against

the bridge rail, his arms spread along its top, "let's be hearing from you."

Dripping before him, I told my well-prepared tale. Henry made no attempt to speak. While I was talking, the sergeant had moved to us and made a cursory search of our clothes. He took out Father's watch, examined it keenly, raised his eyes to mine, and unfastened the albert. He showed the watch and my wallet to his superior.

"Where'd you get this?" the officer demanded, scrutinising the watch.

I told him.

"Forty-six quid," reported the sergeant, after counting. "Papers in the name of John H. Watson, ship's surgeon."

"What about the other?"

"Nothing. Not a penny."

"I have told you the circumstances, officer," said I.

"What were you scrapping over?" he returned.

"It. . . it's hard to explain simply."

"Well, you'd better find some way, because I don't like this. Do you like it, sergeant?"

"Ho, no, sir. Not a bit, sir. Definitely not a bit."

"Look here," I protested, "there is nothing to like or dislike. I have told you that I came to this country in search of my father and brother. My father lies in his grave in Ballarat. My brother, as you might judge from his clothes, I found in distressed circumstances. I am taking him to Melbourne and thence back home."

"Walking it? By this track? I wouldn't take this track to Melbourne, sergeant, would you?"

"Definitely no, sir."

"No. Your brother, you say?"

"That is so. Henry."

"He doesn't look like your brother, any more than you do his."

"Chalk from cheese," contributed the sergeant unasked.

The officer looked at my papers. "Ship's surgeon?"

"That's right."

"Well, now, I may be a quirky sort of chap myself, but there does seem something a little queer about the idea of a ship's surgeon, with money in his pocket and a gold watch, wrestling with a digger in a billabong fifty miles from the coast on a road going neither to nor fro. Would you expect to come across that sort of caper most days of the week, sergeant?"

"Can't say when I did last, inspector." The sycophant lifted the back of his hat to scratch with feigned perplexity at his short-cropped scalp.

"On the other hand, I'd be less than surprised to meet up with a walkabout con-man and his strongarm cobber, moving on from where they took their last pickings."

The sergeant struck his thigh. "That's it, sir! Little difference of opinion on the way. Settling it wi' the dooks."

"You're talking utter rubbish!" Henry said, speaking for the first time; "and you know it."

My heart sank. How often in my life had I been the recipient of that sneering tone and had to fight back the impulse to ram my fist into his mouth. Henry at his loftiest-sounding could have provoked a saint to frenzy.

The policemen merely looked at each other, eyebrows raised.

"Or *two* con-men," the officer corrected himself calmly. "One got up as a gent, his crony as a digger. Ready to take in any sorts who might come their way. Gent wears the watch and carries the cash, of course. 'Here's my pledge and my cash on the nail' line of talk. 'Now, if you care to come in with me on this little proposition . . .' While, for his cobber, it's more a case of 'Help an honest digger wot's bin robbed on his way to the assay office with half a pound o' dust and a nugget the size o' your thumb. Only temporary embarrassed, y'understand. Plenty more where it came from. If ye could jest tide me over, I'll leave ye me note o' hand and send a draft on me bank.'"

His sergeant chuckled appreciatively. "'Aven't we 'eard the likes o' both before, sir?"

"Now you come to mention it, sergeant, I reckon we have."

It was my turn to express irritation. "If you wish to verify what I have told you, sir, I would refer you to Dr. Ramsay, of the Benevolent Institution at Ballarat."

"Oh, yes? Got this cash out of him, did you?"

"He—he lent me it, yes. It was entirely at his own suggestion, though."

"Smooth-talked him, eh."

"Nothing of the sort. He entertained me to dinner in his apartment—"

"A dinkum dab hand, this one, sir," the sergeant offered. His eyes were beady and watchful. My fear was that Henry—or I, for that matter—might say or do something which would give them the excuse to claim we had assaulted them. The sergeant looked as if he would relish that.

"And sent you on your way with a nice loan," the inspector finished for me. "So you thought you'd save the coach fare out of it and walk to Melbourne. But who should you fall in with on the way but your long-lost brother. Then you took the wrong road together, and got arguing about whose fault it was you were lost, and jumped into a handy billabong to punch it out. That your tale?"

The sergeant leered behind him, his hand creeping up to his holster as he saw my fists clench and my foot move. The worst was prevented, though. I heard a sigh and a crumpling noise, and turned in time to see Henry collapse and lie still.

"Come on! None o' them tricks!" the sergeant ordered. I thought he meant to put his boot into Henry's ribs. I got down quickly between them and supported Henry's head. His eyes were shut.

"He is starved and exhausted," I said. "He's eaten nothing for longer than I, and that's long enough. If you choose not to accept my story, be good enough to take us into custody and to somewhere we can get a meal. I beg you, sir," I addressed his superior.

"If you're a doctor, you'll know how to fetch him round," the inspector said brusquely. "Get the nags, sergeant. One up behind each of us into Alexander." He returned his look to me. "If your story doesn't hold up, my lad, you can both look forward to regular meals for seven years."

As I have said, it was rather like one of those nightmares where one is all alone, helplessly surrounded by malevolent forces heedless to one's attempts to explain. I was confident enough that my friend at Ballarat would verify my own story, but he could not speak for Henry. As I rode uncomfortably behind the inspector's saddle, my thoughts raced: the theft of the shot-gun, the hold-up of the coach; either or both might have been reported by now. Dear God, what if he had committed other misdemeanours of which he had told me nothing! Devious as I knew him to be, I could not put anything past him.

Prisoners on separate horses, it was impossible for us to communicate. Irrational fears coursed through me as we bumped along those dusty miles. Suppose Dr. Ramsay, of Ballarat, had dropped dead soon after my departure; or been felled by some crazed inmate and deprived of his memory; or was in some way beholden to the police and willing to perjure himself against me as a favour to them. It could be all up with us then. I thought of my Australian lady friend. She would scarcely welcome being named as character witness for a temporary officer of one of her husband's ships, with whom her acquaintance ought properly to have been on mere nodding terms.

Convicted on a misunderstanding! Consigned to some remote prison settlement, beyond the ken of my few relatives at home, who would at length resign themselves to my having perished in my unchronicled quest for my father and brother. Would captivity embitter me as it had that Wild Colonial Boy? Might it cause the dark side of my character to overwhelm all sense of right, and turn me into a rebel against society upon my eventual release, so that my name should at length pass into Australian folklore:

Ring, ring the cuspidor,
Rattle the spittoon,
And hear tell of Doc' Watson bold
Who made all women swoon. . . .

Hunger must have made me light-headed!

Those were anxious days which we passed in Mount Alexander jail. It was clear to me that no one believed the story I was called upon several times to repeat, nor was even inclined to credit it.

We were confined in a small cell, with barred doors and one tiny window protected by a metal grating. The heat was stifling and the foetid air had to be shared with a procession of other prisoners who were thrust in with us for brief periods while awaiting justice for lesser offences than that of which we were suspected. Their deference to us gave further indication of the standing of bush-rangers amongst the criminal fraternity, but there was no such respect forthcoming from the chief jailer, who had seen a fellow policeman shot down and severely wounded by one.

Day followed upon day without move to release us. My constant enquiries as to whether the inspector in charge had not yet succeeded in corroborating my account were met with dismissive shrugs or, more sinisterly, hard stares and slow head-shakings. I began to suspect that no enquiries were even being made, perhaps so that we might be used as an example that the police were doing their duty by the community, without finding it necessary to go and find a real bush-ranging gang and shoot it out.

For Henry's part, he did nothing beyond lying or sitting listlessly on his straw-filled pallet, staring into space. When he roused himself briefly it was usually to recriminate with me for bringing him to this pass. But for me, he accused, he would be a free man still.

"But for me, you would probably have been shot down or facing a noose by now," I corrected him.

"Word is, you're for one anyways," gloated the newest arrival in our cell. "Old feller bin found throttled in his cabin out near where they says you was took. Bin a stiff for days, they reckon. There's a mob round the jail-front, yellin' for ye to swing."

I had heard the commotion, but now my blood chilled. The effect of the news on Henry was to make him give our half-drunk companion such a look as set him rattling the bars and crying to be moved to a safer place.

"Who cares?" said Henry dully, when I remonstrated with him. "If it suits them to string us up they'll do it. It would solve some problems, anyway."

"We won't have that sort of talk!" I warned him; then, remembering the hopeless way Mother had behaved when all her illusions had left her, I moved to put a reassuring arm about his shoulders, but he shrugged me away.

No less a person than the inspector appeared in response to our companion's pleas; but he ignored the fellow's gibbering and addressed us.

"Come on. Out!"

Two officers stood beside him, thumbs in belts. The mob's chanting became more audible as we passed through to the front office.

"Where are you taking us?" I asked.

He jerked his head. "Hear them?"

"I hear them. But I assure you it had nothing to do with us."

"What hadn't?" he returned sharply, and I realised my error.

"That fellow in with us. . . . Something about an old man being strangled in his cabin."

He let me stew in silence while we were marched into his office, the baying outside growing ever louder. My knees, already weak from apprehension, nearly buckled when I saw a clergyman rise from a chair; but he held out his hand with a prim smile.

"Dr. Watson, you remember me from Ballarat? Copperthwaite—Dr. Ramsay's deputy."

My friend had introduced me to him only briefly, but even in my near-swooning state I recalled his face.

"Dr. Ramsay is unable to get away himself," he went on. "The police insisted on a personal identification, so he asked me to come."

"You so identify this man?" the inspector intervened almost accusingly.

"Yes, yes."

"This is my brother Henry," I managed to tell the clergyman. "He wasn't with me at Ballarat, but . . ."

"Just a minute," the officer commanded. "One at a time. You vouch for this man, then?" he addressed Mr. Copperthwaite.

"Positively."

"Dr. Ramsay confirms he lent him money, and no tricks about it?"

"Fifty pounds, and no tricks, officer."

The inspector gave me his hard look, sucking his lower lip in contemplation.

"All right," he conceded. "He's clear. As to this other . . ."

"Dr. Ramsay confirms Dr. Watson's story in every respect. He had come inland specifically to seek for his father *and* his brother."

"Do they look like brothers to you?"

"We-ell . . ."

"Why on earth should I speak up for him otherwise?" I strove desperately. "I'm well aware that we don't look alike, but that is a long story. I ran into my brother by pure luck. He was exhausted and near-delirious. I took charge, and through my lack of knowledge of the country we strayed on to the wrong road. It was my hope that we might find a coach that would take us up, but none had come along."

"And that fighting in the billabong?"

"My . . . my brother felt he could go no further. He wanted me to save myself and leave him lying by the roadside. I said . . . I said, 'We won't have that sort of talk!' and it came down to a scrap."

The inspector swung on Henry.

"Is that true?"

To my intense relief the answer was a sullen "Yes."

"Well . . . there's things about it that don't ring true to me, but I've other matters to put my time to, what with that crowd out there yelling for Joe Bishop's neck. . . ."

"Joe Bishop?" I could not forbear to ask.

"Swag-man who did in the old squatter not far from where you were taken. Admitted it. They think we've got him in here, only he hopped it the back way before he was got under lock and key. My lads are out scouring the country for him now."

Henry spoke up at last. "Not too rosy for your reputation,

eh, Inspector? Worth a quid or two for us to assure them out there that he's safe behind bars."

"Why, you . . . !"

"For heaven's sake!" I intervened. "Are we free to go, Inspector?"

"Yes. Get out. As for you," he turned on Henry again, "if you try pulling smart tricks of that sort, I'm thinking it's maybe as well this brother of yours did find you in time."

"I don't think I care for that sort of remark, officer."

I seized Henry by the arm.

"Come *on*!"

"Just a tick, old fellow. The inspector at least owes us back the money you had on you."

I would cheerfully have sacrificed it, if only to have got out of there before the policeman changed his mind. But he sighed and pushed a ledger at Mr. Copperthwaite.

"Countersign the order of release, and they can go."

"With our money," Henry persisted.

The bundle of notes was flung on to the desk.

"*And* our father's watch."

It, too, was handed over. I quickly took possession of it and the money myself.

"Thank you," Henry condescended. "And as a token of our esteem, Inspector, we will tell them outside that you've still got your man. Seems the least we can do."

I was never more glad to leave a place in my life.

Rejecting firmly one last proposal from Henry that we should make our way back to the gold-fields and pick up a quick fortune before sailing for home, I got us on to the first possible coach to Melbourne. There I went to the shipping office and enquired if any berth for a surgeon chanced to be on offer. There was none, but the clerk informed me that there were any number of vacancies for ordinary seamen and hands, it being the custom for a proportion of almost any crew arriving in Australia to sign off or merely jump ship and head for the diggings.

Henry had notions of travelling as a passenger. I disabused him of those and signed us both on, aware that he would in all probability be sick and useless for most of the voyage, but taking some delight in anticipating the treatment he would receive from any bo'sun suspecting him of swinging the lead.

I made cautious enquiries as to the whereabouts of the director of the line. He was in Sydney, in the bosom of his family, I gathered. Any personal reunion with that bosom was thus out of the question for me. I had seen enough trouble for the time being, and there were "other faces, other places" in the world.

Besides, I was not keen to let my brother out of my sight. Returning strength had brought optimism in its train.

"We're making a big mistake, you know, Jack," he said. "What's the point of trailing back home with nothing to do and no prospects, when there's untold wealth here for the picking up?"

I could not help being amused by this symptom of that persistent disease which they called "gold fever."

"Harry, think how often we used to go out to Black Head and wait for treasure to wash up. We never saw anything more interesting than that dead dog once."

"Waiting for the sea to cough up is different. Here, you can pick your spot and work it."

"Haven't you had enough of that mug's game?"

"What's life but a mug's game?" he rounded on me passionately. "Stake a claim and scratch away at it all your years. Huh! A hole in the ground's all there's to show, either way."

"It's all poor Dad got. You were a bit luckier."

"You don't understand, Jack, do you? Do you think I'd have gone on playing the bush-ranger? I only wanted enough dough from that one bail-up to pay my way to a place that's a cinch for gold. I know exactly where it is. Come on, Jack. Go there with me. Forty-odd quid, or whatever we've got left, that would get us there and buy us tools and a tent. I'm feeling fit again, and you're strong as a bull. We could clean up between us. Man, it's mad to think of giving up the game just when your number's due."

"Sorry, Harry, nothing doing. The money's borrowed and it's got to be paid back, and not by spending it and having to pop Dad's watch again. We'll find something worthwhile back at home, you'll see."

He argued no more; but it moved me to see the light fade from his dark eyes.

We sailed in the three-masted bark *Salmeston,* 845 tons, in ballast for Sydney. Including ourselves, the crew was twenty strong; there were no passengers. The vessel had been built for carrying tea from the East, but the opening of the Suez Canal had spelt the end of that trade for sailing-ships, almost all the business passing to steam. To my regret for so lovely a ship as she undoubtedly was, and to Henry's disgust at the filthy nature of the work it entailed, the cargo we loaded was two thousand tons of coal for Shanghai.

Often, in later life, I have given thanks for that experience to which adversity had introduced me. It seems a good argument in favour of predestination that those things on which we set our hearts are likely as not denied us, while wholly-unlooked-for advantages are liable to come from seemingly unpropitious circumstances.

My service before the mast was such a case. Life as an ordinary crew member of a fine sailing-vessel, with all its hardships and taxing toil, transformed me once and for all from boy to man. I hauled, climbed, reefed, and furled without thought for anything save the immediate task in hand. It was never spoken amongst us, of course, for we were not consciously aware of it, but the accomplishment of our voyage and the survival of our ship and all of us at our moments of greatest peril depended upon each one of us, from our skilled and seasoned captain and officers to the most utter novice, which latter rôle belonged to my brother and myself. In this respect I must give Henry his due. His experience of living and working alongside men from the lowliest backgrounds and of outlandish habits was far greater than mine. At first, he was as sick as I had expected he would be, and, as I had anticipated, the bo'sun showed him neither sympathy nor mercy, driving him to his work with oath and boot, along with the rest of us. It proved the most efficacious of medicines, and when I had time to notice him, I observed that Henry was acquitting himself splendidly. Not for nothing was the blood of our sailor ancestor so potent in his veins.

Never have I been so thoroughly tested, physically and morally; yet I would not have missed the experience for a fortune. What most men conceive dangerous, I have felt to be of comparatively little consequence. Where there is no imagination there is no fear, they say, and Sherlock Holmes has no doubt justifiably given me little reputation for percipience; but I would aver that the man who is fortunate enough to learn to relegate fear to the place where it ought to belong thereby spares himself much of that self-doubt which precludes bold decisions and inhibits action.

Apart from this, however, my brief sea career provided me with two further benefits of inestimable worth. One was the understanding I gained of basic human nature. Subsisting and working for weeks on end in such conditions, shared with only a score of other men, away from all contact with the artificialities and taken-for-granted comforts of life ashore, left me with a deep respect for the so-called common man, in his ability to serve such sentence as Life has meted out to him with irrepressible courage and hope and a stoic cheerfulness which could be a model for all others.

The other gain which I enjoyed was physical. The weary toil, the lack of rest and proper nourishment, and the having to exist wet-through for days of shivering cold at a time, far from leaving me debilitated for life, gave me a store of rude health on which I have been able to draw ever since. I believe that we can charge up our bodies as well as stock our brains, and that the good health which it has (touch wood!) been my fortune to enjoy throughout a long life was largely generated during this time at sea.

Our passage to Shanghai lasted a few days over one month, which the bo'sun, in confiding mood for once, told us was not bad, considering the weather we had been through. Unfortunately for the shipping line, there was no further charter immediately available to us. It was an irony of ironies at that time that the sailing-ship, which had taken centuries to develop to its ultimate point of technical perfection and beauty, had thereupon been promptly superseded by the steamer, and in little time would be no more. It made me doubly fortunate to have got in my experience, however, and our month's idleness in the bustling port enabled me to enlarge it further, albeit in a different sphere. By the time we sailed in ballast for Hong Kong, four weeks later, I had added certain exotic elements to that other experience which I have been known to boast extends over many nations and three separate continents.

I prefer not to particularise them, but rather reserve them as additions to my list of narratives for which the world is not yet ready, under the headings: The Reckless Encounter with the Smiling Tea-House Proprietress, The Singular Experience with the Retired White-Slavemistress, and The Peculiar Obsession of the Assistant-Harbourmaster's Daughter.

In short, although my milieu at sea was exclusively one of men's men, such was far from the case ashore.

A more sober memory from that period concerns my

brother. We had loaded sugar and cassia and certain mixed goods for London via San Francisco, and sailed for the latter port. Throughout our voyaging we had been members of different watches, therefore on duty at separate times; and when all hands had been called it was invariably in circumstances unconducive to fraternal gossiping. Our chats had been limited mostly to make-and-mend time on Sunday afternoons.

We had little of significance to say to one another. Henry appeared resigned to accompanying me back to London, where, I vowed to myself, I would find him some sort of decent footing and help him rebuild his life. He would scarcely be welcome in Grandfather's household, while I had no wish to appoint myself his keeper. The concerns of land seem far away when one is at sea, though, and we did not discuss them.

In fact, Henry spent less of his leisure time with me than with another hand who had also been a gold-miner; he had returned to sea rather than starve ashore. I suspected that they were harmlessly feeding one another's fantasies, upon which it was none of my business to intrude.

A few days before we reached San Francisco, however, Henry and I somehow got onto the subject of our parents, one which we had been avoiding by mutual consent. With hindsight, I believe it was our nearing America once more which stirred his thoughts, and that he sensed what might be his last chance to unburden his conscience, proceeding to tell me why he had worked upon Father to desert Mother and me in New York and go off with him to the diggings.

"It was for the best for him, Jack," he insisted earnestly. "Ma was all over herself on that skunk Beecher. I reckoned Pa owed himself a life."

"Not forgetting your own interests, of course."

"You know me, Jack. Always restless. Wanting to get on. It seemed the perfect chance, for him and for me."

"I knew you were up to something at the time—shutting yourself away with him, clamming up whenever I came into the room."

"What'd you expect?" he returned sharply. "The least hint and you'd have spilled it all to Ma. You always were her white-haired boy."

I let the jibe go. "So you persuaded him to leave."

"I told him he'd no future with her. He'd already lost her to that Bible-puncher."

"You said that! To our Father about our Mother!"

"It was the truth, wasn't it?"

My fury spilled over once more. I was pulling him up off the fo'c's'le deck, preparing to knock him down a second time, when the mate intervened and curtly ordered me aft. Henry kept well clear of me thenceforward.

I suppose I should have anticipated what duly occurred. If the truth is told, I was too eagerly concerned with adding the continent of North America to my Don Juan's catalogue to give much thought to my brother while our ship lay in San Francisco harbour; but I certainly could not have kept constant watch over him.

I awoke one morning—in my own bunk aboard ship for once—and sensed that something was wrong. It did not take a minute to trace the source to the hiding place where my father's watch and what was left of Dr. Ramsay's money were stowed. The watch was still there, but all the money was gone, with only a scrap of paper in its stead.

> DEAR JACK—No use pretending. It's like the drink was to poor Dad, and I've got to go where the gold is, or die of thirst. Ted and I have gone together. Sorry about the cash, but at least I've left the watch—it seems the least I can do. I'll find you some day and pay you back with interest, out of my millions. Good luck, and don't think too badly of your Brother—
>
> HARRY

So ended our uneasy relationship. I never saw Henry again in my life. The thought of chasing after him again lasted no more than a minute; I recognised that it would be doing neither of us any service.

As to his ever having found that elusive fortune, I doubt it. Had he prospered, I believe he would have traced me, if only to repay that money as proof of his vindication. My guess is that he went down that same hill on which he had been slithering before, only this time reached the bottom of it.

"There, but for the Grace of God . . ."

16

"Your morals don't improve, Watson."

It did not surprise me, on leaving my ship, to feel regret's hollow ache. As I walked away along the wharf at Tilbury, I turned, to pause and gaze on her for the last time. Nothing man-made has ever matched the awesome beauty of a full-rigged sailing-ship.

Rare though it may have been to strike an ideal combination of ship, officers, and fellow crewmen, I had no qualms about considering making the sea my life. I was young, afraid of neither elements nor fellow men, strong enough to cope with any task and to take care of myself against any sort of antagonist. Besides, if I were to complete my medical studies, I should be able to enjoy permanent officer status, perhaps even obtain an appointment as doctor in one of the big passenger steamers plying the Atlantic. I was happy at the prospect of a comfortable cabin, my own place at the head of a table of persons of wealth and distinction, as much as I could wish to eat and drink in luxurious profusion, and—it had not escaped my imaginings—the greatest scope man might ever wish for pursuing his dedicated researches into the ineffable mysteries of the opposite sex.

The prospect of putting out a general practitioner's shingle in some stuffy provincial suburb lacked all allure by comparison. I was realist enough to recognize that I had no medical vocation pure enough to equip me for a lifetime of ministering to humanity at a low ebb. The thought of a hospital post was quite out of the question, as being altogether too demanding, while I could not envisage myself ever aspiring to the skill and status of fashionable consultant or specialist. In short, I possessed no vocation whatever. Pure expediency had led me into medicine, and I might as well make myself as comfortable in it as I could have hoped to be in any other calling.

"As a matter of fact, my boy," replied my grandfather, interrupting the summary with which I deemed it prudent to introduce my proposition, "you have no need to worry your head about your future. I am already preparing the ground for you to take my place here. Your grandmother and I have talked of it a great deal while you were away."

He poured me a second glass of Offley's fine old tawny. We were tête-à-tête once more in his study at Bagshot. The lamps were lit and the fire brightly aglow, for we had recently risen from the dinner-table, over which I had been regaling my grandparents and Aunts Flora and Verbena with a carefully-selected narrative of my experiences since I had last seen any of them.

It was early February, 1878. Snow lay everywhere outside, and heavy frost deepened the fire's redness. Climatically speaking, it was in total contrast with the heat and dust of Australia or the tempestuous Horn; while nothing could have seemed further removed from the bucking yards of the *Salmeston* than the deep leather armchair in which I now luxuriated, with one of Grandfather's Villar y Villars drifting its fragrant smoke in a light haze about me. If ever I was susceptible to persuasion that there was a good deal to be said for general practice after all, I expect it was at this moment.

"Yes," he continued, his silver head resting on his chair-back and his gaze fixed on the mantelpiece, although evidently seeing far beyond it, "retirement has been a good deal in our minds just lately."

"Retire! You, Grandpa!"

Without moving his head, he turned his eyes on me and smiled.

"If I fancy aright, you are thinking that I am neither ancient nor decrepit. Well, you are correct on both counts, and I may assure you that the same is true of your grandmama, God bless her. That is the very reason why, in our wisdom, we think of putting ourselves out to pasture before much longer. Why should we not enjoy what is left to us of our years and health?"

"You have certainly earned it," said I, with an access of warmth which precluded from my mind old thoughts of what a snug and easy-going life Grandfather had contrived for himself, always ensuring that he had a fully-qualified young assistant and a final-year student on hand to undertake all inconvenient and distressing duties, leaving him to receive a select panel of patients of superior wealth and social standing, none of whom was ever required to condescend to the common waiting-room or surgery.

"Well, yes," he conceded, "I flatter myself that I have done my little share to reduce the sum of suffering in this world, which I am sure you are eager to embark upon yourself."

"Oh, yes, Grandpa. Only, I was thinking—"

"Wilkinson is due to move on from here in June or July. Some notion of specialising in disorders of the alimentary tract." He grimaced slightly. "You yourself may hope—I should say *expect*—to get your M.D. at about that same time. It would be ideal for you to come straight here and take his place."

"Yes, Grandpa. Only—"

"A year should see you fully *au fait* with the practice. You will be spared the necessity of building one for yourself. An anxious business, as I well recall. How often used I to stand peering out from behind the curtains of those poor rooms in Croydon, willing some passer-by to be taken faint, and, in catching hold of my railings, chance to notice my plate."

"Did it ever happen?" I asked, amused.

"Only the once. A stout old party collapsed outside the very door. His fall quite rattled the window-sashes. I hurried out to proffer professional assistance, and all I got for my pains was abuse for not having seen to it that the coalman replaced our coal-hole properly. He went so far as to threaten legal action, but happily I heard no more." Grandfather frowned at the recollection of man's ingratitude towards man before continuing.

"As I was saying, a year should be quite sufficient to see you with all the reins in your hand. No doubt you will have got yourself a wife by then, into the bargain. You will find a woman's support and comfort quite invaluable in a profession which can take such toll of the nerves and stamina."

An inch of ash fell from his cigar, smudging itself all over his waistcoat front. He brushed at it with the back of his hand, as if to demonstrate the kind of service which it would be useful to have a woman standing by to render.

"So, if we are to think in terms of, say, twelve months from now, at the outside, John? That would suit, would it not?"

"Grandpa, I ought to tell you—"

"No need for gratitude, my boy. It is the least I can do for my poor darling's loving son. And do not fear that you will have me constantly breathing down your neck. We intend to remove ourselves right away from here, and your aunts with us. We have a great fancy for Scotland; who knows, perhaps that very part whence you came. We have all four of us liked it from those happy visits long ago."

"I'd no idea," was all I could respond.

"It will leave you with neither kith nor kin in England, I'm afraid. But never mind that. We shall be only just up the road from you, so to speak. One more glass now, before we go through?"

There was clearly to be no getting in any word about my seagoing ambitions. I thought I saw my chance, though, when we had rejoined Grandmother and my aunts, and I was pressed to recount the experience of rounding Cape Horn. I obliged with gusto, throwing in every detail and striving to convey the exhilaration which I had felt, both during it and afterwards, and which was still vivid enough in my memory for me to recall every sound and sensation. I must have told the tale impressively, for little shrieks and gasps from my aunts in turn, and occasionally in unison, punctuated it throughout.

"How utterly ghastly!" Aunt Verbie exclaimed when I had done.

"Unspeakable!" from Aunt Florrie. "Living amongst those sailors!"

"No, you see, it was—"

"Never mind, dear John. Terra firma from now on," Grandmama consoled me, placing her delicate snow-white hand on my thick brown one. I loved her dearly, and could not have borne to contradict her; so the issue was never raised.

I returned to Bart's, deciding to let things rest for the time being. There was the small matter of my getting my M.D. at all; Grandfather seemed to take it for granted, but I was far from confident. However, with so much of my training completed, and only another lap or two to go, so to speak, it seemed to me pointless not to spur myself on to the post, and worry in the unsaddling enclosure what I should do with myself from there on.

In the event, I did not make a bad run of it. Experience of the world at large had brought it home to me that human beings were more than anatomical sections on charts. A stomach, a heart, a brain, were no longer to me mere components possessed in common by countless millions, of differing sexes and races and hues. Each and every one of us, I thought, is his or her own centre of the Universe. Whatever exists and happens goes on around *us*, be we emperor or peasant, queen or courtesan. My brain is my brain alone; my heart, my stomach . . . This body and mind are the centre around which all else revolves, and so are those of each of us: a simple enough philosophy, no doubt, but it was enough to make me burn with something which I believed to be intellectual fervour.

The stimulus of it drove me on to consider the position of an individual who shared common inherited traits with a blood relation who was nevertheless physically and morally his opposite; from which point I developed my thesis. I possess no copy of it now, and at this remove cannot retrace my argument and conclusions, or define what exact bearing they had upon the practice of medicine. All I can say is that I was awarded my degree, and that my grandfather congratulated me gravely; although when I later came across the copy I had sent him of my thesis, it seemed to me, judging from the presence of a port stain and smudges of cigar ash upon the first two pages, but on none subsequent, that he had never read it through. Perhaps he, like the examiners, had found my argument so immediately potent that there had been no need to read further.

But I find at this point that I have anticipated myself. The remnants of a certain prudishness tempt me to let the lapse go, and pass straight on to sterner matters; but if this memoir is to be anywhere near to frank, it behoves me to fill in an episode which to some might seem discreditable, but which nevertheless did occur. The patient who withholds some symptom from his doctor cannot expect a full diagnosis or true understanding. Therefore, my association with Sarah Bernhardt cannot be skipped.

"By G—d, Watson, you're looking pretty well knocked up!"

The hearty blasphemer's name was Eddie Waveney-Waveney, scion of the Earl of Eppington and heir to vast estates in the West Midlands, or some such outlandish region. He was living in Mayfair, in considerable style, publicly disapproved of by the more sanctimonious newspaper proprietors and their spies.

"Waves," as he was known to his many friends, possessed the lightest hair and trim beard I have ever seen on a man outside Scandinavia. He was about my age, over six foot tall, broad-shouldered, and beautifully proportioned. At this stage of his life, his excesses had not yet begun to make their visible inroads; I heard that in later years, long after my acquaintance with him had ended, he became so changed as to pass unrecognised in several of his clubs.

I had met him through Rugby football, which he played for Richmond. As I recall him in action, he was a hard goer in a ruck, with an eager pair of hands and a keen eye for an opening.

"Been spending too much time in the saddle?" he said, grinning. We had chanced to meet in Piccadilly Circus and he had drawn me into the Café Royal, in those days a modest establishment in Glasshouse Street, for brandy and soda.

Knowing perfectly well what his remark implied, I expostulated that I had, in fact, been working long hours at my thesis.

"Then it's the other you're needing," he gave me back. "Fancy Paris?"

"Out of the question, I'm afraid."

"Oho! You haven't got, er . . . ?"

"No, I have not! I am hard at work, that's all."

"Need to refresh your mind. Stand back from things for a few days—and stand closer to a few others, what?"

"I'm truly sorry, Waves, but—"

"Cross this evening, shall we? Chuck your tails into a bag and—"

"I haven't any tails."

"No *tails?* Ye gods!" He eyed me calculatingly. "Well, we both carry our share of beef, and I dare say a set of mine will fit you—for as long as you need to keep 'em on. That's settled, then. Waiter! Whistle up a cab, there's a good fellow."

There was little resisting Waves at any time, such was his persuasive good nature. Despite my instinctive reluctance, the prospect of a jaunt to Paris excited me, especially in his company, for unaccustomed cerebral endeavour had addled my brain, convincing me further that the uncomplicated and intellectually undemanding life at sea would suit me exactly. I had never been to Paris, but, of course, had listened to many an anecdote about its allures, not without a certain envy.

If there was any company to be preferred for a first visit, it was Waveney-Waveney's. Generous to a fault, he was always the first in any gathering to take out his wallet, and no other man got a chance to pay his round in his company; he appeared positively aggrieved if anyone tried to insist.

I knew that that was how it would be on our Parisian jaunt, and I will admit that the consideration was not unimportant to me. In a word, I was hard up. Needless to say, the pittance which had been paid to me on signing off from the *Salmeston* had sufficed no further than to treat my erstwhile shipmates in one of the dockyard hostelries. Grandfather had generously recognised that the trip to Australia was bound to have left me out of pocket. He had put me in funds sufficiently for me to repay Dr. Ramsay, at Ballarat, and to set myself up in a new lodging in Holborn, within brief walking distance of Bart's. Even so, I needed to watch my purse carefully.

Waves's incredulity at my telling him I had no suit of tails was, of course, fully understandable. He knew me to be something of a stage-door johnnie, for which pursuit top hat, tails, buttonhole, and stick were absolutely *de rigueur;* the very newest recruit to the back row of any chorus would know better than to entertain the advances of a man not so attired. My friend's breeding, however, would not have allowed him to ask what had become of mine. If he gave it a thought, he would assume that I had pawned them, to see me through temporary embarrassment. He would have been right, in part. In a fit of self-denial, I had told myself that if I meant seriously to give my whole mind to my thesis, I must eschew social diversions. If I had no social diversions, I needed no tails; and if I had no tails, social diversions could not tempt me. To achieve this desirable circle, all I needed to do was pop the whole outfit, which I did, thereby also generating needed cash. It seemed to me a faultless exercise, demonstrating how well my reasoning faculties were responding to the stimulus of scholarship.

It left me without tails, however, and my funds remained low. But there was Waves, giving me his beguiling smile over his brandy glass.

"We-ll," I hesitated.

"Good man. Did my ankle at Twickers last Saturday. Can't turn out this weekend, so might as well find out if the rest of me's still working, what? Wouldn't leave a fellow to get into mischief alone, would you?"

We were in Paris by midnight.

17

"My practice has extended recently to the Continent."

When the proprietress of an establishment we chanced to visit early in the course of our investigation into the social mores of the French capital casually remarked that we should take the opportunity of seeing Sarah Bernhardt perform, Waveney-Waveney responded characteristically by asking where she "hung out." Being of his disposition, and perhaps influenced by the surroundings in which the suggestion was made, he naturally assumed her to be some dancer or *risqué* songstress. His handsome features fell when our charming informant answered, with gestures of agitation, that she referred to the greatest classical actress her country had produced since Madame Rachel.

"Elle est genié!" she declared, beating the air. *"Magicienne! Divinité!"*

"A genius," I interpreted. "Magician. Div—"

"I ain't totally dim, dear chap." He beamed. "Not quite my cup of tea, though, thanks, madame."

It behoved me to reassure her that all Englishmen were not quite barbarians.

"I myself," I said, in careful French, "carry an interest in the theatre. Tell me, if you please, where is it that one sees the Madame Bernhardt?''

''At the Comédie Française, of course, M'sieu'. She plays the *Hernani* of Victor Hugo. *Formidable!* But, naturally, it is impossible to obtain admission. Every ticket is always sold.''

''Alas! Is it that you yourself have not seen her, madame?''

''Oh, *oui*, I have seen.'' She returned the merest smile. ''We have the honour to entertain Monsieur Hugo.''

''Fat lot of use, that,'' said Waves, as we sauntered away, ''telling us we ought to go and look at something we can't get in to see. Just as well we ain't bothered.''

''I wouldn't have minded,'' I replied.

''Fancy your chances round the back, you mean?''

''Waves, there *are* other things in life.''

He halted in his stride, turned to face me, and gazed earnestly into my eyes for some moments.

''*Are* there?'' he said at last, with so droll a countenance that I burst into loud laughter, in which he joined as we went jauntily upon our way.

But I did see Sarah Bernhardt perform that evening, and, in a sense, it was thanks to my friend. We were back in the foyer of our hotel, which, because Waves was the man he was, happened to be one of the most luxurious in the city. The porter's long counter bore the usual collection of playbills, and we had paused to leaf through them, seeking details of the music-halls and cabarets.

''Hard to know where to begin, Waves,'' I said.

''When in doubt, there's always Madame Lecoq's,'' he answered with his wink, and wandered away. The place he referred to was that where we had spent the afternoon. He was obviously well known there.

I lingered for a moment, looking for the Comédie Française bill, more out of curiosity than hope. A voice hissed in my ear: ''M'sieu'—pardon, *milord*. . .''

I looked up, to see one of the porters leaning across to me.

He was a young man, whose uniform's newness and slightly stiff fit suggested that he had not long occupied the post.

"Pardon me, *milord,*" he repeated, and continued in comprehensible English, "Your companion, he is...he is the Prince of Waves?"

New to his calling, he would doubtless be ever alert for his first sight of that other wellknown man-about-Paris, who I now realised Waves did rather resemble. I decided not to disillusion him. Maintaining a straight face, I placed a finger to my lips and glanced about. The boy's eyes shone forth his excitement.

"Not a word," I cautioned.

"Of course, m'sieu'. But certainly. If—if there is any service I may have the honour to perform for his—for—for *Milord*..."

Recent exercise had certainly whetted my wits.

"As a matter of fact, there is one thing."

"Milord?"

"A seat for the Comédie. This evening."

It was a long throw indeed, but to my surprise the ardent youth did not flinch from the catch.

"I will do my best, *milord.*"

"You think it possible?"

"For...*milord.*"

My wallet was half out by this time. "Discretion is everything, you understand. He will be grateful, but will not acknowledge you."

"I understand."

"Excellent. You will deal with me alone."

"Of course, sir."

"The name is Watson. *Mister* Watson." I worked my eyes as I threw emphasis into the prefix, leaving him convinced that I was a viscount at the very least. I gave him a note, and a nod, and left him. Within half an hour the ticket was in my hands, and another note in his.

"Hang it all, old chap," Waves complained when I told him, "we didn't come here to watch Shakespeare and stuff."

I did feel a trifle guilty, under his auspices as I was; but the amiable fellow was easily convinced that if he was intending to revisit Madame Lecoq's house, he would certainly not want me beside him all evening.

"You promise you'll dine with me after your show, though," he insisted. "I expect I'll be famished, and you'll need a drink, with all that old dust in your gizzard."

"It will be my pleasure, Your Royal Highness."

I did not, in fact, see her in *Hernani*, the piece which historians of the theatre tell us established her once and for all as the foremost actress of her day. It had recently ended its run, to be replaced at the beginning of that month—April, 1878—with Molière's comedy *Amphitryon*. The change of bill did not disappoint me: all my life I have preferred the comic to the moving, and the exaggerated "business" in a comedy certainly makes it the easier to comprehend in a foreign tongue.

However he had achieved it, the hotel porter had certainly done well by me—or, should I say, by the "Prince of Waves." The seat he had procured for me was an excellent stall, and I fancied envious glances as I was conducted to it down the long, richly-carpeted aisle. I bore my head high, assuming the air of a man accustomed to nothing but the best; it was as well that Waves's spare tails fitted me so well.

A stout, elderly gentleman stood up to allow me to pass into the vacant seat beside him.

"*Merci très bien, monsieur,*" I thanked him.

"You are an Englishman," he responded in impeccable English.

I gave him a little bow.

"Lavallier," he introduced himself. "Attorney-at-law."

"Watson. Doctor."

He disconcerted me again by laughing.

"It is an irony," he explained. "My poor wife, who should have accompanied me, has been ordered to her bed by her doctor, and another doctor takes her seat, which had to be given up. But perhaps you are not of the medical fraternity?"

I assured him I was, and told him briefly how a friend and I happened to be visiting Paris, and that I had seized the rare chance to come and see the great actress whose fame had already reached London.

"Fame indeed!" He smiled. "But it is a thousand pities for you not to have seen her Doña Sol—her rôle in *Hernani*, that is to say. Or, better still for my money, her Phèdre. My God, a revelation! I tell you, my friend, had she been playing either of those rôles this evening, you would not have had my wife's place, doctor or no doctor."

"Madame's misfortune is my gain, then," I returned.

These pleasantries completed, we turned to discussing Sarah, whose career my neighbour had followed eagerly, claiming to have spotted her greatness in embryo at her debut some sixteen years earlier, when she was a mere seventeen-year-old. By all accounts, he must have been one of very few who did see anything in her at that point, other than striking beauty. I believe it was only the influence of one of her mother's lovers, a duke, that got her an audition; until then, she had been toying with the idea of entering a nunnery.

"She is a complete original," he went on, "a law unto herself. She has made herself great, despite poor rôles and much opposition from managers. Mind you, she has always enjoyed useful *connections*." He emphasised the last word, both with his voice and with a wink.

"A duke of her own, you mean?" I said, in man-of-the-world fashion.

"Better than that: a prince—the Prince de Ligne. She bore his child. He wished her to marry him and forsake the stage, but, thank Heaven, she chose the other sort of contract and went on to earn her fame."

These titbits had whetted my appetite for seeing her perform.

"She has never married, then?" I enquired.

"Never.* She has denied herself none of the more enjoyable elements of the married state without subjecting herself to any one man's whims. She is free to indulge her eccentricities as she pleases."

"Eccentricities?"

"Her menagerie—monkeys, wild cats, reptiles, all kept in her home. Stuffed birds of prey, with skulls in their claws, as ornaments. A skeleton, which she calls Lazarus, but is whispered to be that of one of her lovers whom she poisoned and boiled down—"

"Great heavens!"

"I, a lawyer, and yourself, a doctor, we can perhaps conceive how one so beautiful and fragile can possess such ferocious instincts. They are a sensation to the ignorant mass, however. It has become hard to separate the truth from rumour: how she sleeps in her coffin; how she poisoned two of her monkeys who displeased her, then decapitated one of her dogs in an experiment to determine whether there is life after death. I have it as absolute fact that she has several times visited the School of Practical Medicine to examine interesting corpses. A doctor friend of mine accompanied her and told me that she prodded them with her parasol."†

"What on earth for?"

"In the interest of studying anatomy to help her sculpt. Oh, she is most talented at it; also a painter. She has exhibited in the Salon, you know."

I could almost have wished that we might adjourn to the bar, where I might encourage my lively friend to continue

*A few years subsequently, in 1882, she committed herself in London by marrying an actor, Jacques Damala, but separated from him the following year.

†cf. Holmes beating subjects in Bart's dissecting-rooms with a stick (*A Study in Scarlet*).

such delicious scandal-mongering about Sarah and perhaps other of his notable compatriots; the play seemed likely to prove an anti-climax by contrast. It did not, however —because Sarah Bernhardt was in it.

From the moment of her first entrance I was fascinated; when she spoke, I became entranced. I was close enough to the stage to see that she was much smaller than I had expected of one with such a larger-than-life reputation: scarcely over five feet in height and fragile of build. She wore her own hair, which was fair, inclining to red, or vice versa. Her thin neck was long and her pale cheeks hollow beneath broadly-spaced bones. The nose was long and straight, the curvature of the nostrils seeming to me to denote Jewishness. Her lips were bright red, heightened with paint, and when she smiled, perfect teeth flashed brilliantly forth.

All this was, however, merely the setting for the most alluring pair of eyes imaginable. They were widely separated, long and straight, made longer and dramatically outlined by some black cosmetic. At first sight, I thought the irises were deep blue, but at other moments, as the light played on them from different angles, I should have put them down as green or even gold. Those eyes seemed to seek me out, and my cheeks burned, although I was perfectly aware that I could represent nothing more to her vision than part of the general blur beyond the footlights' glare.

As if her appearance and the sinuous grace of her movements were not enough to captivate me, there was that unforgettable voice. At first it seemed small, a little thin, her one disappointing characteristic. But as the play progressed, and whenever intensity of feeling was called for, it grew and swelled, dominating the space in which we were all assembled, flooding about us like a golden torrent, so that we seemed to be borne afloat on its liquid beauty.

When the interval came, my companion entreated me to

go with him to the stalls bar, where he ordered champagne. To my not-inconsiderable relief, he insisted that I regard myself as his guest, as a visitor to his native city.

"What an actress!" I exclaimed. "What a woman!"

"But alas, not a piece suited to her," he qualified my enthusiasm. "You should see her *en passion*. Blue death, it does things to a man!"

He quaffed his champagne as if needing to extinguish some inner fire, and snapped his fingers for another bottle.

The bell to end the interval was a long time sounding. I noticed several gentlemen frowning at their watches, but my host was happy to extend his anecdotage, accompanied with still more champagne. I had the impression that he was relishing an evening's freedom to let his tongue run loose with the sort of talk which might have earned his wife's censure. At length we were summoned back to our places, and the play recommenced. I soon saw the reason for the delayed resumption: all was not well with Sarah Bernhardt.

No longer did her eyes light their different-coloured lamps for us. Her shoulders drooped, and the lithe grace of her movements had given way to listlessness. The voice had lost its vibrance and become a mere scratchy whisper. I heard murmurings around me.

"Something is wrong," my neighbour hissed.

My inability to translate from the French quickly enough to keep up with the dialogue had me at a disadvantage. This new languor might have been consummately acted, for all I knew of the plot of the play; but her manner clearly had nothing to do with comedy. After some ten minutes of it, she suddenly shook her head violently, flung up an arm to her forehead, and lurched off into the wings. The others on stage stared after her, then at one another, and began to shuffle their feet. One of them essayed what was obviously a brave *ad libitum* attempt to retrieve the situation, but was soon put out of his misery by the closing of the curtains, to the accompaniment of an awed indrawing of a thousand breaths.

A bald, heavily-bearded man stepped out on to the stage, wringing his hands together, and said something which I was too agitated to catch. My neighbour got it, however, and leapt up from his seat to cry "*Ici! Ici!*" Heads were turned, and I realised with a start that he was pointing to me. He seized me by the arm.

"Quick, my friend. They ask for a doctor!"

He hoisted me to my feet and fairly dragged me out to the aisle. The man on the stage was looking my way and holding out his arms as if in supplication. I hurried down towards him, and I fancy I heard a thin spatter of applause.

In all my theatre-going, I had never heard that time-fabled appeal, *"Is there a doctor in the house?"* Once or twice, during dull patches of plays, I had speculated on the chances of its ever being uttered in my presence, and how I might react. Fancy had suggested that, in the event of the request's having to be made on behalf of some popular female star, there might result an unseemly contest between all the medical men in the audience, each envisioning a similar reward for the services needing to be rendered.

Either, on this occasion, there happened to be no other doctor in the theatre, or those who were present were subject to the restraining grasp of their wives; but at any rate, I was the only one available to be helped up on to the stage, into the wings, and past staring cast and stage-hands along the narrow passage at whose end was situated the dressing-room of the greatest actress and most ravishing creature I had ever seen.

She was stretched on a *chaise longue*, her slender body writhing convulsively as she coughed almost without pause. Her handkerchief was clasped to her mouth with both white hands, and I was startled to see the crimson of blood on it, and droplets of it on her costume. An older woman was endeavouring to press a wet cloth against her forehead, while a young man with a wispy, straw-coloured beard knelt beside the couch and made cooing sounds, which were clearly having not the least effect.

It is hard to convey my exact feelings at that time. A few hours previously, it had seemed altogether unlikely that I should be able so much as to set my eyes on her. When, through a fluke, it had become possible, it had been with that gulf between her and me which so many of us bridge in our imagination, but so few ever cross in fact; I refer to the physical and illusory gap which separates actors from their audience. It would not have crossed my mind to ask if she might receive me, or, accustomed though I was to the practice, to buy the most eye-catching bouquet I could afford and join the crowd of stage-door hopefuls. I could surely presume her to be entirely beyond my reach.

Yet here I was, kneeling within the aura of her fragrance, entitled by my calling to consider her under my immediate care and subservient, in theory, to my commands, and able without objection to lay my hands on her and touch her as I would.

I hasten to assure my reader that, if such thoughts did pass through my mind at the time, they were not uppermost in it. My concern was wholly for a woman in suffering and distress. Above all, the blood alarmed me. I wondered whether the coughing spasm had ruptured a vessel in her throat or mouth, or whether, dread thought, the attack was of a tubercular nature. I put my arm about her and pulled her up into a posture which I believed would give her more ease. Her body was tense, but she did not resist me. I commenced gently but firmly patting and rubbing her back, and was gratified to note some diminution in the coughing.

I heard the manager speaking to someone, and, expecting some French doctor to have come backstage by now, I looked round. The manager was conferring with another official-looking man. They were lighting cigarettes.

"*Madame est très malade,*" I rebuked them. "*Défense de fumer, s'il vous plaît.*"

They made no move to comply. The newcomer curled his lip and answered, "*Madame est une grande chienne—beetch.*"

I felt my patient convulse anew, and held her tight. Suddenly her coughing ceased, she hiccoughed severely, then burst into tears. I cradled her to me; what if her blood did stain my clothes—the blood of Sarah Bernhardt!

"*Pauvre petite,*" said the woman who had been soothing her brow. "*Allez-vous-en, espèces d' animaux! La représentation est terminée pour ce soir.*"

"*Au contraire, la représentation est commencée au vengeance!*" sneered the offensive newcomer, with a harsh laugh, and he and the manager stumped from the room, slamming the door.

Madame Bernhardt bent a leg, tore off one of her shoes, and flung it at the closed door, following it immediately with the other, at the same time issuing a string of words which were beyond my vocabulary, but whose vehement import there was no mistaking. I looked towards the other woman for some sign, but she only shrugged.

The young man, who had given up his feeble attempts at consolation, got to his feet, looked at me helplessly, and scurried out. Who he was, or what he was doing there, I could not imagine.

A silence had fallen momentarily. I looked at Sarah Bernhardt and was surprised to see her eyeing me with an expression of curiosity. Her older female companion hurried forward with a dampened cloth and proceeded to wipe the stains of blood away from her mouth and chin. She made no resistance, but grasped the other's hand in a gesture which seemed to express united solidarity against the world of fools. I hastened to introduce myself in my limited French, concluding with a few words to the effect that I was both honoured and saddened to make her unexpected acquaintance in such circumstances. She gave me a gracious little bow of the head and one of the enigmatic smiles which had so captivated me in the course of the play's first act. Seen close to, and directed at me alone, it was enough to make my scalp prickle.

"Tell me, madame, if you please," I continued, "does there exist any condition of the, er, the . . ." The French word for the lungs was beyond me. I could only indicate my chest.

She sighed, and a shadow of sadness dimmed her bright eyes.

"A little," she said, nodding. Then she roused herself, as if determined to dismiss it. "But it is not the trouble. It is the interference of pigs and dogs with my work."

She scowled at the door, and her companion joined her scowl with her own. Sarah's English was pretty well on a par with my French, although her accent was ravishing.

"It is nothing," she went on. "A nervous attack. They criticise and complain, and expect of me that I obey their cretinous directions. I tell them I act as I wish. It is I who knows how to do, not they. They threaten to suspend me. Hah!"

Had it not been for the blood, I should have regarded her symptoms as hysterical, and my assessment had evidently been right. It was not hard to imagine that a woman of such gifts and eccentricities would be temperamental and highly-strung, not to say insistent that she must have her way in all things. The management had for some reason taken her to task during the play's interval, and, perhaps unable to overbear them, she had had recourse to the hysterics which no doubt she could stir up at will. (I read, in later years, that even as a child she would threaten to take her life and leave her mother remorseful at having driven her to suicide by insisting she eat something she did not fancy.)

Thin and fragile though she was—the more so to the touch,

for I still maintained my arm about her, supporting her, and she did not seem impatient to be rid of it—I did not believe her consumptive. It was not beyond the bounds of possibility that she could bleed at will, as easily as she could weep. It was plain, however, that she would not be resuming her performance that evening; hence the chagrin with which the manager and his colleague had left her.

"It will be advisable for Madame to go home and rest," I ventured, fearing a little that she might take no more kindly to my telling her what she ought to do. She sighed again.

"Of course," she murmured. "Florence . . ."

Her woman came forward. "Madame?"

"I will change now."

"Yes, madame."

I prepared to get to my feet. To my surprise, Sarah took hold of my arm and pressed me back on to the sofa, where I was perched beside her.

"You will not leave me?" she murmured, looking me full in the eyes, and I swear to this day that hers had turned the colour of damsons.

"I—"

"You have been so kind, and I have not even your name."

I told it her.

"Then, Dr. Watson, I hope you will give me your escort to my house. Who knows"—she flickered her eyelids at me—"but that I have another attack on the way?"

My mind reeled. I looked up at the older woman and saw a smug smile on her lips. I looked back to Sarah, who was watching me and smiling also.

"I, er, I will be honoured to escort Madame," I said, and it came out in the manner of a croak.

She let go my arm and sprang to her feet, heedless of her recent indisposition. "After all, doctor, it will not be right for me to leave the theatre without some support. Those imbeciles will believe I was feigning if they see me go alone."

I gave her a smile which I hoped conveyed a blend of understanding and willingness to take my share in a conspiracy. "Of course," she immediately dashed my spirits by adding, "Florence will travel with us. It would not do to be seen *sans chaperone*."

"I quite understand."

"On the other hand, we can enjoy our little tête-à-tête when we reach there. I will show you my sculptures."

My heart leapt up again. The thought of Waveney-Waveney waiting his dinner for me did just cross my mind. It crossed, and as swiftly vanished, not to return for the rest of the evening.

18

"The motives of women are so inscrutable."

The French word *hôtel* means, first and foremost, a mansion, and it was a mansion indeed which Sarah Bernhardt had had built for herself on a corner where the Avenue de Villiers and rue Fortuny met; yet hotel in the English understanding of the term it might well have been, judged by its size, its opulence, and the seething activity beyond its portals, which were flanked by two huge terra-cotta representations of apes.

I find it necessary to qualify the above sentence in two respects. In saying that she had had it built, it is correct that several commercial firms had been involved with the work, directed by the noted architect Félix Escalier; but my informative neighbour at the theatre had described to me how Sarah herself had set her own stamp on the work, amending details, dictating designs, carrying out a great deal of the decorative work, and even swarming about the scaffolding to supervise every particular in person. And it was by no means for herself alone that all this had taken place; she had so many attendants and visitors, so much livestock, and so great a store of possessions of all kinds, that nothing less palatial could have sufficed her.

Such notions as I had entertained of a speedy dismissal of Florence, to leave the two of us in the discreet quiet of some parlour, were dashed when, after passing through a crowd which evidently kept constant vigil on the pavement outside, we entered a richly-decorated foyer. Madame, clearly thoroughly recovered by now, strode ahead, inclining her neck regally to left and right as hats were raised and felicitations murmured. Following, I felt it only proper to raise my hat in similar acknowledgement. The envy in the eyes which encountered mine was plain to read.

A rush of people and animals greeted us within. Maids and footmen hurried forward, lithe greyhounds and a Dalmatian skipped and yelped their glee, a monkey danced and gibbered on a perch and proceeded to whirl round and round on his silver chain. A large spotted cat, which I took to be one of the cheetahs of which I had heard, slunk towards me, neck lowered and glowing eyes raised in suspicious enquiry: I forebore to attempt to stroke it.

Pandemonium prevailed, the cries of the animals mingling with the din of everyone talking at once in loud tones. My coat, hat, and cane were taken from me by a handsome young footman, and a dignified butler gestured towards a doorway. I had noticed Sarah say something to Florence, with a nod in my direction, before turning to sweep away up the grand staircase as lightly and swiftly as if she were borne mechanically. Florence came to me and said in French, "Madame says she will be ready for you in half an hour, sir." She gave me that knowing little smile of hers and left me in the butler's charge.

The room into which he ushered me would have accommodated a state banquet. It was long, broad, and immensely lofty, and evidently combined the functions of salon and studio, for as well as comfortable couches and chairs and other drawing-room furniture, I noticed easels supporting canvases in varying states of completion, and, on a dais, a life-size sculpture of a naked woman, with only the head and trunk completed.

The butler gravely escorted me to a chair, and from the contents of a large silver tray on a chiffonier gave me a generous glass of cognac. He opened a silver box of cigars and placed it beside me, and then, with a bow, withdrew.

A stirring in one corner attracted my attention. I saw another monkey on a perch, occupied upon its own person. I got up with my glass and perambulated about the vast space, watching my step after almost putting my foot on a small, humped object which proved to be a tortoise. Something unusual about it made me stoop to peer close: I saw that its shell was encrusted with jewels.

There were objects of interest everywhere: oriental rugs, bearskins, richly-bound books, manuscripts, bronze statuettes, busts in plaster and marble and bronze, oil paintings, water-colours, draped materials of rich hues, the paraphernalia of painting and sculpture, tropical plants, flowers. . . . I saw the stuffed birds of prey with real skulls in their claws, of which my friend had told me. No decapitated dogs were in evidence, nor did I find the fabled coffin; but I did come across the skeleton, "Lazarus," grinning from an easy chair in which he sat with one elbow on an adjoining table and his hand supporting his bony chaps, as though perfectly at ease and ready to share agreeable conversation. I wondered whether there could be truth in her having had him boiled, which in turn gave me pause to consider what might be in store for myself. That message to the effect that she would soon be "ready for me" had had an electrifying effect on my feelings: I thought I had not misread the calculating look she had given me, and Florence's private amusement had seemed to confirm my destiny. Nor did I harbour the least objection to it, provided only that it did not entail any subsequent rendering down.

I was still engaged in my slow tour of this fascinating, cluttered room when the door opened and a slight young man slipped in, closing it behind him. I looked again, and saw that it was no youth, but Sarah herself.

She was dressed in a white silk suit of jacket and trousers—the first time I had ever seen a woman so attired. Great pleats of silk foamed about her neck and at her cuffs, and her white satin shoes were decorated with silk flowers. Her hair was up, its red hue accentuated by the general whiteness, as were her lips, while her great eyes, with their black lining, seemed like charcoal against her pale skin. Her perfume preceded her as she came towards me, smiling. I half opened my arms to receive her.

"Some cognac for me, please," she requested, walking past me to where the cigar box lay. She took one out, cut it dextrously with a jade-handled cutter, and put it into her mouth. She lit it, puffed deeply, and exhaled with a satisfied sigh of a quality which would have turned men weak at the knees. At any rate, that was its effect on me.

"Permit me to remark, madame—" I began, as I carefully poured from the decanter.

"You have been admiring my work?" she enquired, ignoring my opening.

"Oh, yes. Er, is it all yours, madame?"

"Many of the pictures are gifts. And the books. This one here is inscribed from Hugo. That is Flaubert's, and that one is from Dumas. They are all so complimentary."

"Understandably."

I smiled into her face as I handed her the brandy balloon. She looked down into it, went to the decanter, and dashed some more in.

"To your, er, restored health, madame," I ventured, raising my own glass in a toast.

"Pigs!" she snorted. *"Crétins.* To tell me how I must not act!"

It was all the return I got for my genuinely-meant toast,

but she followed it with her smile, which was more than enough reward.

"Here is Loti's book." She indicated a red leather volume. "The dear fool!" She smiled again. "Do you know, he could not think how to introduce himself to me, so he had himself delivered rolled up in a Persian carpet? See, that one there. That is it."

I was conscious that fortune had placed me in a position which the whole world of men could envy. The question of procedure from this point was less easily answered. I decided that one so forthright as she would almost certainly provide the necessary cues.

"Now you must admire my bust," she startled me by saying. "It has been praised by all who have seen it."

This seemed somewhat disappointingly cold, coming from one capable of such intensity; but then, I reminded myself, she was notably eccentric. Her figure was not even very voluptuous.

"By all means," I assented warmly.

"Over here," she said, replacing the cigar in her mouth and carrying her glass, trailing smoke behind like a locomotive.

She paused and turned to me.

"Is it not expressive?" she demanded. "Does it not speak to you of wasted capacity for love?"

"Undoubtedly," I was ready to agree.

"It is of Ophelia, of course," she seemed to find it necessary to add. "Ah, the poor girl—victim of a man's caprice. Some day I should like to play Hamlet, if only to torture him from within for his treatment of her."

To my untutored eye, she was certainly a sculptress of talent. The bust of Ophelia upon which we stood looking down was no conventional one, but a horizontal representation of the girl's dead face and one shoulder and breast showing above the surface of the stream, with her hair and wreath adding their ripples about her.

She led me on around the room, showing me her sculpted likenesses of the playwright Sardou, of the artist Clairin, of some drowning Breton fishermen, of herself as the Muse, crowning Shakespeare and Molière. The large, unfinished figure on the dais proved to be of the sorceress Medea. From contemplating it, she turned suddenly to me.

"It is late, but who cares for time? Take off your clothes."

"Here?" I said.

"You are bashful? Ah, you English!"

"Not at all." I began to tug at my collar and tie. "It makes no difference to me." I felt like adding that I might have expected something a little more romantic, in approach if not surroundings, but I was afraid of provoking sulks or even a tantrum.

"You have done this before?" she asked, watching me remove my jacket and begin work on my shirt.

"Of course. Quite a bit."

"With anyone famous?"

"Well, not exactly *famous.*"

"Then you will be able to boast. You will be able to say, 'Sarah Bernhardt chose me!'"

"You wouldn't mind that?"

"Why should I mind? Ah!"

I had exposed a shoulder. She stepped forward and ran her soft little hand over its curve.

"So firm and noble! I have it! I shall put black on you. You shall be Othello!"

"Anything that will please you—my dear," said I. Now that I came to think of it, I should have felt let down if she had included no manifestation of her eccentricity.

She tugged at one end of a couch, placing it conveniently for me, and adjusted a drape on it.

"Here will do," she said, placing her hands on her hips to go on regarding me as I removed my shirt. I fancied that she licked her red lips.

"Aren't you going to—to get ready?" I suggested, working the tail of my undershirt free of my trousers.

Sarah laughed gaily. "There have been many before you, of many kinds, but you are my first Englishman," she said. "They have always told me the Englishman is so shy. Very well, I will get ready and not watch you."

She moved away towards a table littered with paints and jars of brushes, presumably to seek out the required blacking for my skin. Instead, she unrolled a large sheet of heavy paper and began pinning it to a board.

"What are you doing—*chérie?*" I ventured. She looked up with a frown.

"What are you calling me?"

"*Chérie.* By the way, I haven't told you my name: it's John."

"It gives you no right to use endearments to me."

"Well, I thought in the circumstances—"

"'Madame.' You call me 'madame,' you understand?"

"Oh, all right."

"Such effrontery! Now hurry and get ready."

"After you," I retorted.

"What do you say?"

"I said, 'After you.' *Aprés vous* is good enough French, isn't it?"

She threw down the board on to the table with a crash and came stalking to where I stood, my shirt in my hand.

"How dare you give orders to me?" she stormed. "By Heaven, has the day come when Sarah Bernhardt shall be told what to do by a—a—"

"An Englishman. About time, I'd say."

Her mouth gaped. Her eyes were the size of white-rimmed saucers.

"Now, come along," said I. "That's enough of your games, my girl. Kindly get those things off, and no more hanky-panky."

There came from the depths of her diaphragm an unearthly cry, such as she might well have employed for the agony of Phèdre's rejection by her stepson. Her accompanying onrush bowled me over backwards, so that I fell upon the couch she had prepared. Having grasped at me with both hands, she was naturally borne down with me, so that we sprawled together, she trying to claw my face or exposed chest with fingers which had become talons, I desperate to keep fast the grip I had managed to get on her wrists. For all the disparity between our physiques, she was a formidable assailant. I doubt if I should have come out of it without some scarring had not the door burst open and others rushed in, yelling excitedly. Hands were laid on both of us, and although Sarah went on trying to get at me, we were eventually prised apart. She was heaved into a chair, where she subsided into another coughing fit, while I lay panting on the sofa, conscious of my half-clothed state.

"The police, the police!" someone was shrilling. "Send out for the police!"

"Don't be ridiculous," I managed to gasp.

"Rapine! Murder!"

"Nothing of the sort."

"Perfidious brute!"

"That will do!" I retorted, struggling to my feet to face the man responsible for the insults. He proved to be the straw-coloured young fellow who had been in her dressing-room. His pale face was quite pink-cheeked from his fury, as he almost danced before me.

"You will do yourself a mischief," I told him curtly.

"English savage!"

"Or *I* shall do you one," I warned.

"You call for a fight?" he shrilled.

"If you like. Put 'em up."

I was beyond standing on ceremony. Stripped to the waist as I was, I struck a pugilistic posture. As I did so, Sarah's coughing ceased abruptly and I heard what seemed to be a sharp indrawing of her breath.

The man facing me looked at my fists with some alarm, then drew himself up.

"Gentlemen do not fight with the fists," he said haughtily. "It is pistols or swords."

My prowess at the shooting booth in Cremorne Gardens, on that evening with Aggie Brown, flashed vividly into my mind.

"Pistols," I answered unhesitatingly.

He goggled at me anew, swallowing hard. I heard Sarah laugh.

"Well, Monsieur Jacques?" she asked. "Which do you choose?"

He turned to her. I lowered my hands and followed suit. She was reclining in her chair, with the woman Florence's arm about her shoulder. The butler and the footman and a maid or two hovered in the background.

My antagonist faltered. "I . . . I . . . madame, I merely came here in the hope that Madame would let me read my manuscript to her, as she had promised."

"You did not anticipate such excitement, *hein*?"

"Well, no."

"Consider what rich experience it will offer your writing. There is a certain insipidity about your work which betrays lack of worldly knowledge."

"I am a poet, madame."

"But what could be more poetic than a duel? The dawn light bathing some quiet clearing amongst the concealing trees. The patient horses waiting with their carriages. The grave seconds, supervising the courtesies. The glints of steel barrels or blades. The doctor with his bag. The pale faces of the opponents under their top hats. The watching onlooker, swathed in her furs, wondering to which she shall find herself beholden for triumphing on her behalf. That is true poetry, monsieur, not your insipid shepherds and Columbines." Each allusion was given its appropriate mime and tone of voice. It was all superbly done.

"With . . . with respect, madame, it is not my style," muttered the unappreciative fellow.

"Come, on," I interpolated, "it was your idea. It'll have to be tomorrow morning, though. I've got to be getting back to London."

He looked at me bleakly, and let his eyes fall away. "As Madame pleases."

I looked across at Sarah. She returned my look steadily. Without taking her eyes from mine, she said, "I think you had better leave, Monsieur Jacques. Cultivate an appetite for fire-eating before you essay to write for Sarah Bernhardt."

He gave her a miserable little bow and turned to go.

"And say not a word of what has happened here," she warned him. "If it gets about, I shall know it came from you, and you may be sure that your spineless part in it shall be well published."

He bowed again and went stiffly out. Sarah addressed the rest of her staff.

"You may go, too, and no gossiping, either. There has been a misunderstanding, that is all. *Go,* Florence, I said. Go to bed, and rest assured that I have nothing to fear from Dr. Watson."

They went out. As soon as the door had closed, Sarah burst into helpless laughter. She writhed and wrung her hands, until it turned to coughing again and made her desist.

"Oh, dear me!" she managed at last. "It was the funniest thing I have seen for years."

"I am pleased to have given you some amusement, at any rate," I answered coolly, starting to put on my undershirt.

"Wait," she cried, jumping up. "Not yet. Please get up on the dais and strike that pose again."

"Pose?"

"Like a pugilist. Othello did not quite suit you, and you have given me the solution yourself. Also," she added with a sly look, "it will be fitting for you to retain your trousers."

"You wanted me to pose for you—all along?"

"But of course. Why else do you think I ordered you to take off your clothes? It is rare to encounter a model of such splendid physique."

She went and got the sketching board she had prepared, and a charcoal stick.

"Madame Bernhardt," I said, as horror mounted, "I believe I owe you the most profound apology. I spoke to you outrageously. I thought—"

She stood before me, ready to sketch, and her eyes were that damson colour again.

"I know what you thought. You say you have to go back to England tomorrow?"

"I'm afraid I must. My final examinations are coming up, and—"

"Then we must not waste time. Take up the pose again, please."

I assumed the classic pugilistic stance, fists raised, legs braced apart and slightly bent. She began drawing rapidly.

"The hands a little higher. Perfect! It is a pity you will not be free to pose for me further. A sketch will have to suffice. No, the head still, please. Tell me—John—you would have fought that nincompoop?"

"Of course."

"If he had not been a coward? If he had been a crack shot?"

"I would have taken the risk."

"Why were you so quick to accept?"

"He cast an aspersion on my nationality."

"Ah!"

"And for you—to let you see that Englishmen are not so ungallant as you French believe."

"I should not have thought that of you, John. I know something of men. I have something of a reputation for it."

"I had hoped—" I began, but broke off.

"Yes? Come, you are bold enough in other ways. You must not flinch now."

"I believed you were intending to honour me with . . . But I see my mistake. I have asked you to forgive me."

"And I have asked you to pose for me, and now I have my sketch. See?"

She came to the foot of the dais and held it up for me. Its sweeping black lines made a vigorous effect, which I thought very accomplished and not a little flattering.

"That is one misunderstanding rectified, then," she said, when I had praised her work. "There remains the other. Will you permit me to keep you waiting one half-hour more? Then it will be the large door at the head of the second flight of stairs."

She laid down her drawing things and left the room without a backward glance.

I adjudged myself entitled to another brandy and soda. I made it last half an hour precisely, then went upstairs, having first dressed again for decorum's sake, although I encountered none of the staff. I climbed the broad staircase to the second landing and faced the tall doors. I knocked, heard no answer, so opened them and went in.

The air was heavy with perfume. In what little light there was, I could see that I was in a boudoir, whose further door was open, giving on to the bedroom beyond. I passed through, to be confronted by a vast, richly-decorated four-poster bed. The sheets were turned back, but there was no one between them. I looked about in the dim light, but could see no sign of Sarah.

"John," I heard her voice, in that vibrant timbre which seemed to convey a kiss in every word. "Come to me."

I followed the sound to its source, and found her awaiting me.

She was in her coffin.

19

"The sea air, sunshine, and patience."

There is merely a postscript to be added to this account of my association with yet another of the greatest figures of that later-Victorian era. Occasionally, when "in vacant or in pensive mood," I have thought back to it, and regretted that I was unable to pursue it further; but I know that it was never meant to be.

Waveney-Waveney and I returned to London next day. His own evening had not, I was pleased to learn, been spoiled by my defection.

"Good job you didn't show up for dinner," he told me when we met at breakfast next morning, both hollow-eyed and listless from lack of sleep. "Madame was feeling frisky and fancied me for herself. Carried me off to her private apartment and gave me the most gigantic meal, apart from everything else. Kept serving up fresh courses all night." He gave me his wink over his coffee. "Had a good time yourself?"

"Pretty lively."

"Got yourself one of the cast, did you?"

"You could put it like that."

Of course, I often read about Sarah in the newspapers in

the months which followed. She created another of her sensations during the Paris Exposition that May by impetuously making a flight over the city by balloon, together with one of her lovers, eating *foie-gras* sandwiches and drinking champagne. And in the early summer of '79 she paid her first visit to England, with the Comédie Française company, for a season at the Gaiety Theatre which drove all London wild. I saw several of her performances, although I was not in the country during the earlier weeks, and duly sent my card up to her and into the house when she was staying in Chester Square, but got no response. I scarcely expected any; and when I visited the French Fête at the Royal Albert Hall in early July, in aid of the French Hospital in London, and saw how close an attendance the Prince of Wales was dancing on her, I knew she was forever beyond my reach.

Almost of more interest to me than her performances was an exhibition of her sculptures and paintings in a Piccadilly gallery, which I believe was the first one-woman show ever held in London. It was a private affair, so I was unable to attend, and felt not a little thankful that no one who knew me would be likely to be there, either. When the newspaper accounts of it appeared, though, I could find no reference to a figure or painting of a pugilist. I have sometimes wondered what became of it.

I used to smile to myself when the Sarah Bernhardt fever was at its height, and people were clamouring for photographs and medallions of her, and all the ladies were sporting replicas of her famous hat. The tale I could have told them would have been beyond their capacity for belief. If she never did immortalise me in bronze or stone or paint, she had certainly done so in her coffin.*

*My reader will readily appreciate my amusement—albeit undisclosed—upon listening to Holmes's account of how he had deduced the solution to the case of "The Disappearance of Lady Frances Carfax" from the abnormal size of the coffin in which we found her alive in the nick of time: "Why so large a coffin for so small a body? To leave room for another body."

I have said that I was absent from the country early in 1879. I had, in fact, been away since the middle of the preceding summer, following my attaining at last the full status of Doctor of Medicine. I had presented my aforementioned thesis in the May, and thankfully reached the goal of my long and—save for diversions—tedious period of medical study at the end of June, 1878, which was also the end of that academic year.

"Well, Jack—ready to drop anchor in leafy Surrey at last?" Grandfather congratulated me, raising his glass of John Exshaw (Yellow Label).

I drank in response, then relieved myself of the utterance which I had been carrying prepared and rehearsed since hearing my result.

"Grandpa, if it's all the same to you, I prefer to go back to sea."

"Back to . . ." Astonishment swiftly gave way to suspicion. "There's no sort of bother, is there? You can confide in me, you know."

"None at all. It's just that I don't feel ready to settle down."

"But . . . but you're twenty-six. The hard part of doctoring's behind you now. From here onward it is a downhill canter all the way. The practice to step into. Nothing to trouble you there. An excellent list of patients, in the habit of paying on the dot. This house, which will be a trifle large at first, but not for long, I'll be bound, eh? Most of the servants with it to look after you. What more could you want?"

"It's most generous of you, sir, and I dare say I could become very comfortable. Only, I don't feel altogether ready for it yet."

"Not . . . ! Bless my soul, what will your generation come to?" And the bewildered old sybarite drank off his brandy at a gulp and poured again.

"I sometimes think it a mercy that poor Violet is in her

grave,'' I overheard one of the maiden aunts say to the other after I had announced my decision, which had had the effect of casting a heavy cloak of gloom over my grandparents' household. ''One son a scoundrel; the other an ingrate.''

''I told you there was bad blood in *him,* the first time she brought him to our hotel in Stranraer,'' her sister answered. ''It's *him* they got it from, not poor Violet.''

''I must say I'm surprised at John, though. I believed him to be the steady one.''

''Still waters run deep, you know. The next thing we shall hear, he will be paying attention to *women.*''

''Dear me! Yes, poor Violet is well out of it.''

What blushes I could have painted on their maidenly cheeks! But I conducted myself with decorum, said goodbye to them all, and took myself off to sea again. Grandfather sold his practice soon afterwards and they all went off to Scotland, to sustain him in retirement from his life of unremitting toil.

As I had envisaged, I was able to get a berth as assistant doctor in a liner without difficulty. Not many medical men, it seemed, shared my love of the sea, so such posts were quite easy to come by. I could have taken up a good engagement on the trans-Atlantic run, but decided against it, on the ground that the relatively short voyage, and the crowded vessels, with their large complement of sickly emigrants, would afford me little leisure to explore those social relationships which loomed large in my attraction to the life. Instead, I signed on with the Pacific & Orient, in their service to the Far East.

I do not propose to detail my travels, which were almost wholly agreeable, albeit with certain bizarre interludes, which I might example by, in India, The Abominable Occurrence of the Nautch-Girl and the Pearl, and in Japan, The Confusing Incident of the Geisha who did Nothing in the Night-time.

In these and adjacent regions of the Orient I found myself in many a fair port, enlarging my knowledge of the world and of life all the while. I revisited Australia and was able to travel up to Ballarat and inspect my father's grave, now graced by a simple but finely-chiselled stone, for which Grandfather had paid; and also to pass an evening's reunion with the good-natured Dr. Ramsay, at which the Reverend Mr. Copperthwaite looked briefly in. I also saw something of New Zealand—that lovely, lonely outpost of the furthest flung empire left in the world; and all the time hobnobbing with the fashionable, the worldly, and the beautiful, the nature of my appointment placing me on equal terms with all.

The one passage which I must describe in some detail, for it was to prove germane to my entire life, was from Bombay to London in the spring of 1879. I had taken the opportunity of a few days in port to accept the invitation of one of the surgeons at the Military Hospital at Poona to pay him a visit. We were at war again in Afghanistan at that time, the Amir having defiantly accepted overtures from the Russians, between whose country and India his mountainous domain lay as a buffer zone vital to our Eastern Empire's defence. Many of our passengers, both outward and homeward bound, were officers and their families, and I had struck up some happy friendships.

"Ever fancied the Army?" my Poona friend had said to me, as we neared Bombay at the end of the passage bringing him back from home leave.

"The sea suits me well enough, thanks."

"Pretty dreary sort of life, I'd have thought, cooped up in the same surroundings."

"They change with each new lot of passengers."

"Damned bores, a lot of 'em, surely?"

"There's always someone."

He gave me a comprehending smile. "Still, nothing to compare with the life up the passes. Seeing the dawn light on the peaks. *Chota hazri* in the open air at six A.M., with no pampered old biddies chattering at you across the table. The rising heat, the smell of the dust, the British Other Rank, damn his lovely soul. The wily Pathan, best enemy a man could fight. The mess silver under the stars. Ah, it's a life-and-a-half for a fellow!"

I admitted I could conceive of its attractions; but I was rapidly becoming entrenched in my comfortable ways. I had put on a stone in weight since having to relinquish Rugby and exchanging my student's diet for three substantial meals a day and a great deal of drink and snacks on the side. The dawn lighting up the wave-tops, glimpsed from some lady passenger's state-room window as I prepared to hurry back to my own comfortable cabin, was sight enough of Nature's artistry for my eyes.

"At any rate," he had said, "come out to Poona next time you're in port. It'll give you a taste of mess life."

So I had gone there, 119 miles from Bombay by Great India Peninsula railway, climbing to almost 2,000 feet above sea level at a place where two rivers converged. I found it a delightful spot, which I have often recalled to mind when reading Kipling's Indian tales. Ancient temples and palaces faced elegant modern public buildings of gleaming stone; and everywhere gardens of perfectly kept lawns, borders, and palm trees.

I enjoyed indeed the mixture of ritual, stiff formality, and boyish games which constituted a mess night. I lingered on to join in a cricket match next day, consequently getting back to my ship with less than an hour to go to sailing-time.

The passengers were all aboard, so I was deprived of my customary pastime of leaning on the upper deck rail to watch them embark and assessing the relative attractions of those females who appeared to be without male escorts. A ship's doctor's work generally keeps him fully busy for the first twenty-four hours or so, attending to any chronically ill passengers, seeing the invalids made comfortable, and reassuring those of both sexes who feel it the required thing to become seasick at the first slap of a wavelet against the hull. It was not until dinner time on our first evening out from port that I was able to view my companions in the first-class dining-saloon *en masse*.

They seemed the usual mixture of red-faced old buffers, military and civilian, and their imperious memsahibs, either tiny and fierce-eyed, with sharp voices, or vast, booming baritones; the bachelors, quiet-mannered and decent, or over-hearty and inconsiderate; the pairs of spinsters, never out of one another's sight; and that rarer well-dressed lady keeping mysteriously to herself—and always looked for by us officers.

As my bearded superior, the senior doctor, made the general introductions from his end of the long table at which he and I presided, and our dozen of the passengers bowed to one another as their names were read out, my eyes alighted on one in particular. She would be in early middle age, well formed and comfortably built, with pink cheeks in an otherwise very pale face which contrasted starkly with the blackness of her hair, fetchingly touched with the merest threads of silver at the sides, and the duller black of her mourning dress. Her eyes were downcast, and I could see readily that she was ill at ease. I marked her down as a recent widow, and wondered that she had not kept to her cabin, as most such tended to do, in my experience. By unspoken consent among the officers, the newly widowed were regarded as "out of bounds," with no attempt made to take advantage of their vulnerable state.

"Lady Greene," announced my chief, and she obediently raised her eyes, to flicker her gaze and a brief, wan smile around the company in silent acknowledgement. Her look was in my direction for no more than a second, giving me no time to make her my bow, had I even been able to manage it. But I recognised her: she was Aggie Brown.

She was three places away from me, between one of the

bluff old colonel types and a pair of the spinsters, who had declined our steward's attempt to place them separately, setting the whole seating pattern at our table awry. The chief doctor was a hearty sort, always urging passengers to mix and make friends, and so take their minds off imagined seasickness, and I saw he had spotted the disparity. He spoke to the steward, but the latter's headshake told me that the spinsters had already proved implacable and that nothing could be done to move them apart. Consequently, I was forced to eat that long meal situated too far from Aggie to be able to address her, though knowing that, in any case, anything we should have to say to each other could not be in anyone else's hearing.

I noticed that she answered when spoken to by her neighbours, and ate quite well, not refusing the wines, which was at least a good sign. She did not look my way, thereby convincing me that she had identified me as readily as I had her. What on earth she could be doing masquerading as a titled lady, and why in mourning, baffled me. I thought how well she looked the part: handsome and straight-backed, confident and poised. Insofar as I was able to ponder it amongst the meaningless conversation which I was forced to keep up with my own immediate neighbours, my only guess was that she was travelling as the mistress of some man who was in all probability sitting at some other table, for discretion's sake. The mourning clothes would be part of a scheme to keep other men at their distance from her, and curious women from pressing their questions too closely. I resolved to speak to her as soon as possible, if only briefly, before her gentleman came to claim her, and reassure her that she need feel no fear that I might give them away or embarrass them in the slightest.

We all rose from table together, the unaccompanied ladies heading for their communal salon, or their cabins, the bachelors and some of the other gentlemen making eagerly for the conviviality of cigars and port and brandy in the smoking saloon. I tried to espy Aggie, and saw her lingering in the foyer outside the dining-room. I determined to get in my quick word before her gentleman joined her.

"Lady Greene?"

"So it's *Doctor* Watson now!"

"Aggie, I knew it was you. You can't think how glad I am to see you again."

She gave me her full smile. "I could feel you lookin' at me all through dinner, like in them old times."

"I'd look at you anywhere, Aggie. I've thought about you so often." This was quite true. The man who can forget his first woman, or girl, can have little sentiment in his soul.

"Well, I've thought of you—sometimes. Wondered how you was gettin' on. You married yet?"

"Oh, no. But... but you... I mean..."

My look indicated her widow's black. The expression she returned me told me at once that it was not part of a deception.

"No, I ain't married," she answered, though. "Might have bin by now, I suppose. I dunno."

"Are you... with anyone? Travelling, I mean. You can tell me, Aggie. I wouldn't split."

"I know you wouldn't. No, I'm on me lonesome. Funny ole world, ain't it?"

"Then you're not Lady Greene?"

"Green, all right. I just never thought of it happening, that's all."

"What happening? Look, Aggie, if you're on your own, can't we have a chat? Somewhere less public than this."

"Yeh," she said with resolution. "I'd like that. I reely would."

My thoughts naturally flew to her cabin. I said instead, "Out on deck? It'll still be warm, in spite of the breeze."

"All right, then."

"Ah, Watson! Coming in for a few rubbers?" The hearty greeting was from the First Officer, a fanatic for bridge who liked me to partner him, for we understood each other's play.

"I'm afraid not," I returned. "I've had the unexpected pleasure of meeting with an old friend. Mr. Clements, Lady Greene."

He bowed over Aggie's hand, and she gave him a polite smile. I noticed his suspicious glance at me before he turned to go. My reputation as a ladies' man was not unknown, and I fancy he suspected me of poaching on forbidden land; but I faced him out and offered Aggie my arm in formal manner. Nor did I let it go when I had got her out on to the boat deck, to a point where we could stand beside the rail, shielded by one of the boats from the rush of the breeze, yet able to benefit from its passing breath on the warm air. The bow-wave glowed with phosphorescence, and all the stars and a perfect oriental crescent moon were on display over the dark Indian Ocean. The strains of the ship's band playing lilting Strauss blended agreeably with the sea sounds.

She left her arm under mine, staring out ahead of her into the darkness as she told me her story.

"You remember him? 'Uncle' I called him at first, and you was took in."

"Talk about green! That was me, then."

"An' I was Brown. Fancy!" I was pleased that she could manage a little laugh. "Anyways, I told you he was going to see me right, when I found I was in the family way. He took nice little rooms for me in Fulham. Enough for me and the nipper. Didn't mind me entertaining a bit, but wouldn't let me go to the Gardens no more."

"I should think not. I wish I'd known where you were."

"I did think once of letting you know. Wouldn't have minded seeing you, once you was out of that school. Only, I reckoned you'd start wantin' to look after me, or something. I didn't want that, for me or for you."

"You should have, Aggie. I wouldn't have pestered you."

"You'd your own life to make. I'd made mine, and I was happy enough. He was a good old s—d, bless 'is heart."

Her voice trembled a little under this last, and it occurred to me that her mourning might be in some way connected with the silver-haired protector whom I remembered vividly from our one evening at Cremorne. She sniffed and continued.

"Last year he got news that his brother had snuffed it out in India. Been living there for donkey's years, and blowed if he wasn't a baronet, so Frank—that's 'Uncle'—had to take up the title and came into all the property. It's all in India—something to do with supplying the Army and Navy, which was why he'd got his title. Old Frank fancied he might make a try at keeping the whole bang-shoot going, and when little Frank got old enough he could step into his boots."

"He'd married you, then?"

"No. We'd talked about it, to give the boy a name and that, but Frank had his own business in the City, and his clubs and his friends, and I told him I'd never fit in. I didn't want to think of them nudgin' one another behind his back and whispering how he'd married a tart."

"You'd have adapted to it, Aggie. I saw the way you carried yourself at dinner."

"Oh, I know me manners, and I can speak posh. You would scarcely know me, doctor, were you to hear me conversing amongst ladies. I mean, you got a title, you got to blooming live up to it."

"But I thought you said—"

She sighed. "It was like this. He wanted me to marry him at last and come out to India. With a handle to me name, and him having taught me how to behave meself in public, I wouldn't have felt out of place. There's plenty of chaps higher than him marry girls lower than I ever was. Anyway, if you've got plenty of money to chuck about, anyone'll kowtow to you. Do you want me to speak posh all the time for you? I can, if you like."

"No, no," I protested, laughing. "I prefer you as I've always remembered you."

She gave my arm a little squeeze. "You're a good 'un. Cor, that was a night of it we had, wasn't it?"

"If you can call an hour a night."

"But what an hour! Kept in practice since, have you?"

"Aggie—"

"Anyway, as I was telling you—he wanted us to marry, but I wasn't sure. I didn't reckon much on going to India, and having to live la-di-da, and watch meself as I'd have to, whatever he said otherwise. And he said we couldn't take young Frank with us. He'd have to stop at school in England till he was old enough to come out, except for a few months a year. I didn't fancy that. Still, old Frank had been good to me, and he said he didn't want to go out on his lonesome, so we agreed we'd give it a try. I'd go with him, pretending to be his wife, and see how I fancied being Lady Greene to everybody, and whether I'd like India. But we wouldn't get really spliced yet, in case I didn't like any of it, and wanted to go home, and he'd stay out, with no hard feelings on either part."

"A very civilised chap, your 'Uncle Frank' sounds."

"He was. Generous to a fault. Took to the baby from the start. Was going to leave me and little Frank everything he had, if I went through with it. Even if I didn't, he promised he'd set us up for life."

"But you didn't like it? You've decided to come back. Why in mourning, though? Is it to help him save his face in some way?"

She gave a sharp sob, and gripped my arm convulsively.

"It ain't no game. We hadn't been five minutes ashore at Bombay. The poor old b——r took his hat off to wipe his brow, and the sun got him and he dropped dead on the spot."

I let her sob, holding her to my side. It would not have done to have placed my arm about her; for one of the ship's officers—not least one of the doctors—to have been seen behaving so in public would have been considered scandalous.

The naïve notion of an elderly baronet pausing on the Bombay dock-side to mop his brow and thus exposing himself to the malevolence of the Indian sun would have raised a guffaw in any smoking-room. Coming from Aggie, my senior in years but so genuinely artless still, it moved me deeply. Her benefactor's heart failure, on the very threshold of a strange continent and a way of life totally unknown to her, must have given her an immense shock. He had been her protector in the broadest sense, her most intimate companion, and her child's father. As her tears proved, her widow's weeds were no mockery.

When she had recovered herself, which did not take long (for she was obviously still the self-sufficient Aggie Brown beneath her sham title and expensive clothes), I observed gently, "Well, Aggie, it's hard for those who are left behind, but we should be glad when they go as quickly as that. Think what he may have been spared, and you, in a strange land, without relatives or friends—"

"Oh, he had relatives, all right," she interrupted me. "They'd just met us. His other brother and his stuck-up wife. Now he's Sir Whatever-it-is Greene, and she's Lady, and every brass farthing Frank thought he'd been going to own is theirs."

"You... you don't say he hadn't put you in his will!"

"I *do* say. He never would make one. Always said it was tempting Fate. His lawyer, when he got the title and had to sign papers and things, wanted him to do it, but, you see, he didn't know about me and little Frank. He drew one up for him, leaving everything to his younger brother, as would have been proper, but Frank told me he'd make a what-d'-you-call-it...?''

''A codicil.''

''He'd make one of them after we'd got to India and I'd decided whether I was going to marry him and stay, or go home. Didn't seem any point in maybe having to keep changing it. Anyway, it never got done, so—there you are.''

''This is dreadful! You mean you have nothing?''

''A few dresses and things. Some ear-rings and beads and that. Keep me going for a bit.''

''His brother and his wife—didn't they offer to help?''

''Give over! He hadn't told them about me. Pretended we'd met on the ship. 'Miss Agnes Brown,' if you please. When they saw how I carried on after he'd dropped down, it didn't take them a minute to add up two and two. They took me in front of their lawyer and made me swear on my oath that I wasn't married to him in secret, or anything.''

''What about the will?''

''He'd brought that with us, so's to have it handy for changing, according to whether I wanted to stay on or not. Course, they took possession of all his things, and found it there. You should have seen their looks till they'd finished reading through it and didn't find me in it.''

''But didn't you tell them everything—how close you and Frank had been for so long? The boy, too? Surely they'd have made some provision.''

''You haven't seen them—or heard 'em. They'd always thought bad enough of Frank, because he spent his time gadding about London, and then for him to have got the title and everything on top of it. They told me the sooner I packed off home to where I came from—and you can guess what they meant by that—the better. The lawyer was a decent sort, though. He sent his Indian clerk after me to bring me back, and kept me in a waiting-room till they'd gone. He said I was entitled to keep my clothes and things, 'cos nobody could say I hadn't paid for 'em meself."

"Your jewels, too?"

"I hadn't many. I asked him about them, and he just winked and put his finger to his lips. Decent cove. He arranged to sell some of 'em for me, enough to buy me a ticket home and some cash over. I've kept a few pieces to pop in Uncle Joe's in the Fulham Road when I need to."

"So all this was very recent, I take it?"

"Two weeks today. Quick as that. The lawyer bloke told me, 'If I was you, Miss Brown, I'd take the first boat home. Don't waste your time and money sitting in a hotel, wondering what to do.' I reckon he was right, don't you?"

"The best advice he could have given you. And it's my luck that you fetched up on this of all ships."

"Well, I must say it makes it easier, finding somebody I know."

"Someone who's kept the fondest memories of you, Aggie. I'll do anything I can to help."

"Ta. I expect the 'Lady Greene's' a bit of a cheek, but I reckoned to meself, if I'd decided to come home without him dying—and I reckon I soon would; I didn't care for the look of the place—then I'd have travelled in style. So why not treat meself while I can? Seeing the poor old codger drop dead like that made me think how you never know when a treat's going to be your last one, so make the most of what you've got and let tomorrow go hang. I came out as Lady Greene, and that's how I'm going back, first-class starboard cabin."

"Number?"

"Hey-up!"

"Your own words, Aggie: 'make the most of what you've got.'"

"'Let tomorrow go hang,' eh? You sure you wouldn't get into trouble?"

"Not if we're discreet. I'm sorry about your friend—truly

sorry. But life goes on, and I can truthfully say there's no woman in the world I'd sooner have met at the start of a voyage."

"Well, it'd take my mind off a few things. Listen, though . . ."

"What, my dear?"

"You're going to give it about that we're old friends, are you?"

"That's right. So we are."

"Then don't you reckon I ought to know your name?"

"Eh. You do."

"Dr. Watson? That doesn't sound like old friends. I mean your first. You never told me it."

"It's—"

"Wait. Let me guess. You're a little bit Scotch, aren't you?"

"A great deal, though I didn't think I sounded it."

"It's just the way you say some things."

"Or do them?"

"Cheeky! James—that's it. I reckon you're a James."

"Wrong, but not far. John."

"John. Johnnie. Jack."

"John in front of others. On our own . . ."

"What?"

"Anything that comes to mind."

"Something does. Deck A, Cabin 31. Here! What's bloomin' funny about that?"

"Thirty-one. Aggie, my dear, you're my old school locker number!"

20

"The whole procession of his ancestors."

I need scarcely add that, throughout the weeks of that passage, I spent as much time with Aggie as I could; and the most blissful voyage in all my life it has remained.

For discretion's sake, I had to keep up my share of social intercourse with the other passengers, and partner other unattached ladies in the various games and entertainments. I fancy I caused one or two disappointments by not pressing my attentions where they were invited, but there was no longer any question of it.

I was glad, though, that I could not monopolise Aggie. I could see it doing her good to play up to her rôle as ''Lady Greene,'' making the utmost of what, without the reassurance of my presence in the background, would have been an uneasy and apprehensive time for her. It was uncomfortable to me to watch other men making up to her, especially after she braved the disapproval of the more elderly ladies by modifying her mourning attire. Still, she kept her nights for me.

''Wearing all black reminded me of me school-maid's uniform,'' she told me as we lay resting in her bed.

"I always fancied you in that," I reminded her.

"You spent enough time ogling me in it, saucy monkey."

"I've always thought about you in green, though. You were all in green, that evening at Cremorne."

"That's right! And I finished up Lady Greene—well, nearly. You said then I looked fit to be a duchess."

"So you are. Many a duke would prefer you to what he's got."

"Reckon I'll find one, do you?"

"There aren't any aboard here."

"Too late, then. 'Less they come hunting around the halls."

That brought me sharply up on to one elbow, to stare down at her in the dim, shifting light.

"What do you mean? You're not going in for that sort of thing again!"

"Face facts, Johnnie. I'm no chicken. Not many more years before I'm old boiling fowl. I'll get some sort of job, enough to keep me. But there's young Frank. He's going to have the best chance, if I have to earn it on me back."

"You're not to talk like that."

"I'll talk how I please, ta," she flashed. "I'm not yours, any more than he is."

"You little fool! I care what happens to you. I want to help you."

"Don't you go starting that again."

But her look suddenly softened and she reached up to kiss me. She looked almost girlish in the half-light, her fine dark eyes moistening slightly from emotion. I thought how much worthier she was than someone like Sarah Bernhardt, with her spoilt tantrums and self-centred existence. Sarah, too, had to bring up a fatherless son, and had evidently done so with love and such responsibility as she was capable of; but how differently circumstanced the two women were, and how I longed, with sudden intensity, to be of help to Aggie.

An idea began to form, though I knew I had to be careful in expressing it.

"Aggie, listen. There may be no actual ties between us; but if you'll only let me help, I'd like to very much. No, please don't interrupt. I have a pretty good life of it, for as long as I care to. I took it up because I like the sea, but also because I'm lazy and haven't any particular ambition. With every year that passes, I'll grow more idle and comfortable. Only, meeting you again has made me start to see what an aimless sort of existence it is. A man should make more of himself."

" 'Take what you can while you can get it, dearie.' "

"Not if you don't want it any longer."

The fact was, I was beginning not to want it. When I was alone with my thoughts, especially in those first waking minutes of the day when one is apt to review one's situation and prospects in the most critical and pessimistic light, I had begun to see in myself that disposition towards fecklessness and waste which I had found in my family. Father had taken refuge from his unfulfilment, first in alcohol, then in a mindless fool's quest for gold. My brother had squandered his undoubted talents, and perhaps by now his life, after that same objective, with nothing to justify its being termed Adventure. Grandfather had idled away his years, enjoying his complacent status, never troubling his conscience about the sick and needy whom he had been trained to help. Our womenfolk had been no better: aimless, ungiving, content to exist uselessly while accepting the protection which they took for granted.

Now here was I in my turn, with nothing more on my horizon than continued easy and luxurious circumstances and an unending procession of women. I, whose young imagination had been stirred by the epics of exploration, of voyages into the unknown, of comradely sacrifice in the face of hopeless odds, of single-handed courage in defiance of every form of evil. I, with an ancestor who, for all his dark faults, had offered his life in his country's supposedly glorious cause.

It was as if those weeks aboard that liner, sharing with Aggie Brown the only form of frank and prolonged intimacy I had known with any woman since my mother, changed me. With hindsight, I see that my almost frenzied pursuit of women up to that time had been an unwitting search for a renewal of my mother's lost love. In Aggie, my senior by a number of years, I sensed I might find it.

My heart thudded, and I was aware of the dryness of my mouth as I went on.

"Aggie, I'm as alone in the world as you are. Why not share?"

She stared at me in silence. I babbled on.

"At the end of this trip, I'll give in my papers and get a practice somewhere on shore. You'd be set up for life, and your little boy would have the father he needs."

"You'd . . . you'd do that for me—for us?" she whispered wonderingly.

"If you'll let me."

"Daft ha'porth." She smiled suddenly, and pulled me down to her.

Some time later we were able to resume the conversation. It was Aggie who returned to it.

"Now, you listen to me. It's nice for us like this, and I don't say it's the only time I like being with you. When we're just strolling about respectable it's nice, too. I'm proud to be seen with you."

"And I with you."

"I reckon any kid could grow up glad to have a dad like you."

"A boy needs a father. Well, then?"

She was shaking her head. "I could keep up a show, for you and for him. But it'd all be pretend, Johnnie. It wouldn't be me. I don't want to spend the rest of me life pretendin' to be what I'm not."

"You wouldn't have to. You'd change. You'd forget what you used to be. I mean—"

"I know what you mean. It's not an insult. Fact is, though, I don't want to change, any more'n I want you to change to help me. I know you, Johnnie Watson, and it's why I wouldn't tell you where you could come looking for me after I left the school. Offering to stand by me! How old were you then—seventeen?"

"That was different. It was when I thought the child might be mine."

"Same thing, though, isn't it? Ready to chuck your life away regardless, just to do the decent thing. No, Johnnie, ta all the same. I wouldn't have it then, and I won't now."

"But the boy. Never mind what you don't want for yourself, and don't want for me. What about him?"

"He'll be all right. The one thing Frank did before we went to India was put down enough money for him to stay at boarding-school. He's paid for till he's sixteen."

"Well, that's a relief, at least. But what about you?"

"I'll find a place. Somewhere just big enough so's he can come on his holidays. Who knows, another feller may take a fancy to me yet."

"*I've* taken a fancy to you."

"What did you say you lot call widow women on the boat—'out of bounds'? That's what I am to you after we go ashore. I mean it."

"But, Aggie—"

"Any more buts, and I won't even have you in me cabin again, let alone in me bunk."

I could tell from the look in her eye that she was determined. And when, next morning, I awoke in my own cabin, to spend as usual my ruminative few minutes staring at the low, panelled ceiling, I felt more unsettled about my future than I had for many a day. More than ten years had passed since Aggie had initiated me into manhood; and when I looked back over them, I was alarmed at how little of importance I could discern, how few significant milestones marked my progress through a trivial wasteland. Her return into my life, however brief that promised to be, seemed to me to symbolise another form of initiation, and I determined that even if she would not let me take full care of her, I should do as much as I could, and should set about amending my own way of life in the process.

It came to our last day of the voyage. After a disappointingly (to me) calm passage through the Bay of Biscay, we were steaming into the English Channel. It was a warm summer's evening, and the moist green smell of England already perfumed the air, bringing sweet refreshment to the returning India hands. A grand farewell banquet and dance took place. I watched with mixed emotions as our lofty Captain, resplendent in his braid, danced with "Lady Greene," drawing admiring looks from all.

Her white neck and shoulders seemed almost luminous above a peacock-blue gown, revelatory of her buxom charm. Her cheeks were pink with energy and health. Her lovely hair shone like polished black steel. I knew that I should be the one privileged to spend the latter part of that night in her arms, as much to her pleasure as to mine; yet a hollow apprehension pervaded me. Like the Cinderella story in reverse, she would all too soon cease to be Lady Greene and turn back into ordinary Aggie Brown. She had made it clear that she would accept no glass slipper from me; but if I could not be her Prince Charming, I was determined at least to watch over her and, by stealth if necessary, give her and her little boy what help I could.

"Well," she said, when we were alone in her cabin at last, "it's bin nice while it lasted, hasn't it?"

"You know I don't want it to end like this," I made my last try.

She put her arms up about my shoulders.

"It's been so perfect, specially coming just as the bottom had seemed to have dropped out of me world. It was a bit of a lark bein' Lady Greene for a time, but I never got so used to it that it'll be hard goin' back to plain Aggie Brown."

"Never 'plain,' Aggie."

She kissed me on the lips.

"You always say the right things to make a girl feel good inside—and, what's best, I know you mean 'em. Cor, somebody's got a good hubby to look forward to. When you reckon you'll start thinkin' of settling?"

"I'd settle the minute this voyage is over if you'd say the word."

I looked for that change in her eyes which I so longed to see, but found not even hesitation in them.

"Don't spoil it, Johnnie. I'm too old for you. Too out of me class. There'd come the day when you'd have to admit it to yourself, and feel you was saddled with me—"

"Never!"

But I think I knew she was right. My father's example alone should have been enough to underline her words. She released me and turned her back for me to begin the familiar yet always delicious task of freeing her from the constriction of gown and stays. It was unthinkable to me that this should be the last time.

"Aggie," I asked over her shoulder, "will you at least let me see you still?"

This time there was a moment's silence before she responded.

"I'd sooner not."

"You can't mean that."

She turned sharply to face me again, the movement causing her released gown to fall about her legs.

"Course I don't *mean* it, but it's what I've got to say. You go on seein' me and you're bound to go on asking me. Either that, or you'll get sick of me, and I don't want that neither. Oh, Johnnie, can't you get it into your loaf that it's best for both of us to stop now?''

"Why? Why? 'Take what you can while you can get it'—our own words. Who knows what's round the corner for either of us? Why throw away happiness?''

"Because, lovey, as you'll find some day like all of us do sooner or later, happiness is like a golden guinea just out of the mint. The more it gets spent, the more the shine goes off it.''

"What are guineas for but spending?''

"Saving. Just one or two. Special ones, to keep and take out and have a look at now and then, bright as the day they was made.''

She stepped abruptly free of the folds about her and placed her hands firmly on her broad hips.

"All right, then. Course you can bloomin' see me when you're passing, so long as you want. But there's to be no more talk of changing your life on my account; and the day it don't suit you to come visitin' me no more, you just stay away and nothin' said, 'cos I'd sooner not know. Out of sight, out of mind—that's got to be the rule for us both. Agreed?''

"With all my heart, Aggie!''

"Then come bloody on! These stays is sawin' me in 'alf.''

I resumed my work with a will, my spirits soaring within me, my body ardent, and my mood for reformation forgotten. And so to bed.

In fact, her circumstances were by no means so bad as I had pictured them. Against the possibility of her not fancying life in India, and taking up his offer to come home, the late baronet had paid for her rooms in Fulham to be kept for her, with her things still in them, under her landlady's care. I could not claim to be a true assessor of the value of jewels, but those few which I had seen her wear on the voyage had looked to me to be worth enough to keep her in relative comfort for some time. All the same, I insisted on taking her straight from the docks to my branch of Cox and Co.'s Bank, at Charing Cross, where I opened an account in the name of Miss Agnes Brown. I had kept my intention from her, and it was not until it had been accomplished that she realised what I had done. By then it was too late; her specimen signature had been secured, and she was too dazed by the august setting and the discreet assistant manager's deferential handling of the transaction to protest.

"I'll never touch a bloody penny!" she raved as the cab bore us Fulham-wards. "Of all the cheek, goin' round opening bank accounts for folks!"

"I don't 'go round' doing it, Aggie. It's a little gesture, that's all."

"Think I was a bloomin' whore, takin' money from blokes!"

I did not answer that directly, merely did my best to explain it as a contingency fund for her to turn to should emergency ever arise.

"Don't worry, my dear, you'll never find a fortune in it to insult your precious pride. There will be little enough paid in; only I couldn't go off for months at a time knowing there was any chance of your getting into difficulties."

"Dunno why you're so concerned about me, I reely don't. Here, this isn't some dodge to get me to wed you, is it?"

"I promise not. You've only to say the word, though, at any time—"

"I wouldn't wed you if you was the last bloke still breathin'. You're too good to deserve a ball and chain."

Her apartment proved to be in a quiet street of modest terraced houses off the King's Road. It was simply furnished and equipped, the most luxurious item being a large bed in the principal of the two bedrooms. She saw me contemplating it.

"I don't bring fellers here, if that's what you're thinking," she told me. "Frank was different, of course, and you can be, so long as you behave yourself."

"What does that mean?"

"No more talk of wanting to get wed. Any of that, and out you go."

"As you say, my lady." I bowed.

"And none of that, neither. I'm Aggie Brown again from now."

"Does your landlady know the story?" I wondered. That wall-eyed old lady had welcomed Aggie home as unconcernedly as though she had been gone for no more than a few hours' shopping, and scarcely glanced at me.

"She won't ask, and I won't tell her. She takes the rent, serves up breakfast, and dotes on little Frank when he's home. That's how it'll stay."

"Speaking of Frank," said I, "I hope you'll give me the pleasure of meeting him."

Aggie shrugged. "Depends if he's home from his school when you happen to come. And no hanky-panky in front of him, remember!" she cautioned with wagging finger.

"Really, Aggie! Where is he at school, by the way? Not Epsom, by any chance?"

"I did think of tryin' to get him in there for the lark of it," she admitted, "only Frank said it would go hard on the poor kid if someone found out his ma had been one of the maids there. He's at a place down in Kent. There's boarding-schools galore there."

"Perhaps we could go down and visit him, now you're back."

"No thanks. Fine thing it'd be for me to turn up with

another bloke to tell him how his pa had snuffed it in India since he last saw him.''

''I see your point. Well, I hope he grows up to be as considerate towards you as his father seems to have been.''

Aggie frowned. ''I keep hoping so. His reports isn't too good. He's sharp enough, they give him that, but he seems a bit of a handful.''

''A handful?''

''Wild, like. Bit of a trouble-maker. Doesn't get on much with the other lads.''

''I'm sure he will if he grows up like his mother.''

''Cheeky s—d! Look, here's a photo of him, took on his last holiday.''

I took the silver frame from her and glanced at the sepia print. I glanced, then stared at the slight, sailor-suited figure posed beside a potted palm against a backdrop of drapes and columns.

I was looking at a double for my brother, Henry.

21

"I had come to an entirely erroneous conclusion."

"Try pulling the other one!" she mocked.

"I tell you, it is!"

"Garn! I knew you when you was a kid, remember? You was a bit older than my Frank is, but I remember well enough what you looked like. He isn't a scrap like you."

"I know he isn't. Nor was Henry—my brother. There's a Spanish strain in our family, the male side. It goes back generations, to the Armada. It misses some and comes out in others."

There was absolutely no mistaking it. The dark eyes, dark hair and brows, the narrow face, and that arrogant high nose added up to a spitting likeness. Aggie looked again at the photograph, which she had seized from my hands when I had exclaimed aloud.

"There ain't one detail alike," she pronounced. "A great bull like you and a weedy little thing like him. Yes, a weed. I don't care if he is me own kid, it's the only name for him. Comes of having a dad as old as his was. Their juices aren't what they used to be."

"Don't be absurd, woman!" I snapped, more impatiently than I should have allowed myself.

"And don't you start 'womaning' me! See what it would have been like getting wed?"

"I'm sorry, Aggie. But you'll be thinking twice about that before long, I promise you. I tell you this is my son."

"Stuff! You're trying to use it to talk me round. I shouldn't have let you come here."

"I'm very glad you did. Great heavens, I might have gone through my whole life never knowing he existed!"

Despite her protesting wriggles, I got my arm round her and drew her down to sit beside me on the bed.

"Aggie, Aggie—my dear, dear Aggie. You and I, that marvellous evening at Cremorne—"

She returned an expletive too coarse to record. Her face was red with angry emotion, and her eyes burned, yet I sensed that tears were not very far behind. It occurred to me that perhaps she had known all along.

"Did you know?" I asked gently.

"There's nothing *to* know. I tell you he's not your kid, and you can stop trying to talk me round that he is."

"The dates fit—your coming when you did to tell me you were in the family way."

"I'd been knocking around with Frank ages before that once with you."

"But he never gave you any children, did he? Come on, Aggie, I do happen to be a doctor."

"It don't prove nothing. There was other chaps, too. Even one night a week adds up to quite a few."

"But you told me it was his—Frank's."

"Wasn't none of your business."

"And you wouldn't let me know where you were going when you left the school."

"You needed to get on with your work. Anyways, Frank

wouldn't have wanted you knocking about after me all the time."

"He didn't object that evening."

"Wasn't none of his business then. It was only after he took me up, put me in this place, that he had a right to say who I could see."

"Aggie, please stop fighting me about this."

"I'm not fighting, just telling you to stop being so bloody silly."

"What's silly about wanting to acknowledge my own child?"

"He *isn't* yours."

"I'm telling you, in all honesty, that he is."

"Because you want to hook me into getting wed to you, and you reckon you've seen the way. Well, it won't wash."

"A boy needs a father. You've admitted he's turning out a bit of a handful already. What's he going to be like in a few more years, with only his mother to bring him up?"

"There never was a feller yet I couldn't handle, and I don't see why he should be different. Besides, when he hears his pa's died, he'll feel he wants to help me."

Not that one, I thought, but did not say it. The resemblance to Henry at the age of ten or eleven would be more than one of features and physique. "Sharp enough . . . wild, like . . . trouble-maker . . . doesn't get on much with the other lads. . . ." Her description of Frank would have fitted Henry exactly.

I said, "I lost my own father, Aggie. I know what it's like for a lad."

She gave me a keen look. I was convinced she was scrutinising my features.

"Bet you didn't give your ma much trouble."

Realising my mistake, I could not pretend that I had. A better inspiration came to me. "Suppose I prove to you he's mine."

That startled her. "You can't—because he isn't."

"I say he is. The only thing in doubt is whether you know it, and are hiding it out of some cock-eyed notion that it's best I shouldn't know."

"I've got nothing to hide. I showed you his photo, didn't I?"

"That's true. So I suppose I must believe you really think I'm wrong."

"Ta very much. Cor, we should have called it quits last night. I knew you'd be trouble for me."

"On the contrary, Aggie, all I want to do is convince you that your Frank is my son—our son. To hear you acknowledge that would give me the happiest moment of my life. I venture to hope it would be the same for you."

She sat silent for some moments, looking at me. I wondered if she were framing some words, and did not interrupt; but all she said at length was, "Well, sorry I can't oblige."

I got to my feet.

"You going?" she asked, rather too hopefully for my liking.

"Yes. And when I come back," said I, lifting her by her hand and compelling her with my arm to stand close so that I looked down into her eyes, "I shall bring with me the proof that even your dear stubbornness will not be able to deny."

"What proof? What can there be?"

"A photograph album. My grandparents will have it with them in Scotland. I'm going to fetch it and show you how my Henry and your—*our* Frank are as alike as peas in a pod. Then, Aggie Brown, you're going to change your tune about a thing or two."

And, before she could speak or move, I had crushed her to me and kissed her lips. Without a word more, I strode from the room and the house, and made my way to King's Cross Station.

As the train bore me northward, I pondered the position. I was convinced that I was right. There was no denying the source of those darkly arrogant features which had stared at me from the photograph. It was a look I had lived with for years, whose supercilious hauteur had made my fists clench a thousand times, and occasionally strike out.

I have chronicled my dislike of my brother. It might be supposed that I could hope to find little to attract me to this copy of him. A more prudent man would no doubt have accepted Aggie's denials thankfully and made himself scarce, rather than pursue a responsibility which I might well live to regret. Whether or not she knew the truth, she had had the sense to separate herself from me, convinced of my determination to stand by her. It had evidently not occurred to her that she was depriving me of a right as well as a responsibility. I had never been aware of any urgent wish to become a father; yet knowing that I was one had set me afire to have it acknowledged.

Mother's photograph album, which my grandparents would certainly have kept, could not fail to settle it. Even Aggie would have to agree on the boys' likeness, and all I then had to do was persuade her that I was not offering marriage as some sort of charitable gesture. As to what our collective future should be, that could be worked out. It seemed prudent to let the lad finish his schooling in familiar surroundings, by which time I should be well established in medical practice and Aggie would be accustomed to being my wife, in a comfortable environment into which he could take his place with ease.

The question of how he was likely to turn out, as inheritor of the Henriques strain, did not daunt me. Knowing what to look out for, I fancied I could counteract it. In a way which I suppose owed something to selfishness, I even welcomed the challenge. I had wanted a purpose in life, and here one was: to extend the study on which I had based my doctoral thesis, by demonstrating that if awareness exists of the origins and nature of inherited characteristics, steps could be taken to anticipate and divert them. The scope of such a science seemed boundless. How many persons possessing undesirable or unfortunate traits might be saved from themselves by case studies and the application of the methods I should postulate? The population of our jails and asylums might be halved in the space of a generation! *Watson on the Identification and Interpretation of Inherited Tendencies, with some Observations on Their Segregation and Diversion:* I could envisage the very lettering on the spine of that epoch-moulding treatise. I saw myself in demand to address the premier medical bodies of Europe, the British Association, the Royal Society; stepping up, gowned and mortar-boarded, to receive parchment scrolls, gold medallions, honorary degrees with accompanying Latin orations; perhaps there would come a baronetcy of my own, a peerage even.

There were a few obstacles, not the least of which would be to achieve acknowledgment of the high-principled purpose of one who, it could not fail to become known, had fathered his own son at the age of fifteen on a school maid and part-time prostitute not a few years his senior. Still, might not even that circumstance be turned to exemplary effect? The mighty Tolstoy's moralising was the more awesome for his having been a rake. I, too, had passed through the fire, in whose searing heat there had been hammered out the weapons with which I was girt for my campaign. . . .

I broke off the composition of speeches of thanks to consider whether, in telling Grandfather my domestic intentions, I should give him all the details. On the whole, I thought I had better not. There would be some pain to him to be told without preparation that he was great-grandfather to a ten-year-old, conceived while I had been still a schoolboy.

"Well, I'm delighted to hear it," was his complacent

response to my bare statement that I proposed quitting the sea forthwith and settling down in general practice. "You've had your share of the roving life. Besides"—he leaned over to tap me on the knee with a long forefinger—"your grandmama and I have our hopes of you in the nursery line before much longer."

"Oh, ah, yes," said I, a trifle startled. "There is that, too."

The ladies were not present. I had thought it best to give him the news first, in the privacy of his sanctum. He cleared his throat and looked at me keenly, and I sensed that he had caught some hint of the guardedness in my reply.

"You, are, er . . . you are not by any chance . . . that is to say, well, coming out with it bluntly, as man to man, not averse to the other, er, sex?"

"By no means, Grandpapa."

He gave a deep sigh of relief.

"That is good to know. Not that there is anything about you which might suggest . . . What I mean to say is that we have wondered, just occasionally, if in choosing the sea, you were, so to speak, running away. You catch my meaning?"

"Absolutely. Nothing like that." I thought it might be carrying reassurance too far to tell him what had been one of my principal motives in going to sea at all.

He gave me a contrivedly roguish smile. "You have, ah, sown the odd wild oat, I imagine?"

"The odd one, yes," was as much as I permitted myself.

"Good, good." He smiled. "So you will not keep us waiting too long, then."

"Oh, no. Not too long."

I received the keen look again. He was quite perceptive, in spite of his indolence.

"Would it be hoping too much to suppose that there might be a particular lady already, John?"

"Well, er—"

"I see." He smiled again. "I shan't press you, then. Your grandmama will be delighted. We have always been so disappointed that your aunts . . . But we won't go into that."

Indeed, the aunts entered at that moment, twittering of tea, and I was spared any further interrogation. I feared some heavy hints on Grandfather's part over the tea-table, but there were none. He must have spoken to Grandmama, though, for she came up to me afterwards to press my hands and look into my eyes and say quietly, "God bless you, John. We are so pleased."

I obtained possession of the photograph album, at the cost of having to spend an entire evening going through it with my aunts and listening to their painfully biting comments on every representation of my poor father. They blamed him for everything, making Henry out to have been some species of corrupted angel. The more I saw of the old pictures of my brother in boyhood, the more my conviction was reinforced that Aggie's boy was my kin.

Anxious though I was to get back to London with my proof, I was expected to linger a full week with what was left of my family. It was odd being in Stranraer again, re-treading the walks which Henry and I had made so familiar, thinking to myself that, if all went well, I should be able to come back again before long, accompanied this time by a living image of him as he had been in those days.

I went out to Black Head, and spent a full hour lost in contemplation of those swirling waters and jagged rocks where our saga had begun. Had I possessed any poetic talents, I might have been moved to come up with something appropriate, but my mind could produce nothing more than "A Black Head and a swirling sea," which sounded faintly familiar and in some way ludicrous.

At length I was able decently to take my leave. There was

no longer any question of my being able to join Grandfather's old practice at Bagshot; in the disappointed aftermath of my preferring to go to sea he had relinquished all interest in it. He offered various other introductions, but I told him that I should prefer to look about and make my own way. It was in my mind that my domestic circumstances were bound to be in some ways delicate, and I wanted to establish myself in a place where my background would be quite unknown and Aggie could "talk posh" from the outset, and her past never be discovered.

Bearing the treasured album, I took an overnight express to London and was there next morning. I had not yet even troubled to find myself any sort of lodging; my possessions remained at the left-luggage department at Charing Cross railway station, where I had deposited them when accompanying Aggie to my bank. Nor did I concern myself with such matters now, but made straight to the little street off the King's Road.

The wall-eyed old lady answered the door. I had put down my overnight valise, retaining the heavy album under my other arm. I raised my hat and gave her a smile designed to unlock those askance features.

"Good morning, Mrs. Capper. Is Miss . . . er . . . Lady . . . er . . . at home?"

I had suddenly realised that Aggie had not told me under what name "Uncle Frank" had installed her there.

"No, she's not," came the uncompromising reply.

"Do you happen to know when she will, er—?"

"She won't."

"Won't?"

"Be back. She's gone."

My mind reeled. "Gone!"

"Never bothered to move back in. After you was here last, she took herself straight off to a hotel and said she'd send for her things. I kep' her rooms for her, as instructed, and another three weeks paid up still to go, but she said she wouldn't be wanting 'em. Gave her the push, did he?"

"Er. . . ?"

"His nibs. Him who paid for her. Her uncle, he called himself, but you can't pull wool over my eyes. Gone off, I expect, and she's had to find somewhere cheaper."

"You don't know where she's gone, then, Mrs. Capper?"

"Not a sniff."

"But—what about her things?"

"Cart came for them, day after she left. Didn't say where they were taking them, and I didn't ask."

"You mean you haven't even a forwarding address?"

"Forwarding address? She never got letters—'cept just one or two from that poor mite of hers."

"Her little boy?"

"Smart little chap, though I can't say I cared for the way he would keep getting at my Tiddles when he came here."

"Your. . . ?"

"Tiddles—cat."

"Ah." An idea intervened to interrupt this unsatisfactory exchange. I opened the album at a marked page and showed it to her.

"You've got his picture, too, have you?" she remarked impassively. She peered closer. "'Henry'? I thought he was called Frank."

"A nickname." Her offhand recognition had given me all the confirmation I wanted. It left my mind far from easy, though.

"She didn't give you any idea at all where she was going?"

"No."

"No message—for me?"

"No."

"If you wanted to find her, where would you begin looking?"

She shrugged. "I don't, so I wouldn't. She was paid up

here and still three weeks to run. Told me to keep the change. Rooms are let already, so why should I grumble? She owes you, that's your lookout.''

''It's not a matter of money. It's more to do with Frank—er, Henry.''

The sideways look was focused on my features. ''Not saying he's yours, are you? Nothing like.''

''It's not that so much, but I must find them. Do you know where he's at school, for instance?''

''Kent.''

''But where in Kent?''

''I dunno. None of my business.''

''You don't remember any markings on any of his letters—anything like that?''

''What you take me for!''

I took up my bag and left. My very soul felt numbed. I walked as in a daze. I had no doubt at all that it was because of me that she had left there: that stubborn, misguided conviction of hers that my life might be blighted through her. Had she recognised the truth about Frank after all? Had she—heady thought—found herself falling in love with me despite herself, and decided that this harsh parting would provide the antidote?

Whatever lay behind it, I knew that looking for her would be a hopeless enterprise. I had not the faintest idea where she might have gone. Beyond the fact that Frank was at a boarding-school in Kent, I had nothing to go upon. Even in those days, the Kent coastal hinterland bristled with boarding-schools, almost all of them privately owned, accommodating anything from a couple of dozen boys to a hundred or two, some registered, many not. It was beyond question for me to essay a search amongst them, looking for a pupil whose name might be Brown or Greene, who did not know me, and with whose life I had no established right to interfere.

One point of contact remained open: the trust fund at Cox & Co.'s Bank. I made my way there at once. To add to my frustration, a supercilious clerk refused me any information about the state of Miss Brown's account. I protested in vain that I myself had been responsible for opening it only a week before, and had effected the standing order which was to provide it with funds. What happened to those monies—whether they were drawn out in full or in part, or left untouched—was none of my concern, once they had been paid over, he lectured me sternly. An appeal to the assistant manager who had so attentively conducted the opening formalities for me proved fruitless. He was coldly aloof, giving me the impression that he suspected some underhand contrivance in the transaction. For two pins, I would have cancelled the arrangement there and then, and transferred the business to some other bank; but then, how could Aggie know where her money lay, should she come to need it? I was certainly not going to go back on my promise.

So I crept away, to stand in the street with teeming, hostile London about me. Never in my life had I felt so lonely and bereft.

The shipping office was not many minutes' walk distant. I had only to go there to be sure of a welcome and the offer of an appointment, perhaps even reinstatement in that which I had recently given up: my familiar cabin, my colleagues and friends, a fresh company of passengers, with perhaps one amongst them, some lady capable of enchanting me out of the dull despair which at present weighed upon me like a suit of chain-mail. But, whoever such a one might be, she would not be Aggie Brown.

22

"I had neither kith nor kin in England."

I did not go to the shipping office. The idea of absenting myself from England just then was unthinkable. Feeling cheated and frustrated, I mooned about London, looking for Aggie.

The shortest odds on my finding her seemed to me to lie in this same district where she had been living. The days of the Cremorne Gardens between it and the river were over by now, but the fact that she had chosen Fulham for her abode suggested that she favoured the area and perhaps had friends in it. Accordingly, I took a modest furnished room off the Fulham Road for my base. I saw little of it. As I had done when searching for Father in Ballarat, I roamed the streets by day and night, endlessly looking, too agitated to sit indoors for fear of missing her.

It was not a comfortable situation. A man cannot expect to perambulate a neighbourhood, however populous and raffish, with no other evident purpose than to peer under bonnets, without inviting hard looks and the interest of officers. There were many more constables about the streets of London in those days, and they were less dependent upon scientific methods of crime detection than upon sharp eyes and keen memories. I was stopped and questioned several times, most of them after dark. I took to carrying my small medical bag with a few items in it as a means of identification. Almost a decade was yet to pass before Jack the Ripper's reign of terror, and that at the further end of London, but I have no doubt that, had my prowling coincided with his, I should certainly have been taken in for investigation, and the fact of my carrying the appropriate instruments would have given me some hard explaining to do.

It seemed prudent, therefore, to keep myself a good deal off the streets, yet still in places where I could maintain my vigil. Aggie had shocked me with her mention of resuming her old part-time trade, using the music-halls as her venue, so I took to visiting them. They were many, and widely scattered about the metropolis, for that was their golden age. I remembered her mentioning Collins's, at Islington, and Gatti's, under the arches off the Strand, but my quest took me to many more: the Canterbury, the Oxford, Weston's, Wilton's, the Pavilion, and others less salubrious where I almost dreaded to find her. She was at none, however, respectable or low.

My researches naturally exposed me to the overtures of the other girls. Somehow, my inclination towards that sort of thing on any casual basis had faded since my reunion with her; nevertheless, I needed to ingratiate myself with them, on the off chance that one of them might help me find her, so the least I could do was treat them to refreshment. I found none who knew her, though, and after two or three weeks of hard searching, with its attendant drinking and constant late nights, I was beginning to feel jaded and hopeless.

Angry, too; for the more I brooded upon the matter, the more I began to feel cheated and betrayed by her. It bore in upon me that she had no right to hide herself and what I was wholly convinced was my son from me in this fashion. Perhaps I had alarmed her by my discovery of the truth about him, and my eagerness to possess them both. Perhaps she believed genuinely that she was acting for my good by keeping me from them, so that I should concentrate on making something more substantial of the life which was still before me. All the same, I came to know that ignoble emotion self-pity as I reviewed the number of times I had been abandoned and betrayed: by my father, for leaving me without taking me into the confidence which he had so readily given to Henry; by my mother, for her infatuation with Beecher, which had wrecked our family unity; by Sarah Bernhardt, for taking me up for her brief plaything, then tossing me aside like any unwanted toy; and now by Aggie, for whom I had felt what I took to be true love.

It was anger which saved me. Anger, and disgust at the maudlin state into which I had let myself drift. I recall distinctly the moment when, slouched on a bar-stool with a glass before me and a wheedling girl's arm drooping about my neck, I became aware of my reflection in the plate mirror in front of me. My top hat was pushed carelessly back on my head; my eyes were half-shut, with dark pouches under them; my cheeks were puffy and unhealthily flushed, my shoulders abjectly hunched. Any latter-day Hogarth catching sight of me would have whipped out his pencil and pad and got himself a splendid study for a nineteenth-century *Rake's Progress*.

Suddenly, in that moment, I knew true anger. It came surging up from that black reservoir which I had always been conscious lay within me, and its bitterness nauseated me. In one movement I shook the girl from me, and with a sweep of my hand dashed the glass and its contents from the bar. Not caring that a hush had fallen on the room, and that all eyes were on me, I stood sharply erect, fished a coin from my waistcoat and tossed it on to the counter, picked up my stick, and strode out.

I marched into Whitehall and down it towards Parliament Square, where another public house occupied a corner site, whose other permanent feature was a group of massively-proportioned men wearing scarlet jackets with glistening buttons and sergeants' chevrons, broad-striped blue trousers, and tilted pillbox hats, and carrying white gloves and slender, silver-mounted canes. There were five of them there as I approached, and they did not lounge against the public-house wall, but stood stiff-backed and barrel-chested as they chatted with a police constable.

All their eyes examined me from head to foot and back as I presented myself before them.

"I wish to join up," said I. "Kindly tell me how to go about it."

The reader will not, I fancy, have formed an impression of me as a type of man given to headstrong whims or dramatic gestures. I am aware that the image I have acquired over many years, particularly in contrast with that of my mercurial friend Sherlock Holmes, is of stolidity and phlegm, which in some accounts has been represented as dullness of both enterprise and wits, an interpretation on which it is not my place to comment. My precipitate decision to throw off feckless habits and join the Army must therefore appear sensational and out of character. In fact, it was not quite so impulsive as it might seem.

I have described how frustration at the loss of Aggie Brown had led to desperation, despair, self-pity, and finally anger; and I believe I have given sufficient account of my inheritance to imply that it was always on the cards that some day I might commit unsocial behaviour and even violence. My ancestor had, after all, been a fighting man, going forth to war as a member of a great and daring enterprise which happened to fail. At least he had answered a man's calling, and to that extent had fulfilled himself. Introspection had convinced me that I had not. I had had my little adventures, and proved myself equal to the hard life of the ordinary seafarer, before qualification as a doctor had presented me with softer options. I had "knocked about," as the saying is, tested my strength and courage and not found them wanting; while that traditional gauge of manliness, a capacity for attracting and dealing satisfactorily with the opposite sex, had not found me a sub-standard specimen.

I had done nothing magnificent, though; nothing heroic, of which the son for whom I was searching would be proud to boast, and would take example from himself. The notion of the great treatise on inherited characteristics had somehow subsided, and anyway it would not have been what could be termed manly work.

Casting about in my mind for some purge for my growing desolation, I had thought of the Army. The brief experience I had had in Poona came back to me, together with the persuasive words of the military doctor who had introduced me to it. True, he had shown me only the pleasures of mess life, and the picture he had painted for me of campaign conditions had been wholly hedonistic. My restless state in London during this unhappy period called out for something more than another escapist experience. That capacity within me for violence demanded an outlet: something through which it might burn itself out, a refiner's fire from which I might emerge cleansed and calmed, and in a mood to settle down to that course through life which was regarded as normal by men with natures less unsatisfied than mine.

Unfortunately, there had been no such opportunity offering. The most ardent warrior cannot go off to war when there is no war being waged, which was the case at this time, and I appeared to have missed that particular boat.

As I have already recounted, the brief war to depose the hostile Amir Shere Ali Khan of Afghanistan, together with his Russian friends, and make his country secure against further Russian incursion, had been going on during my visit to India. It was now over, under a treaty with the new Amir, Yakub Khan, and our forces were firmly established in control of the Khyber Pass and other strategically vital territory. This was all very fine for those gentlemen who, having enjoyed their taste of action, could now content themselves smoking their pipes at sunrise on mountainsides until some Afghan tribe or other should offer a little violent sport, but it was not what I was seeking. So, having mulled over the idea of joining the Army as a means of assuaging my restlessness, I had rejected it.

Suddenly, however, things had changed. On the morning of the day in which my outburst in the taproom occurred I had opened my newspaper to read that Afghanistan was aflame once more. On September 3, the Kabul mob and mutinous Afghan soldiers had massacred the British Resident, Major Cavagnari, and all of his European staff and escort. Without doubt, it heralded the resumption of war; and in that instant of unwelcome recognition of my present self in the bar-room mirror I perceived that my tide was at the flood.

I stood before the recruiting sergeants' appraising stares, with the policeman looking on more mildly.

"Fair specimin," remarked one of them in an Irish accent.

"Nae bad," answered the one with the tartan decoration to his cap.

"Hoccupation?" demanded the biggest of them.

I had already resolved not to reveal that I was a doctor. It was well known in my profession that the Army was always short of medical men, not least because they tended to be poorly paid. This was not my own objection, which was that as a surgeon behind the lines I should have no chance of the kind of active service which I needed like an antidote to my ills. I did not even particularly aspire to be an officer. I merely wished to be taken far away and sent out to fight somebody whom I did not know and therefore need not trouble my conscience about.

"Bit of this and that, you know," I answered, roughening my accent a shade and essaying a friendly wink.

"Ah, shure," responded the Irishman.

"Och, aye," confirmed the Scot.

"How long?" asked the Englishman, a Grenadier Guardsman who seemed to be the group's president.

"How long what?"

"D'ye want to serve? Twelve year? Twenty-one?"

"Oh, no!" said I, aghast. "The duration of the war, perhaps?"

This seemed to be quite the funniest thing any of them had ever heard, to judge from the immoderate way they laughed. They almost reeled about, forgetting their dignified bearing.

"Oh, come on in for twenty-one, do," said one of the others who had not yet spoken, affecting an effeminate tone.

"'Duration of the war.' Will yez listen to him?"

"Oughter try the Marines."

"Or the Band of Hope."

"I am not jesting," I told them furiously. "There is a war again in Afghanistan; British subjects have been massacred. I have a right to offer my services to my country without being mocked."

That stopped their mirth. Their spokesman leaned towards me menacingly.

"Listen, sonny, fighting wars is sojers' work—real sojers, not any Tom or Dick what fancies a bit of a lark. Do the likes of you good to get taken in for twenty-one, and I wish I'd the sergeanting of you."

"Aye," agreed his Scottish confrère. "Tak' the shillin', or clear off."

They closed around me, chests protruding.

"Just a minute, just a minute," interrupted a lighter voice. It was the police constable. He wanted nothing in comparison of stature against the sergeants, and his uniform, though drabber, was as imposing in its way. Besides, he was ruler of the street, and they deferred to him.

"What's your game?" he demanded of me.

"My game?"

"You told me you were a doctor last week."

There was no answer I could make. I had not recognised him, but his trained eyes had remembered me.

"What's in that bag?"

I had overlooked the medical bag in my hand. I opened it and displayed the contents.

"That's yours?"

I sighed and admitted my identity. The soldiers were quiet with genuine curiosity as I went on to tell the policeman my circumstances.

"You should of said," said the Grenadier Guards sergeant. "You being a doctor, you'll get in for as long or short as it suits you, won't he, Mick?"

"Aw, shure," the Irish Guardsman confirmed. "Come and go as they chuse, not like sojers at all."

"But you don't understand," I persisted, "I want to get into some action."

"Och, ye'll be in action a'right if them Pathans get near ye," said the Scots Guard. "Them kind don't ask if ye're a damn' doctor before they'll stick a spear in ye."

"You really think I'd stand a chance?" I addressed their president.

"Look at it this way, mate, it's the only chance you'll get, 'less you sign on proper. Then it might be five year before they send ye abroad. Put yourself forward as a doctor, and they'll give ye a fancy uniform and ship ye straight out."

"In that case," said I, brightening, "I reiterate my question—where do I go to enlist? But perhaps you gentlemen would care to give me the information indoors, over a glass?"

"Shan't say no to that, will we, sarn'ts?" beamed the Grenadier, and got a unanimous vote.

"Bloody soldiers gets it all," grumbled the policeman, and tramped off on his lonely, temperate beat.

My elation was destined to be short-lived. When I presented myself that afternoon at the office to which they had directed me, I was received with interest and courtesy, and granted an immediate interview with a distinguished-looking old gentleman in a frock-coat, and a uniformed officer, whom I recognised as having been a senior Bart's man in my early days who had shown me a small kindness or two. They assured me that there was no question but that my offer of my services would be accepted, then proceeded to dash my hopes by explaining that I should have to undergo a four-month course in military medicine at the Army Medical School.

"But the war could be finished in that time," I protested.

"There will always be war, on and off, out there," replied the older gentleman. "Russia has her eye constantly on India, and possession of Afghanistan remains her first ambition. These tribal wars are more than local uprisings. They are backed as part of a greater plan."

"You can't expect just to sail out there and put up a shingle saying you're an army doctor and all patients welcome," said my Bart's friend, laughing.

"You must realise, doctor," his colleague went on, "that battle wounds are far different from anything you have been taught to deal with in the normal run of the profession, not to mention certain diseases and hygiene problems prevailing in the East. Your impatience to serve does you credit, but I am afraid you must first go through the course."

I hesitated. The whole purpose of my taking this step seemed to be negated by the prospect of yet another dreary period of study, with my problems unresolved and my need for violent occupation unfulfilled. They saw my uncertainty.

"You come at an excellent time, for both yourself and the Service," said the older interviewer. "There are only two courses a year at the school, and the first begins next month. You can hope to be through with the least possible delay, and possibly on board the first of next season's troopers, say in March."

"Are there still vacancies?" I asked.

The younger man laughed again. "And to spare. The course takes forty-five, and we haven't two-thirds of that number, even though we ran no courses at all last year, when things were quiet. You understand, Watson, that the pay's far from great; but you get a commission, with all its privileges and plenty of fun."

"I do not think the doctor's motive in coming here is to seek fun," his senior rebuked him mildly.

"He knows what I mean. Anyway, you won't find Netley a drudge. Quite a Rugger man, aren't you? Plenty of chance to let your steam off there."

"Not to mention," persisted the graver one, "an excellent opportunity to extend your medical experience at the country's expense. You'll be under such distinguished men as Longmore, for surgery, and Campbell Maclean, medicine."

"The New Forest in autumn. Perfect time of year. You won't notice the weeks pass."

"Very well," said I. "If you will take me, I will come in."

We rose to our feet and they shook my hand. So it was that I embarked upon another phase of my life which the fatalist in me tells me was preordained to present itself precisely how and when it had.

23

"What was I, an army surgeon . . . ?"

The Royal Victoria Military Hospital at Netley, in Hampshire, occupied the most impressive building I had seen in my life, in terms of sheer size. Its frontage extended for more than a quarter of a mile, and the great premises served as a grim memorial to the huge numbers of casualties suffered in the Crimean War, or rather to that relatively fortunate minority of them who survived to reach these modern premises, built especially to receive them. I could not help feeling that the sentiment inscribed on the picturesque abbey ruin nearby—"Approach with reverence, for there are those within whose dwelling place is Heaven"—might have been equally suited to the principal military hospital of the Crimean period.

Thanks to the lessons learned through their suffering, military medicine had progressed in great bounds in the forty years preceding my time there, and I found everything brisk and efficient. In personal comfort it was wholly satisfactory: we were not yet officers, but were treated as such, with comfortable quarters and messing, soldier servants, and plenty of time for leisure. There was indeed a thriving Rugby team, and with the season having recently begun when I arrived, I was able to get some games. The somewhat erratic nature of my life since my Blackheath days had slowed me a good deal, and I had put on weight, but I began to feel fitter than I had for many a day, and more purposeful in general, and thought that my destiny's arrangements for me could have turned out far less agreeably.

As my friendly interviewer had predicted, the New Forest was in its autumnal glory. I made many excursions across Southampton Water to explore its deep glades, arched with every hue of copper and gold. I roamed the shingle at Southsea and explored bustling Portsmouth, going also to stare at the birthplace of the great Charles Dickens in that town; and I traced the progress from Beaulieu Abbey to Netley of that thirteenth-century White Company of monks seeking a place to found a new community.

Even my studies seemed more to the point than in the past. There was something eminently useful about learning to extract a bullet or shell splinter, or treat an infected spear wound, which had been lacking from my earlier tuition. I think, at bottom, I had always felt that any profession in which my easy-going grandfather could enjoy prosperity by doing almost nothing at all ought not to be considered wholly sincere, whereas tending a fallen soldier under fire must represent about the most unequivocal service that could be imagined.

My course at Netley represented a period of renewal of my health and self-respect, lifting my spirits considerably. I got on well with my colleagues and took to the army ways as easily as I had to life at sea. There was much discussion amongst us as to our future, should the fighting end decisively. I found myself leaning towards a desire to make the Service my career, come what might. Our semi-enclosed world of tradition, custom, active occupation, and easy camaraderie, not wholly isolated from the greater world, yet separated from it by barriers which none but the invited might pass, had begun to seem an ideal state. It offered me security and membership of a uniquely privileged society; yet it remained open to me to make such forays into other spheres as I might wish, comfortable in the knowledge that a line of retreat lay open and the citadel would be always there to welcome me into its sanctuary.

In course of time I might marry (my colonel's beautiful daughter, perhaps) and found a Service dynasty, retiring at length with an honour or two, to act the role of benevolent patriarch while filling my days with my London clubs, croquet, rod and line, and the penning of memoirs: the writing inclination, which had lain mild hold upon me in boyhood, still made itself felt from time to time, though I had lived too restlessly ever to face up to its disciplinary requirements.

As to Aggie, I had almost ceased to think of her. She preferred to live without me, and to go her own way; so be it. The urgency to be brought together with my son had dwindled, too. We should be strangers, and if his nature was as like Henry's as his appearance, I doubted that we should find much in common. My conscience was not over-active upon the subject. Men had had mistresses and begotten children by them since the world began, without plaguing their minds unduly. I gave instructions to the Paymaster-General's office that my pay and allowances should go to Cox's Bank, Charing Cross, where the order in Aggie's favour stood. The least I could do was to continue that; but, all things considered, it was also the most.

I qualified at Netley at the beginning of March, 1880. We clustered about the notice-board, eager to learn our postings. Not all of us hoped to go abroad; many of our number looked for home service. It was to my infinite relief, though, that I read of my attachment to the Fifth Regiment of Foot, the Royal Northumberland Fusiliers, for I knew that they had long been stationed in India. Sure enough, I was summoned by the Adjutant that same day and ordered to prepare myself to sail from Portsmouth in the trooper *Euphrates* on the sixteenth of the month.

"Short notice, old boy, but you have kept on about wanting to get out there. Doesn't give you much time for embarkation leave."

"That doesn't trouble me. I have no close family."

"Hm. Well, just nice time to get yourself kitted out, then. Actually, there's a ship sailing a week today, the *Jumna,* but I understand the officers' accommodation has been pretty well all allocated. No point in sacrificing comfort for the sake of a few days."

"No, indeed. The sixteenth will suit me admirably."

So, on the morning tide of March 16th, I sailed from Portsmouth, conscious that in doing so I was travelling in the footsteps, so to speak, of Nelson. As I watched the ramparts recede, and the cries of the large crowd grew faint, the wish in my heart was not for "Glory or Westminster Abbey," but that I might do my duty well and have an interesting time in the process. I little foresaw how interesting it would prove.

I disembarked at Bombay on April 12th and went at once to the Army Medical Department, where, I had been instructed, arrangements would be in hand for me to join my regiment.

After an almost farcical hour of being shuttled between one official and another, none of whom had any papers relating to me and who all seemed to disbelieve that I even existed, I at last found one who seemed interested enough to try to solve my problem. The upshot was that I was sent back to the very first of them, bearing a memorandum which made his pale cheeks flush angrily. He was gaunt and light-haired, and looked as though he had never been near the tropics.

"How the devil was I to know who the devil you are?" he demanded accusingly.

"I gave you my name and appointment," said I mildly.

"*Assistant* Surgeon," he retorted sarcastically. "No such rank. It was abolished years ago."

"I'm afraid I didn't know. What should I be, then?"

"*Acting* Surgeon. Those damned Whitehall-wallahs!"

"Does it make any difference to me?"

"Quite a bit. Acting rank means . . . acting—temporary, that is—though, strictly speaking, *Temporary* stands for something else."

"I don't see how I can be a temporary surgeon. Either I'm one, or I'm not."

"Yes, yes. It's a technicality, that's all." He enumerated on his fingers, "Acting, Temporary, Substantive. Once you're Substantive, they can't take you down a peg."

"What's in a name?" said I lightly. "I don't suppose any wounded man is going to draw the distinction."

He gave me a withering look. "You'll be lucky to see a wounded man. The Sixty-sixth have had exactly one casualty in several years."

"The Sixty-sixth? Surely that isn't my regiment, the Northumberlands."

He smote his papers. "That's just it, too. You're not *for* the Northumberlands. You've been mis-posted. Damn' headquarter-wallahs!"

Resenting being treated as some officially non-existent interloper, who had appeared with the sole purpose of disrupting his leisured routine, I snapped back, "I have it in black and white on my Movement Order: 'You will proceed to India on attachment to the Northumberland Fusiliers.' The paper is in my kit, if you wish to see it."

"I dare say, I dare say. Only some damn' headquarter-wallah boxed it up again. The Northumberlands are fully up to strength with doctors—always have been. You're wanted for the Sixty-sixth."

"Who are they?"

"The Berkshires. Damn' fine body of men."

"I hope you're not about to tell me they're on garrison duty back in England—Reading, or somewhere?"

"Wouldn't have put anything like that past those Whitehall-wallahs. No, they're up on the Frontier."

"Then that's all right. They are in the Khyber Pass?"

"Not exactly."

He proceeded to give me a curt summary of the Afghanistan situation. There were two British-Indian forces up amongst the passes, deep in the enemy's country: a northern one under Sir Sam Browne, V.C.,* with Sir Frederick Roberts† in command in the field, and a southern one under Sir Donald Stewart. The former was based at Peshawar, with responsibility for the Khyber Pass and Kabul; the latter had recently moved up to Quetta, to operate in the southerly passes to Kandahar. The Northumberland Fusiliers were part of the northern command; the Berkshires, of the southern.

"And I suppose you will tell me that all the action is in the north," I said.

He gave me a pale smile at last. "Can't wait, can you? Give me a headquarters desk any day, but it takes all sorts. In fact, you're wrong. It's been pretty hot work in the north until recently, which is why they've had to take troops from the south to go there as reinforcements. The current betting is that this new Amir chap, Ayub Khan, who thinks he ought to be top dog on their side, won't be able to resist proving it by taking his chance against Kandahar, now that its garrison is depleted."

"Then the sooner I can get there, the better," I declared.

He laughed out loud. "Leave tomorrow, if you wish. Mere fifteen hundred or so miles. Shouldn't take you more than a month to six weeks."

*The inventor of the shoulder-belt which bears his name.

†Later Field-Marshal Earl Roberts of Kandahar, Pretoria, and Waterford ("Bobs").

I suspected him of ribbing me, but he was not quite the ribbing type. In the event, his estimate was only a week out, each way.

Fully anticipating the thrust by the Amir Ayub against Kandahar, the high command were despatching troops and supplies to that region with all haste. A steamer was leaving Bombay next day for Karachi, on the first and least uncomfortable leg of that long trek, and I found myself aboard her in the company of many other officers who had come out with me in the *Euphrates*.

Several days at sea were followed by several more in a slow, suffocating railway train as far as the railhead at Sibi. Deprived of the sea breeze, we suffered intensely from the heat, and as one of only three medical officers on the train I was kept constantly busy. It had no corridors, of course, and whenever it stopped, which was often, I was anxiously summoned to yet another foetid compartment where some man had succumbed to the heat or to the onset of that stomachic distress which the very air of India seemed to have brought on wholesale. Scheduled halts were made at certain stations, where the locomotive took on water and coal or was exchanged altogether; and at these the men detrained as one and lay on the platforms like corpses in rows, while opportunist native boys and girls moved amongst them with containers of water and fruit. Before commencing the journey, the O.C. Train had given strict orders that such offerings were not to be purchased or consumed, but the craving for moisture of any kind over-rode these, resulting in further waves of digestive disorder as we progressed. I was almost too busy to think of my own discomfort, which, I supppose, was very much to the point of my having come out to this place at all.

From Sibi we marched and rode, according to rank or duty, in a long convoy of stumbling, red-coated men, mules, bullocks, and carts both military and civilian. Our dusty, stony track began to ascend, as the awesome mountains reared before us. Now, although it continued hot by day, it became almost freezing cold at night, presenting new demands on our limited resources. We had not enough tents to go round, even though we had lost scores of men on the way, so that many poor devils were forced to get what rest they could in the open air. We marched from daybreak to long after nightfall, day in, day out. It was at the end of May, five weeks to the day from leaving Bombay, that we arrived at the ancient, much-fought-over city of Kandahar.

The army was quartered in a tented cantonment a short distance from the mud-built, square-proportioned city which rose from fertile surroundings more than three thousand feet above sea level. I was cordially welcomed by the Adjutant, and after the usual period of watchfulness and veiled hostility to which proud regiments were wont to subject newcomers to their midst, I found Colonel Galbraith and other officers friendly enough company. Although they had themselves only arrived there a short time before me, they had reinstituted all their mess procedures, with the silver, fine wines, and other paraphernalia giving the impression of long occupancy. I remarked as much to my genial chief, Surgeon-Major A. F. Preston, my senior by quite some years and a patient instructor to me in their rituals.

"Wherever a regiment goes, it carries its tradition with it, like a snail its shell," he said. "On the march, even if the table has to be of ammunition cases, you'll find the silver brought out at dinner-time and the old toasts proposed. It is such blind acceptances that enable one to face up to all eventualities, and permeate down throughout the ranks."

"They seem a good set of men."

"First-class. There has been nothing much to do so far, but when the time comes they will not be found wanting."

Amongst my fellow officers was a quiet-spoken, withdrawn young lieutenant, who was introduced to me as Will Gale. He carried one arm in a sling. The regiment not having been in action, I assumed him to have been the victim of some sporting accident. He visited our dispensary not long after my arrival to have his dressing changed. My chief attended to it personally, and I was struck by the odd deference which he showed towards his young patient.

"Nicely on the mend, but still some way to go," he pronounced, after the subaltern had submitted to the usual tests. "The muscle needs to strengthen more before I can let you throw away that sling."

The young man thanked him shyly, addressing him as "sir," instead of the more familiar "Doctor," clicked his heels to attention, and marched smartly out.

"You know who that is, of course," remarked Preston to me.

"Will Gale? I tried to chat with him in mess, but he's hard to draw."

"The best of them are. He's up for the V.C., you know."

"The Victoria Cross! But I thought there had been no action."

"He didn't win it with us. Not been with the Sixty-sixth much longer than you. Posted from the Norfolks."

"Posted away from his own regiment?"

"He was a sergeant there. Couldn't stay on with a commission."

"But he looks scarcely old enough to have been a lance-corporal, let alone a sergeant."

"Ah, but his has been no ordinary career. The only survivor of the Kabul massacre, I think. Before that he'd been in a half-dozen scrapes, wounded several times. Roberts commissioned him in the field, and, d'you know, it was only a year to the day since he'd first enlisted."

"Extraordinary!"

"You'll see something equally extraordinary in mess this evening. Colonel Ripon is coming in to dine. He's political and military adviser to Wali Shere Ali, the Governor of Kandahar.''

''What am I to expect?''

''Wait and see, and tell me what you think over a pipe afterwards. Let's see what you deduce.''

My appetite thus whetted, I could scarcely wait; and when the time came for us to assemble, and I was taken up by the Adjutant to be introduced to our distinguished-looking visitor, I could have fallen back with astonishment. Save for the difference in age, and other slight discrepancies, Colonel Ripon and Lieutenant Gale might have been doubles.

Each was about six feet in height, broad-shouldered and muscular in build. The configuration of their noses and brows was identical, and save for the effect of difference created by the Colonel's moustache being grizzled, their mouths were also alike. But it was in their eyes that there was the greatest similarity: the eyes of both were grey and of nearly the same striking shade, simple, straightforward, and kindly, topped by straight and rather heavy eyebrows. Even their voices were not unalike, though the Colonel's was clipped and militarily precise, while I had noticed that Will Gale's held a less-cultivated tone, as might have been expected from one who had come up from the ranks.

''Well?'' asked Preston with amused-sounding interest after we had retired to our shared quarters much later that evening, and were sitting side-by-side in our canvas folding chairs, with our pipes and whisky-sodas, beneath the diamond-like stars.

''I never saw such similarity in my life,'' said I, although my thoughts that evening had travelled to the photograph album left behind in the box in my bank vault.

''Would you say the boy's his bull-pup?'' my chief enquired.

''His what?''

He laughed. "I'm sorry. His son. It's an old family expression of ours,"

I forebore to ask him how they termed their daughters.

"They seem very close, certainly."

"Ah, well, the Colonel owes Gale quite a debt of gratitude. The boy saved him when he was set on by some Afghan thugs in the city. The old man would have been cut down but for Gale, who happened to be near. He put a revolver bullet through one's head and the rest were dealt with by some soldiers; but Gale caught a nasty *tulwar* slash, hence his bound-up arm."

"A man of action, indeed," I said. "But there is no known connection between him and Colonel Ripon?"

"I doubt it. The old man seems a pillar of rectitude in all things. Sheer coincidence of physical types from differing backgrounds and circumstances. If you ever do pursue that theory of yours, you'd better make provision for coincidence. With the millions of folk on this earth, there are bound to be a few *Doppelgängers.*"

It was not until a good many years later that I learnt that Colonel Ripon and Will Gale, V.C., were in fact father and son, separated in the boy's infancy, a fact not known to either. The full particulars were recounted by the writer and traveller G. A. Henty in his book *For Name and Fame: or, Through Afghan Passes.*

A further passage in that same narrative, although it does not single me out for mention, was to recall to me, upon first reading it, the searing experience through which I was about to go, and which would leave its marks upon me in more senses than one, serving as that refiner's fire whose clarifying flames I had been awaiting.

24

"I served at the fatal battle of Maiwand."

My fear that I should reach my regiment to find that there was neither action nor immediate prospect of it had been realised, but those weeks at Kandahar were too occupied with settling myself into its many routines for time to hang heavily. Although the climate of our elevated station was temperate after the searing heat through which I had travelled to get there, there were the usual hygienic precautions to be enforced, and daily sick parades held to deal with that strange variety of ills which the British soldier seems to carry with him to any part of the world to which he finds himself posted. I was kept fully employed, yet found time for agreeable leisure, taking part in a number of games of cricket on the dusty *maidan,* the necessary equipment having been amongst the earliest items of supply to have come up.

The 66th were the only British regiment at Kandahar at the time. Brigaded with us were units of Indian cavalry, infantry, and artillery, among them the 3rd Scinde Horse and 3rd Bombay Light Cavalry, the Bombay Grenadiers, and Jacob's Rifles, each with its mixture of British and Indian officers. We also had the support of Afghan soldiers of our presumed ally Wali Shere Ali, whose army was supposed to assume control of Kandahar when the time came for the British-Indian force to move on. Talk in the mess, however, gave little credit to this indigenous army.

"They'll cut and run at the first shot," I was assured. "That is, assuming they ain't crept off and left us in the lurch before even a shot's fired."

The latter was, in fact, what occurred. Word having reached us late in June that the massed forces of Ayub Khan were marching on Kandahar, intent on ridding Afghanistan of all British influence, our modest force struck camp and marched out to meet them. There were those in our mess who fervently advocated making our native army march without its weapons in case it should be tempted to defect to Ayub; but our commander, Brigadier-General Burrows, who struck me as an officer of no great resolution, replied that such a course would be an insult to Wali's men. So we marched out towards the Helmand River, intending to intercept Ayub on his way to Kandahar; and before we had been gone several days, we had lost the whole of Wali's force. Taking their arms and supplies with them, they had streamed off to throw in their lot with the advancing enemy.

Our regimental officers were incensed at this treachery, and were all for sending the cavalry after them, if necessary to cut them to pieces. General Burrows was reluctant to order anything so offensive, but at length consented. By then it was too late to catch up with the entire force, but at least our cavalry managed to retrieve six artillery pieces which the defectors had taken with them. Since we had only six guns of our own, this was reasonably gratifying. Even so, our entire remaining force was only 500 cavalry and 1,500 infantry, and every rumour had it that Ayub's army was at least 30,000 strong, many of them fanatical Ghazis, whose known thirst for infidel blood was fearsome even to our British lads.

"When it does come to a scrap, whatever you do, don't get captured," Surgeon-Major Preston counselled me gravely. "Those Ghazis are amateur anatomists to a man, and they prefer their subjects alive."

"Ugh! I had heard some things."

"I'm perfectly serious. Keep the last round in your revolver for yourself."

"What about the wounded?"

"We do our best by them until we can do no more. After that—well, I think it comes down to one's own conscience."

Nothing I had heard in my life had so chilled me as that.

No exact information about Ayub's movements, or the strength of his army, could be got. All that we did hear was that the officer commanding in Kandahar, General Primrose, flatly refused to send out any more troops to reinforce us. So it was that, when we came at last into contact with our enemy near the village of Maiwand, in the valley of that name, he outnumbered us ten to one.

He came upon us in the valley, with ravines running along both of our flanks, and ranges of hills beyond, so that he could command us with artillery from the heights and send his foot warriors sneaking up the ravines almost into our midst. Add to this that his fighters were fanatically indifferent to losses, and it was soon evident that we stood little chance.

We continued our advance, however, in the early hours of July 27th, presumably on the assumption that a bold display would dishearten our opponents. The 66th were on the right of the line, with Jacob's Rifles on the left and the Bombay Grenadiers in the centre. The cavalry waited in the rear.

Throughout the morning the battle was largely an artillery duel, with the enemy able to fire on us from several angles, with more guns and clearly more plentiful ammunition than we possessed. Nearing midday, we saw the approaching horde of men on horseback and foot, and a fearsome sight they were. However, our Martinis spoke volley after volley, causing the advance to falter within half a mile of our position.

Our casualties had been steadily mounting throughout the day. Preston and I slaved in the heat, with gore to our elbows, needing orderlies to whisk continually at the swarms of flies which sought a bloody feast at our makeshift operating-tables. All the time, there was the forlorn realisation that, unless something little short of a miracle should happen, the poor devils we were tending were merely being saved for an even more painful and terrifying fate. Still, while hope remained, it behoved us to do our best for them.

Scenting his ascendancy, the enemy crept closer, beginning to fall upon our men in swift dashes from the cover of the ravines. It was the Indian units which bore the brunt of these raids, the sepoys being hacked to pieces by the long, curved *tulwars*. The reports gasped out to us by our own wounded, most of whom were suffering from gunshot, were that Jacob's Rifles had crumbled and fled in amongst the Bombay Grenadiers (who until then had been holding firm), reducing them to similar confusion.

"Where the devil are the damned cavalry?" groaned an officer whose left arm had all but been taken off by a shell splinter. "Why don't they attack, *attack?*"

"Burrows is holding them off," said another, awaiting his turn for my attention. "Keeping them as a last reserve."

"Last reserve, after the rest of us are done for! He's mad. A British charge against a native army never failed to turn the trick in all history. *Attack!*"

They were the last words the poor young patriot ever spoke. The orderlies removed him from the table with little ceremony, for his colleague to take his place.

It was becoming apparent, from the steady stream of casualties, that the 66th's losses were going to prove terrible, whatever the outcome of the day. Late in the afternoon there occurred a loss which we could least afford: Surgeon-Major

Preston himself, bending over a soldier whose wound he was probing as calmly as if he had been in a hospital operating-theatre, gave a sudden sharp cry and crumpled to the dusty ground. I interrupted my own work and rushed to examine him.

"The back!" he gasped. "Thank God, not the spine, I fancy."

A swift examination proved him right. The stray bullet had missed his backbone and passed only through flesh and muscle; but he was clearly finished so far as further work was concerned.

"Never mind me," he murmured through his pain, as he heard me instructing my own orderly, Murray, to clean the wound for dressing. "The poor devils only have you now, Watson."

"Nevertheless," said I, "I propose to patch you up and pack you off to the rear at once. You will live to treat many more yet, and it is my duty to ensure that you do."

Against further protests from him, I got him into fit shape to be borne away on a curtained stretcher, and told off two of the native bearers to make all haste with him. I learned much later that after carrying him a short way they set down the *dhoolie* and fled, relieved for their own skins' sake to have been ordered to the rear and anxious to make their escape unencumbered. A passing horse-artillery wagon fortunately took him up and on to the safety of Kandahar.

He was one of the luckier ones on that tragic day. It was late afternoon when he received his wound, and the Battle of Maiwand was all but over. Our Indian formations had fled in rout; the cavalry, to its eternal disgrace, had ridden away without so much as drawing a sabre in anger*; and what re-

*The cavalry concerned have always insisted that they received no orders to enter the fray; presumably none of their own officers felt able to take the initiative.

mained of the 66th, with some remnants of the Bombay Grenadiers, had fallen back into the village to make that last stand which has passed into history as one of the epics of British arms. Exhausted, parched, and deafened by the non-stop firing, those Berkshire men fought the shrieking horde for every foot of open ground, every house and hut, every inch of cover. They stood erect, man by man, firing and bayoneting until the dead and dying were piled around them; but inevitably, one by one, they were overwhelmed and triumphantly butchered. No honourable recognition of bravery was shown by that enemy.

The 66th's heroic stand made possible the escape from certain slaughter of several hundred men. General Burrows had given the order, long overdue, to retire, though by now "retirement" meant retreat and every man for himself. Will Gale came rushing to me. His face and uniform were cordite-blackened and blood-streaked, but he seemed to be unwounded: luckily for him, he had been allowed to discard the sling from his arm only a few days before the action.

"You've got to get out, sir," he panted. "I'm having three carts brought up now to take as many as we can get into them."

Following my wounded superior's example, I continued to concentrate on the wound I was just then seeking to contain.

"Is this Colonel Galbraith's order?" I asked, using my teeth to sever a length of surgical thread.

"The Colonel is dead, sir. Captain Fletcher's in command of the rearguard, and I'm staying with him. His compliments, sir, but you can be of more use on the line of retreat than lingering here."

"For God's sake, Gale," I expostulated, gesturing towards the mass of groaning figures all around me, "there are far more than any three cartloads here, even piled on top of one another."

"It's all there are available, I'm afraid. There's general panic among what are left of the native troops, and they'll seize the carts for themselves if we delay."

"Gale, I can't leave any of these men."

"There is nothing you can do for those who cannot travel. As to the rest, they will have a chance if you will go with them, sir." He bit his lip and added, "So, sir, will you."

The bearers rushed in at that moment, urging in their rapid, high-pitched voices that the carts were outside and would not wait. I indicated those men who were the least severely wounded, and would have some chance of recovery if we could get them to safety.

Through all my days, I have remembered the eyes of those whom my choice passed by, and who were still capable of understanding what was happening. I saw not reproach, but a realisation which was terrible to recognise. By passing them over, I had as good as affirmed that their state was hopeless. It was probably no more than they already knew: what struck horror into me, though, was that they knew the fate far worse than death which awaited them should the enemy find them still alive.

Young Gale hissed into my ear, "Isn't there something you can give them, sir? Something quick?"

There was nothing. Our little stock of opiates had long since been exhausted. There was an alternative, though. I ran to where Preston's and my own revolvers lay on a chair, with their ammunition belts. I unbuttoned the holsters, noting with acute pain the widening of one man's eyes as he saw the action. I gently shook my head and laid both weapons on the ground amongst the wounded men.

"I'm sorry, lads," said I. "It's all I can do. There—there will be nothing to be ashamed of in your Maker's sight."

I heard the sob in Gale's throat as he seized me by the arm, propelling me away, shouting to Murray and the other orderly to follow. Pausing only to drag on my tunic, my eyes so blinded with tears that I could no longer make out my surroundings, I stumbled from the entrance of our rude shelter.

The noise was terrific: the rattle of musketry, the banshee shrieking of the attacking tribesmen, the cries of the wounded. I tottered forward. Gale—I took it to be—clapped a hand on my shoulder. . . .

That I survived the massacre at Maiwand is self-evident, in that I am here, so many years later, to describe it. The reader of my narrative entitled *A Study in Scarlet* is already acquainted with the brief, if not wholly accurate, particulars of how I reached safety, thanks to the quick thinking of Murray, who, when I fell unconscious from that bullet in my shoulder, which I had thought to be no more than an encouraging clap from Will Gale's hand, had the presence of mind to throw me across a pack-horse and lead me, unconscious, away from that dreadful place.

Ten officers and 275 men of the 66th had perished there. I have stood, in humility, gazing up at the remarkable memorial to them and to other men of the Berkshires who fell in the Afghan campaign: a gigantic statue of a roaring lion, in Forbury Park, at Reading, the county town. But for the grace of God, I could well have been one of those commemorated by it. I have no doubt at all that, but for incredibly determined resistance kept up by our rearguard, under Captain Fletcher and Lieutenant Gale, we should have perished to the last man. Though they were shattered and worn out from a whole day's fighting, they kept to their task, and it was the enemy who faltered and gave, no longer having the heart to pursue us and doubtless expecting that we had reinforcements on the way. Their losses had been five times ours, and sheer lust for blood was not incentive enough to urge them on still further as night fell.

I recall very little of that night and the following day. Consciousness ebbed and flowed, with dream-like interludes of shouting, firing, and agitated movement all around. Most of my waking time was a dull awareness of pain in my left shoulder and arm, the jolting motion of the animal carrying me, and a raging, feverish thirst.

It appears that our pathetic column of survivors, gallantly protected by the rearguard of Berkshires and Bombay Grenadiers, somehow covered no less than sixty miles in some thirty hours, to reach the safety of Kandahar. I have often counted myself one of the luckiest of them, saved by unconsciousness from the worst pangs of thirst and hunger which drove many half mad, and not having to stay awake to fight. Although the enemy did not pursue us as a body, we were constantly subjected to raids by opportunist villagers whose settlements we passed. All the menfolk possessed *tulwars,* and many owned locally-manufactured copies of our Lee-Enfield rifle, liable to explode in the user's hands after the first few rounds, but dangerous enough while they lasted; while the older men favoured the purely indigenous long musket, fired from a crooked rest like our old arquebus. These were charged with home-made missiles combining nails and metal scrapings, and were known as *jezails.*

Towards the end of the nightmare trek, I became aware also of pain in my right heel, which suddenly became intense and no doubt caused me to faint again, for I knew no more until I awoke on a charpoy in a cool, mud-walled room lit by a field lantern. I heard myself groan involuntarily. A voice nearby promptly called, "Murray!" and within a few moments that splendid fellow was tending to me.

"Where are we?" I asked him through stiff, sun-cracked lips. "Peshawar?"

"No, sir. Kandahar. Peshawar was too far off for us to make for there."

"You're all right, Murray?"

"Thanks, sir. One of the lucky ones."

"Major Preston?"

"Here, Watson," called the other voice. "Next bed. Glad to see you conscious at last. Feeling much pain?"

"Not so much in my shoulder," said I. "My foot, though. The heel..."

"*Tendo Achillis*. Took a *jezail* bullet in it, Murray says."

"That's right, sir," the orderly confirmed. "While you was slung across the horse. One of the b——'s shot you from behind a wall. A Grenadier picked him off in his turn, though, you'll be glad to hear."

"Is the bullet out?"

"Most of it. They're made up of bits and pieces, and there's probably some left in yet. Your shoulder's clean enough, though."

"Grazed subclavian artery," my chief informed me. "Painful enough at the time, I dare say, but it'll be right as rain."

"But how about you, sir?" I saw that he was lying face down, moving only his head.

"Oh, I'll soon be about. Missed the spine, as I thought. Trouble is, we're holed up in this God-forsaken place until some relief can get through—if they trouble to send any, that is."

While Murray was dressing my foot, the Surgeon-Major gave me the tragic details of the past battle and the retreat to Kandahar. We wounded had been brought straight into the citadel. The cantonments outside the walls were being hastily dismantled and everything fetched in, in preparation for a siege of unforeseeable duration.

It lasted, in fact, for more than a month, and a weary time it proved. The enemy made no effort to storm the city, content to lob in occasional artillery shells and to fire muskets at anyone showing himself on the walls. All supplies from without were cut off, and there was little enough in store to feed the army and civilian populace. It was an intensely hot time of year—the temperature over one hundred degrees by day—and conditions of hygiene deteriorated rapidly. Whether it was the result of eating unwashed fruit, or drinking tainted water, or perhaps from contact with an unwitting carrier amongst the native hospital orderlies, I had no sooner found myself able to limp about the wards than I was laid low again, this time with a fever which rendered me incapable of recognising day from night.

It seemed to last for months, though in fact it was for just three weeks. In those days we called it enteric; now it is known as typhoid.

My recovery from it more or less coincided with the arrival on the last day of August of the relief force under General Roberts, after a magnificent forced march all the way from Kabul. Their coming could not have been more timely. The hospital room which I had originally shared with Surgeon-Major Preston and two other wounded officers was jam-packed by then, as were all adjoining rooms and passages. Medical supplies were exhausted; rations of food were at a minimum. Morale was at the lowest imaginable ebb: Roberts himself is said to have remarked disgustedly that the defenders of Kandahar had not even the spirit to fly the Union Jack until they saw his force approaching.

I can make no claim to have stayed impervious to this despondency. Already weakened by my wounds, I had been dragged down by the fever to depths I had never before plumbed, leaving me emaciated and helplessly weak. I have been taken to task for asserting (in *A Study in Scarlet)* that my life was despaired of for months, when at the most it could have been for a few weeks, and I can only offer that up as a reflection of my recollected state of mind. As to my life having been despaired of at all, it certainly was—by me.

Doctors do not necessarily make good patients just because

they are better informed about what is happening to them, and might happen further if things turn worse. Typhoid was a dread disease in those days, and a doctor's qualifications conferred no dispensation from it. The very experience of being ill at all was almost unknown to me, therefore all the more alarming. I am certain that, but for that reservoir of stamina which I have already spoken of having accumulated in my sea service, I should not have pulled through.

As serious as my physical condition, though, was my state of mind. As I lay through those endless days and nights, in that baking, stenchful room, in a semi-swooning state between awareness and oblivion, I thought again and again of my questionable future, and what little I could make out was unrelievedly gloomy.

That my service days were already at an end, I was convinced: so brief had been my adventure, and so calamitous. Presumably I should get a pension of some sort, after being shipped home by a grateful government, but then what? The question answered itself: my long-deferred submission to the status of general practitioner would have to be implemented. I must regard my irresponsible years at their end, my oats sown. The time had come to seek out that groove along which I must henceforward trundle for as many years as would be permitted me before age and infirmity propelled me down the final slope.

Looking back, I had not much cause for regret. I had lived pretty fully, experienced much, and, if I had still not achieved anything singular, I had sampled more in my twenty-eight years than most did in a lifetime. Nothing could have been further from my imagination than the great, glowing adventures which have subsequently been my unique lot. All I could see was that I must be thankful to have survived Death's onslaught, and must make what I could of what was left to me within the context of the respectable, potentially comfortable profession for which I had qualified. It ought to be enough; but to my depressed, enfeebled mind, it represented all sorts of endings, and no kind of beginning at all.

25

"I'd ha' known you without a question."

It has often been represented to me that my several references to my wartime experiences and their legacy are not wholly consistent with one another. I accept that this is so, but assure the reader that the version here presented is the correct one.

In the brief account of my military service which accompanies the particulars of my first meeting Sherlock Holmes and of our first shared investigation, *A Study in Scarlet,* I referred to having passed my time in hopsital at Peshawar, not Kandahar. Had the editor who accepted that narrative troubled to send me a proof of it in printed form, I should naturally have corrected the error. That he did not accounts also for its appearance bearing the subtitle: "Being a reprint from the Reminiscences of John H. Watson, M.D. late of the Army Medical Department." My letter accompanying the piece had referred to the possibility of his publishing *extracts* from my *proposed* reminiscences, which I had in mind to publish piecemeal and then draw together, should they prove substantial and popular enough to warrant it. The consequent assumption that they existed in some original form has produced many enquiries over the years from readers flattering enough to wish to find copies. The result has been disappointment to them and embarrassment and irritation to me, and it will be noted that I never again published with that same journal.

I repeat, I was in Kandahar, the nearest base to Maiwand. Peshawar was far distant, and the wounded who received treatment there were from the Kabul region only. It was a silly error, which could and should have been corrected before seeing print.

As to my wound itself, I have been accused of vagueness in not being able to specify whether it was in my shoulder or leg, or whether I was shot once, or twice, or even shot at all! Here I have been the victim of my own attempt at diffidence.

When a man speaks of his war wounds, I believe that any hearer is entitled to think in terms of substantial injuries, probably sustained on different occasions in a prolonged period of service. I myself saw but one day's action in my army career, a day in which hundreds died or suffered the sort of terrible wounds which I helped to treat. I received but two, both minor: the one in the shoulder as I was about to join the retreat, and that in the foot at a time when I was barely conscious of where I was, but far from the scene of the recent action. It would have been anathema to me to have represented myself in any way as a much-wounded veteran. My pride in having served in Afghanistan is to have seen the British soldier in the heroic rôle in which our story-books portrayed him, and which today appears to be regarded with abhorrence by certain elements amongst us. With what I hope will be accepted as fitting humility, I have sought to make as little as possible of my part, and in referring to a wound, rather than wounds, have consequently trapped myself into inconsistencies of reference.

I trust this sets the record straight at last, and that it will be recognised henceforward that these present reminiscences make up the only true and full account of that part of my life which led up to what I might term my re-birth as the companion and biographer of Sherlock Holmes.

The medical board before which I was summoned found emphatically for my being sent home without delay. I protested that my injuries were healing and that a spell of leave would have me fit again for duty.

"Well tried, old boy," said the president, smiling, "but you'll never put weight back on those bones out here. English air and plenty of good square English meals are the only thing that will set you right. You'll go with the next convoy to Karachi. There's a ship waiting at Bombay, the *Orontes,* and you'll be on her."

I sailed on October 31st, in company with seventeen other invalids and the first contingent of returning British troops. General Roberts having defeated Ayub Khan before Kandahar and captured his entire equipment and baggage, the rebel leader had fled, and peace descended once more on Afghanistan. Save for a brief outbreak a year later, the tribes have remained more or less faithful to the Governments of India and Great Britain, although the North-West Frontier has ever remained a sort of playground for skirmishers.

The *Orontes* called at Malta on November 16th, and eventually reached Portsmouth ten days later, November 26th. We disembarked at Troopship Jetty, at the south end of the Royal Dockyard, close to the Royal Naval College. So it came about that, only eight months after leaving the Royal Victoria Military Hospital, Netley, to begin my great adventure, I found myself back there, a convalescent pending discharge from the Service.

I had naturally communicated my situation to my grandparents, and duly received an invitation pressing me to go and spend as long with them as I might desire. However, after the heat of the East, the prospect of Scotland in December was intolerable, not to mention the notion of passing

Christmas in the proximity of my aunts, with their disapproval of anything approaching levity and that temperate zeal which drove Grandfather to the refuge of his study when he wished to smoke or drink.

The paternal government had notified me that I should have nine months' allowance of eleven shillings and sixpence a day to enable me to restore myself and set myself up in life before going on to half-pay, which would constitute my permanent-wound pension. I determined to make the most of it, for what that amounted to, in one last fling in London, that great cesspool into which all the loungers and idlers of the Empire are irresistibly drained. It should be my last attempt at finding Aggie; she and young Frank were again much on my mind, especially now that my attempt to turn my back on a conventional way of life had failed. After that, I would throw in the sponge, get myself a practice—Grandfather had offered to advance me the initial capital—and sink into modest oblivion.

I remained at Netley one week before gravitating to London. I had thought of making my lodging once more in the Chelsea neighbourhood, but decided instead on something more central. The streets radiating off the Strand abounded with small, inexpensive hotels—the Craven, Horrex's, Scott's Private, and their kind—and in one of these, I forget which, I found myself a room at six shillings and sixpence a day for bed, breakfast, and attendance, which was all my need in the way of a base from which to conduct my largely aimless meanderings about town.

Determined to get the question of Aggie settled as soon as might be possible, I went to Cox & Co.'s Bank and enquired about her account. Beyond confirming that my payments had been made into it regularly, they declined information, leaving me none the wiser as to whether she had had any recourse to it yet. I thought of discontinuing the payments, with the idea that if she had become at all dependent on them, and suddenly found herself deprived, she might come enquiring, which would at least have served to flush her from cover; but it seemed an ignoble tactic, and I did not adopt it.

I made the round of the music-halls once more, again in vain, but leading to a chance encounter which was to prove significant.

"Cor!" exclaimed one of the girls at the Canterbury one evening. "Don't I remember you, you great pillock!"

"I beg your pardon?" There was nothing familiar to me about her puffy features. She was more quietly dressed than the others, small, and with the still-comely plumpness, although she would be in her forties. She sidled up to me and appraised me hard.

"Yes, it is you. Thinner, and you didn't have a moustache then, but I'd know you. Opéra Comique. *Sorcerer.* It was you got poor Perce the push, bobbing up like that before you ought, and old Gilbert seeing you."

I peered hard at her. Surely this could not be the relic of the fetching little thing who had coaxed me into that adventure whose recollection could still send shivers through me.

"I was one of the extra chorus, looking on," she explained. "Saw it all. It gave us a real giggle while it was happening, but we were sorry for poor Perce afterwards."

"He had rather himself to blame. I was only trying to do him a favour."

"I know, dear. Very grateful he was, at the time. That Gilbert, he's a sarcastic old cat. Clever, I grant you, but they say he gargles with acid before he starts the day."

"Well, I hope Perce found something else."

"Did he! Went back into the pub for a bracer, after the tongue-lashing he got, and walked slap into a manager whose eccentric dancer had had a stroke that very morning. It was always Perce's strong line, more than chorus work, and he got the job there and then. Never looked back—'well, hardly ever,' as they say."

I laughed and invited her to have a drink. She accepted a glass of hock and seltzer, in which I joined her.

"Are you still, er . . . ?" I asked, uncertain as to the capacity in which I found her.

"Now and again. I was in *Pinafore* for a bit, but with Perce on his feet there wasn't any more need, and I couldn't stand that so-and-so Gilbert."

"Oh, I see. You and Perce are, er—"

"Took up with him a while ago. Drunk or sober, he's an old love. I do the rounds with him every night, to keep him on the straight and narrow. S'pose you thought I was here on the game?"

"No, no!"

"Go on! No, I like to watch him from up here, with a drink in my hand, and the girls are friendly enough, once they know you're not after their trade."

"He's on here tonight, then?"

"Next turn. Then off to Collins's. Stop and watch him, if you're not too eager to get on with what I suppose you came here for."

"Not at all. I'd prefer your company, if I may have it."

"So long as it's all you want."

"Will it insult you if I say it is?"

"You're a bit of a duck. I'm Gladyce, Glad to pals."

"And I'm John."

She shook my hand formally with her pulpy gloved one. "Pleased to meet you, John. Have another with me, while we watch old Perce."

We leaned on the rail at the back of the amphitheatre, tall glasses of hock in hand, and watched as the tootling band played off the wobbly soprano, to whom no one had been paying much attention. The chairman made a lot of noise with his gavel and facetiously announced, "Your own—your *very* own—*Percy Forbes!*" I was pleased to hear a small cheer and a rattle of applause. Gladyce turned and smiled proudly.

The orchestra struck up a chirpy tune, and from the wings came a whirl of colour, comprising a loud, over-bright check suit and the red face of Perce under a brown bowler, which he doffed elaborately as he stalked grotesquely to and fro in a double-jointed way, seeming to take two steps back for every one forward, yet contriving to advance in a manner which I recognised at once. I had seen him perform before, but had not connected him with the inebriate whom I had sought so ineffectually to help through that Gilbert and Sullivan rehearsal.

He was perky and inventive, and clearly a favourite with the audience. He sang a droll song in a grating voice, did a series of exaggerated parodies of the styles of walk of members of well-recognised professions, and took his exit after a final dance whose climax was a gyrating movement seeming likely to screw him into the stage. He was warmly applauded.

"Very good," said I.

"Bless his old heart!" Gladyce exclaimed. "You'll come round and have one with us? He's often said how he'd like the chance to shake your hand."

Without awaiting my reply, she seized my hand and whisked me, with almost breathless haste, through an exit door and into the backstage labyrinth, where the usual mêlée of costumed performers and bowler-hatted stage-hands filled the cramped space. She thumped once on a dressing-room door and marched in without pausing for permission.

It was a cramped little room, lit by gas, with a narrow bench-top along each side, with mirrors over, and a great deal of theatrical litter. A man in evening dress and with an Irish-looking face, whom I took to be the mandatory sentimental tenor, was sitting reading a racing paper, from which he spared only the merest nod and smile to my companion. Perce himself, jacket off and with a towel round his neck, was hovering as if impatiently awaiting her coming. I recognised his features now. His hair was grey under some fading gingery dye, and his cheeks were darkly red, in a way not attributable to cosmetics.

"Look who I've brought," Gladyce exclaimed. "The *Sorcerer* bloke."

Perce's surprised features cracked open in a broad smile and he stepped forward, hand outstretched to shake mine.

"How do, lad. Reet glad t'see thee again. I've kep' saying to Glad, haven't I, old girl . . . ? Come on, then."

This last was addressed to her, and I saw him lick his lips as she drew open her capacious handbag and produced from it a half-full gin bottle and two glasses. Watched keenly by him, she poured careful measures into them both, and then, to his evident horror, handed one to me, keeping the other for herself.

"Hey up!" he cried. "What about t'workers?"

She smiled teasingly and gave him her glass, pouring some more for herself into a mug lying on one of the dressing-tables. Then we raised our drinks in a mutual toast. Perce gave out a great sigh of relief after his first sip.

"First tonight," he assured me, with a wink.

"And it's all you're getting till later," said Glad.

"I'll tell thee what, lad," he said to me. "Never tek up with a good woman. Tha'll never have owt thi' own way again."

"Just you get your things on, you old boozer," she rejoined. "You're fourth on at Collins's, remember."

He gave me a rueful look. "Like I say, I allus hoped I'd see thee again to say a word of thanks and have a bit of a crack together."

"It's a pleasure to meet you again. I gather all turned out for the best."

"The old bag's told you, has she? Yes, it did, ta, thanks to thee. Here, you doing owt tonight?"

"Nothing in particular."

"Come on to Islington in the cab with us. Keep the old girl company while I'm earning the spondulicks, then come round to our place for a bite of supper. We only live behind the Holloway Road.''

I looked to Gladyce. She was beaming approval. ''We've got plenty in, and you're more than welcome.''

For the first time in days, I felt my spirits lift. ''I will come with pleasure,'' I told them.

''Champion!'' cried Perce. ''We'll have another on that.''

''Oh no we won't,'' retorted Gladyce, removing his empty glass from his hand. ''You've had your ration for now.'' She gave the glasses the merest rinse under the single tap in the room, shook them out, and stuffed them and the bottle into her bag. Perce gave me a wry wink.

''No bloody justice,'' he observed. ''You and her standing out there boozing your heads off while poor old muggins does all the work. No justice, is there, Paddy?''

''There is not,'' answered the tenor, without raising his eyes. ''Good night.''

''Good neet, lad.''

Our passage between the two music-halls was a jolly one, our shared reminiscence of the *Sorcerer* débâcle given added spice by the unceasing exchange of Perce's dry northern wit for Gladyce's cockney forthrightness. They insulted one another outrageously, and it was obvious that they were devoted to each other. I gathered that, having ''taken up'' with him, she had appointed herself his protector from himself. Despite his mock-ferocious threats of what he would do to her if she did not allow him another nip of gin to sustain him on the cab journey, she kept her bag firmly closed, not to be opened again until we reached our destination, when she doled out one more measure.

Afterwards, however, it was different. Once Perce's last performance of the evening was done, restraint was lifted, and we all went drink for drink. Who could blame them, I thought, glancing round their cosy, tidy little parlour in the narrow terraced house, redolent with the odour of the steak-and-kidney pie, peas, and mashed potatoes which their all-purpose servant-girl had ready for their return. I well knew the insecurity which hung over their way of life, and the ever-present likelihood that the luck in which I had played an unwitting part could desert him as swiftly as it had come. Common prudence, I suppose, would have had them putting aside every penny against that day, but it was not in their nature, and would have done nothing for their essential spirit in the short term. Moralists would look down on them for their free and easy ways, their drinking, their living "in sin," yet under all that they were as cosy and respectable a couple as might be found. Considering Sarah Bernhardt's extravagances and open defiance of convention, which exaggerated her talents to make her a legend, I thought that Perce and Glad deserved all the happiness they could press out of the modest rewards they got from that artificial profession, of which an eccentric dancer represented as integral a part as a tragedienne.

Like all theatrical folk, they were night-owls, accustomed to talking long into the early hours and sleeping it off by day. We ate and drank prodigiously, and I spent what remained of that night on the *chaise longue* in their parlour. I awoke bleary and broken, and would have crawled off to my own lodging, but the servant insisted on making breakfast for me, although it was close to lunch-time, and before I had finished eating it, Glad had appeared, dressed in a wrapper but with her face and hair done, and looking and sounding as bright as a bugle. We got into conversation again, and then were joined by Perce, who launched into a stream of North Country anecdotes which had me helpless with laughter. By the time I was able to go home late that afternoon, I realised that I had enjoyed myself more than for many a long day.

So began a friendship of a kind which I should more accurately term "comradeship." Both Perce and Glad begged me to keep close with them, insisting that I was the best company they had enjoyed for years. I cannot think that I contributed much beyond that receptiveness which is what stage folk most value in others. I was "a good audience," attentive, appreciative, and offering them by my brief responses that encouragement off which they feed. Typically, they kept asking me about my own life, and when I had barely started to reply, found some cue in my words to set them off on another story about themselves. However, when I told them at last about Aggie, they heard me out with interest.

"Tek thi example from me," commented Perce. "Poor downtrodden b——r. Thee keep thi independence."

"Just you close your silly trap, you underdone Yorkshire pudding!" rejoined his ever-loving. "You'd have been drunk in some gutter by now, without me to wet-nurse you."

"Aye—'appen so," he acknowledged with a serious nod. It was no doubt true. Freely as she drank with him after his working day's end, she watched him beadily at all other times, doling out his liquid rations, keeping him sober and capable.

"I'll keep my eyes and ears open for you," Glad promised me, apropos Aggie. "If she come hanging round any of the halls, I'll find out."

Sunday was Perce's evening off, and I was pressed to spend it with them at home. We started carousing early, and by nine o'clock we were all a little flown on the whisky which I had insisted on bringing with me. Glad decided she could fancy some jellied eels. It was their little servant's evening off, and Glad insisted on going for them herself, to the horse-drawn stall in Seven Sisters Road, no doubt anticipating that if she had asked Perce to go he would have nipped into the Nag's Head on the way, met a crony, and needed rescuing from the resultant pub-crawl. He and I were left together, I under stern orders not to let him get too many drinks ahead before she came back.

He did not, however, make at once for the bottle, but sat forward in his fireside chair, staring thoughtfully into the little grate.

"You're looking for wrong 'un, John," he surprised me by saying.

"Wrong what, Perce?"

"It's not your mam you want. It's your dad."

He reached automatically for his glass, paused, and looked at me seriously.

"It's me who wanted a mam to pick me up when I'd tumbled down and couldn't get meself up. It's me needs somebody standing over me saying, 'Now, our Perce, you've had enough,' and 'Just one extra tonight, on account of being a good lad.' It's me, in a few years, when me joints is gone all stiff, who'll be looking out for somebody by me to say, 'Nay, lad, don't thee fret thiself, 'cos tha'll allus have me to look after thee.' Me. John, not thee."

"All men miss their mothers, Perce."

" 'Appen; but not all need 'em. Great young chap like thee doesn't want his mam standing over him measuring out his bottle. He wants his dad, to lake at games with him, stand up to him and see who's best, smoke a pipe and take a drink and talk men's talk."

"I happen to *like* women—for the usual reasons."

He grinned and drank at last. "Anybody can see that. I wouldn't trust thee and Glad alone in t'dark."

"Get on with you!"

"Oh, she's got you measured up, has Glad, and no mistake. Read you like a book. They can, women."

"Are you trying to tell me that in looking for Aggie I'm wanting to make up for losing my mother? That *is* what you're getting at, isn't it?"

" 'Appen so."

"And Glad sees me like that, too?"

He nodded. "Her and yon Aggie."

"Aggie!"

Perce picked up the bottle. "Sup up and have another fill, then I can tell thee before my nerve goes."

"You've *seen* Aggie?"

"Glad has. Found her through one of the girls at Collins's. Nay, don't look like that. She's not on the game. She's taken up with this feller, and he wants to wed her, and she's happy, and—oh, humma, have a drink, do!"

I was only too glad to oblige him, and refilled my own glass. The effect of strong drink on me has always been to calm rather than to enrage, and perhaps they had seen as much, and had cunningly chosen their moment and their method; for I had no doubt at all that Glad's excursion to the eel-stall had been prearranged, with poor Perce under motherly stricture to do his duty, man-to-man, in her absence. The relief on his face told me as much, and he admitted it when I taxed him direct, scanning my features anxiously for sign of wrath or distress.

We heard the street door, as Gladyce returned, and I could have laughed out at the way she strolled into the room, carrying the eels in their newspaper wrapping, humming a street-organ tune, and trying to look nonchalant.

"Perce tells me you're madly in love with me and want me to take you away this very night," I said. "Are you going to eat your eels first, or bring them with you?"

Her round-eyed stare would have been an asset to Perce on stage.

"How many have you two been having?" she demanded. Then it was my turn to stare, as she turned back to the door and beckoned—and Aggie walked in.

26

"Woman's heart and mind are insoluble puzzles."

"Aggie! My dear, dear Aggie!"

I had leapt to my feet so violently that the little table nearly went flying. Perce lunged desperately for the bottles and glasses and hugged them to him.

" 'Ullo, Johnnie. My, you've lost some weight. I like the 'tache, though."

She herself was aglow with health and vitality, handsome as ever and smartly dressed. She accepted a glass of whisky and sat down next to me on the horsehair sofa.

"I hope you told him," Glad said accusingly to Perce. He made the gesture of crossing his heart.

"Thank God for that. Come on."

"Where?"

"Kitchen. Help me eat these eels."

Perce grinned comprehendingly and made to follow her. As an afterthought, he turned back for one of the whisky bottles, gave me a broad wink, and went out.

"Aggie—" I began, as soon as the door was closed. She put up her finger to my lips.

"Listen to me, Johnnie. Perce has told you I got another feller? Yes, well, he's a widower, just gone fifty—"

"Fifty!"

"Yes, fifty, which suits me to the ground. He's in the drapery, own little business and house over. I knew him and his poor missus through old Frank. Thoroughgoing decent sort—the sort I want and who wants me."

"*I* want you, Aggie."

"No you don't, no more than I want you. No, listen! We had our lovely fling, and no girl could have wanted better. Only, what I could see and you never could, was that when it comes to settling down you don't want no older woman, no more than I want a younger man. A pretty young wife's what you need to look out for, Johnnie, love—someone who'll dote on you like she does her dad."

"I don't know where all this stuff's sprung up from," I groaned. "Perce, and now you."

"It's plain common sense. I could see it all along, only I didn't like to hurt your feelings, and I was enjoying meself while it lasted."

"So was I." I could not keep a hint of bitterness from my tone.

"You do see, don't you, love?"

"You're . . . quite sure it's what you want, Aggie?"

"Certain. Time I settled down proper. You've got all your life before you still."

"Hah!"

"Plenty of it, anyway. Come on, buck up! You ain't done yet."

"Well . . . But what about Frank?"

Her expression grew more serious.

"I bin thinking about him. What you was trying to make me believe—"

"It's the truth. I told you I had the proof."

"Yeh, well, I thought it was all along. Only, I knew you and the way you were. I wasn't having you messing your life up all on account of one lovely tumble at Cremorne. It worked out nicely with poor old Frank, who was happy enough to go along with it. The kid's right enough where he is. No blessed good telling him how the pa who snuffed it wasn't his pa at all. What'd that make him think about me, I ask you, and what chance'd it give me and Albert—that's my new one—what chance'd it give us to make anything of him?"

Although my lips were framing an argument, I could not in honesty deny that she was right.

"Ask yourself the truth," she persisted, seeing me hesitate. "Does he mean that much to you really?"

"I... I think it was chiefly because he was part of you, Aggie. Not so much for himself, but because of what you and I... what I hoped..."

I was unable to go on. I bit my lip, then took a fierce swallow of whisky. Aggie refilled my glass for me, squeezing tight my hand with her other.

"I'll see he's a credit to you, Johnnie. Only, well, like, I've let Albert think he was old Frank's, too, and it could be awkward for me if... D'you know what I mean?"

I nodded. "You don't want me to see him at all."

"Would you mind, Johnnie—for me?"

I shook my head.

"Ta, love. There'll be other little Johnnie Watsons yet."

"But never another Aggie Brown."

I seized her and crushed her to me. She gave me her lips unstintingly, and for long silent moments we remained locked together in a farewell embrace. At length, Aggie drew gently away and got to her feet, smoothing out her dress.

"By the way, Johnnie, I never touched none of that money."

"Will you let me do one last thing, Aggie?"

She gave me a suspicious look. "What?"

"Will you let me go on paying it until Frank is eighteen? Will you save it up for him? It isn't right that your—that Albert should have to find all the money, and you can tell him it was something left you by your late husband."

"I don't see the point."

"I do. Just let me do that one thing, Aggie. Please."

"All right, then. Ta. Like I say, I'll do the best with him for you. Ta-ra, Johnnie, love. And thanks."

She went swiftly out, leaving me standing in the middle of the little room. I realised that I was trembling, and that I wanted to cry. I reached my arms out to the mantelpiece and sank my head between them, staring down unseeing into the fire.

After I know not how long, there came a tap at the door from the kitchen. I was aware of it opening and someone coming tentatively in.

"All reet, lad?" Perce asked softly.

"All reet," I mimicked back and turned to face him.

"Glad fetched another bottle with her. Reckoned happen we might need it."

"We do," said I. And we drank every drop of it.

EPILOGUE
"The wonderful chain of events."

This memoir approaches its end. It is common property from here on how a chance encounter, occurring only two weeks following the events just described, transformed my life from bleak hiatus to a purposeful progress which has never since lacked for interest and excitement. A few words, to clarify the details that are already well known, seem to be called for.

In letting it be believed that I decided to leave my modest hotel in the Strand in quest of another less pretentious and expensive, I have been guilty of a mistruth. The fact of the matter is that I was required to leave there by the proprietor, lest my behaviour should bring his establishment into ill repute.

My state of shock occasioned by the emotional experience of my last farewell to Aggie, together with the amount of whisky with which my solicitous hosts spent the rest of that evening consoling me, freely encouraging my tears and shedding sympathetic ones of their own, reduced me to a condition which is better left to the reader's imagination than described. I awoke in my room next day unable to retain the slightest recollection of having returned there. Stumbling at length downstairs, I encountered only hostile glares from the proprietor and his wife, and the curtest of responses to my proffered greeting.

Thoughts of Aggie were flooding in upon me already, and I hastened to the nearest hostelry to seek that means whereby they might be dulled, with the result that I was soon close to incoherence again and had to be helped back to my hotel by a pot-boy. I spent the rest of the day asleep in my clothes, until, waking after nightfall, I sallied forth again and repeated the process.

So I continued for several days, topping myself up whenever approaching sobriety's gleams began to re-illumine those thoughts which I desired to keep drowning until they should rise no more. Gladyce called to enquire after my well-being and, having Perce's gin ration about her, made use of it to console me in my room, where we were discovered by the landlady's wife, who burst in dramatically and ordered my respectable visitor off the premises as though she had been any woman from the streets. Forgetting all notions of politesse, I told the woman what I thought of her, and was immediately afterwards visited by her husband and told to pack and get out.

I deposited my belongings at Charing Cross left-luggage office and groped my way across Trafalgar Square and up the Haymarket to the Criterion, in quest of a hair of the proverbial dog. The "Cri" was but a few years old in those days, elegant and fashionable without being exclusive, the haunt of resting actors, journalists, theatrical agents, and the brotherhood of the Turf, from jockeys to tipsters. It was already said that one need only spend a half-hour in its vast American Bar before meeting somebody one knew, or could strike up easy acquaintanceship with. It was New Year's Day, 1881, and I felt, in my forlornness and rejection, that I could not bear to drink alone. Glad and Perce would be pleased to welcome me at Holloway, I knew, but he would be performing that evening and I did not wish to obtrude my present mood upon them at the risk of inciting him to drink prematurely.

I nodded to the two vast doormen and crossed the marbled saloon to the American Bar, with its patriotic design of the national eagle with bolts of forked lightning in its talons, all splendid in gold leaf not yet tarnished by years of tobacco smoke. The long bar extended down one side of the narrow room, with chairs and marble-topped tables along the other. The room was only half full of all-male company, bowler-hatted and greatcoated against the outside cold, but would soon become and remain crowded and companionable until late at night. It was the place for my present mood.

I ordered my glass of whisky and water, and quickly began to feel restoration creeping over me. It being the first day of the year, I endeavoured to turn my mind to resolutions. At last, it seemed to me, the time had come to offer my concession to life—not so much to go on to the retreat as to make my tactical withdrawal to a secure position. Perhaps I should not seek a new lodging after all. The great expresses to Scotland left from King's Cross around the middle of the night. I could be on one of them, and sleep my way northward towards an interview with Grandfather which should mark both a capitulation and a rebirth.

So, we'll go no more a-roving
So late into the night,
Though the heart be still as loving,
And the moon be still as bright.

For the sword outwears its sheath,
And the soul wears out the breast,
And the heart must pause to breathe,
And love itself have rest. . . .

A hand clapped my shoulder, the wounded one, making me wince and turn sharply, to see the smiling face of young Stamford, who had been a dresser under me at Bart's.

"Dr. Watson, Mr. Sherlock Holmes": such was that same Stamford's simple introduction which was shortly to mark the most important of all my life's transitions. Coming so unlooked-for, and at so seemingly low a point in my fortune's ebb, I saw none of its significance that afternoon in that chemical laboratory at Bart's Hospital. All I saw was a prospective fellow-lodger, whose company I fancied I could tolerate companionably and economically for what little time it might take me to decide my future.

That the immediate years of that future should prove to be so determined by that singular being's whims and activities did not, of course, then occur to me, let alone that the entire remainder of my life would be in varying degree bound up with his; that through him I should experience adventures such as I had never imagined, and achieve what I might with modest justification term literary fame.

Least of all did it dawn upon me then that in finding him I had discovered the father substitute for whom I had been so long and unwittingly seeking. Hindsight has shown me that without question. I had sought a mother, and found a father: and his name was Sherlock Holmes.

"How are you? You have been in Afghanistan, I perceive. . . ."